THE KILLING VOTE

Dedication

For all the activists who are working diligently and constantly to keep the government and the health care industry from legislating how and when a human life should end.

THE KILLING VOTE

by

Bette Golden Lamb
&
J. J. Lamb

Two Black Sheep Productions
Novato, California

Other Books By
Bette Golden Lamb & J. J. Lamb

The Gina Mazzio RN Medical Series:
   Bone Dry
   Sin & Bone
   Bone Pit
   Bone of Contention
   Bone Dust
   Bone Crack
   Bone Slice
   Bone Point

By Bette Golden Lamb & J. J. Lamb:
   Sisters in Silence
   Heir Today...

By Bette Golden Lamb:
   The Organ Harvesters
   The Organ Harvesters-Book II
   The Russian Girl

By J. J. Lamb (Zachariah Tobias Rolfe III P.I. Series):
   A Nickel Jackpot
   The Chinese Straight
   Losers Take All
   No Pat Hands

The Killing Vote

www.twoblacksheep.us

ISBN-13: 978-0-9984643-4-3
ISBN-10: 0-9984643-4-1

Cover Design: Sue Trowbridge
www.Interbridge.com

Chapter 1

Denny scanned the letters on the large storefront window. He read them again, threw his head back, snorted, and spit on the sidewalk.

CORPS
Coalition of Older and Retired Persons

Shit! There's only one Corps. The U.S. fucking Marine Corps!

He spit again.

Man, they even used the stinkin' red and gold colors.

He looked around for something to smash in the window, then stopped.

Be my ass if I pulled a friggin' stunt like that.

He used his index finger to trace each letter of *CORPS,* then spun around and leaned hard against the glass.

Punk-ass job. Who cares about the stupid Coalition of Older and Retired Persons? Not this ex-Gyrene.

He pulled out an old-fashioned pocket watch that he'd lifted off a smashed suit at the bar last night.

Late! Pays shit, then he's late!

Restless, he stomped down to the corner, looked up and down Market Street, then over to Twelfth before slowly crossing to the other side of Franklin. He stood there for a moment, surprised at how much traffic there was in San Francisco this early on a Friday morning.

He started back toward the storefront, this time walking with more purpose, his arms swinging from the shoulders in an I-know-a-girl-who-lives-on-a-hill cadence.

Damn Marines!

Tossed my ass.

Eleven friggin' years in The Corps. Would have gone twenty. Hell, maybe even thirty.

The dishonorable discharge had hurt. Still hurt. They didn't give a rat's ass about some grunt and the medals he'd earned in Iraq.

"Respect this, motherfuckers," he growled, spinning around to give a digital salute to every sentry-straight lamppost in sight.

He stopped opposite the CORPS building and stared across the street at the plate glass windows. He was supposed to wait around the corner, but he'd wanted to see the place they were going to do. More like a hole-in-the-wall pizza dive. If it'd been his call, he'd have tossed a couple of Molotov cocktails through the window and let it go at that.

But he was just a grunt. That's all. Just a friggin' hired grunt.

* * *

Myra Jackson needed to get to San Francisco's CORPS offices early. There was a big mailing to get out before the weekend started and she was stuck with training a new batch of volunteers. Thinking about it made her cringe.

She waited until the #41 Muni bus came to a complete halt before leaving her seat. She knew the delay aggravated the bus drivers, but a near-disaster after a jerky stop one morning made her change her habit of trying to be the first one off.

She tucked her purse under one arm, the strap over her head and across the opposite shoulder; her free hand gripped a shopping bag—**Coalition of Older and Retired Persons** was emblazoned in gold and red on both sides. An overhead Hallmark advertisement made her smile and remember the surprise 75th birthday party the volunteers had held for her last week, and how she'd never let on that she was really 78.

Arthritis gnawed at every joint as she inched her way to the rear door. She waved her thanks to the driver as she carefully stepped down through the bi-fold doors.

* * *

Denny checked his watch again, saw it was time to get back to the meeting place. When he got there, Al was waiting, leaning against the right front fender of his beat-up, black Sentra.

"Neat ride, huh?" Denny said, pointing to an orange three-quarter-ton utility company rig he'd driven to the site. **South City Electric** was painted on both doors and the tailgate.

"Hell, Denny, why didn't you buy a friggin' neon sign and set it up out here?" Al said. He pulled at his graying beard and walked around the truck, shaking his head back and forth with each step.

"What was I gonna do, man? My beater truck died yesterday, so I boosted this one. Got tools, supplies, everything in one package. Cool, huh?"

"You dummy! What if a nosy cop runs a check on it?"

Denny strapped on a tool belt. "I only took it last night." He dangled the stolen watch by its gold chain and tapped the face. "It's gonna to be at least another hour before anyone even knows the damn thing is missing."

"I hope to God you're right." Al hoisted a backpack from the trunk of his car. "Let's get moving." He looked again at the garish **South City Electric** truck, scowled, and motioned for Denny to follow.

They walked quickly down the narrow alley behind the row of buildings that fronted on Franklin. When they came to the back door of the CORPS offices, Al reached for a large ring of keys attached to his belt by a retractable cable.

"Let me pick it," Denny said, pushing forward. "I need the practice."

He had a slim leather case already in his hand.

"Those things take forever, even for someone who knows what he's doing." Al elbowed him aside. In less than ten seconds he'd found a master key that let them inside the offices.

"Coulda done it."

"Yeah, yeah! Maybe next time when we don't have a big orange billboard announcing we're in the neighborhood."

"What billboard?"

"Just find the goddam fuse box and get started. I want to be outta here in less than twenty minutes."

"Shoulda started earlier. I was here on time."

"Put a lid on it and do your thing, will ya?"

"I'm doin' it. I'm doin' it." The gray metal box hung next to the archway they'd just come through. Denny raised the latch, swung open the door, and stared at the fuses and circuitry. "Piece of cake." He reached out and turned off the master switch. A refrigerator whirred into silence.

"Everything dead?" Al asked.

"I think so. Let me check."

"You do that."

* * *

Myra stood on the street corner and waited for the traffic light to change to green.

There were so many cars these days and the drivers were so mean and pushy. Seldom used her Ford Taurus anymore—only for an occasional weekend trip to visit friends in Monterey or Mendocino.

She watched her bus move away from the curb and into the traffic.

Everyone complained about the Muni system. But it brought her downtown just fine every weekday morning. Her half-day-mornings job at CORPS was perfect; it gave her the rest of each day to herself. Not only that, she really loved working with the CORPS director, Nathan Sorkin.

She sighed, thinking about the busy day ahead of her. She needed to get moving if she was going to get fresh, hot coffee ready for the volunteers, and for the meeting Nathan had scheduled with Ted Yost, who was helping them with the Washington thing.

The familiar clock on a nearby bank told her there still had plenty of time to stop at the corner deli and pick out some fresh bagels and Danish to take to the office with her. Nathan frequently chided her for spending her own money for the morning snacks, but she enjoyed watching him and others smile as they picked out a favorite treat to go with their morning coffee.

* * *

Al pressed a small wad of C4 into the narrow space on one side of a wall electrical outlet, the last of six in the small suite of offices. He pierced the explosive with a tiny detonator and tied it into the wiring, then replaced the faceplate.

"How'd you set it up, Denny?"

"Sequential. Flip any one light switch, then everything triggers—one after another. Whole fucking thing shouldn't take more than two or three seconds."

"Good!" He screwed the faceplate back onto the switch. "Help me fasten the rest of these."

"Yeah, okay. But I hate even looking at this boom-boom shit." Denny started to turn away, then saw a packet of the explosive flying through the air toward him. He scrambled to catch it, almost landed on his ass.

Al laughed. "It doesn't do squat until it's triggered. How many times do I have to tell you that?"

Denny stared at the small, grayish brick of C4 in the palm of his hand. "You can tell me a million fucking times and I'm still not going to like this goddam stuff.

"But you'll play around with enough voltage to electrocute an army."

"Electricity's my thing, man."

"My point exactly."

"What?"

"Never mind. Let's finish up and get the hell out of here."

* * *

Myra waited for the illuminated walking man sign to let her know it was safe to cross the street, but as she stepped off the curb, a bright orange truck almost sideswiped her. She watched as it accelerated up Franklin, gone in a blink. Her heart was still racing as she unlocked the CORPS office front door.

Nathan wasn't here yet. She smiled.

First, for a change.

After turning over the Open/Closed sign, Myra locked her purse in the lower drawer of the reception desk.

She paused for a moment and looked around the empty offices. The semi-darkness had a calming effect, which she enjoyed for a moment. Instead of turning on the lights, she walked back to the break area, spread out a clean napkin on the counter, and made an arrangement of the bagels and Danish.

Going first to the reception area, she then went through each room, gathering up dirty coffee cups that had been left on desks, tables, and the floor. She rinsed the coffee pots and washed the cups in the cramped bathroom's tiny sink, then got everything ready to make coffee and tea.

As she measured out the coffee, she looked up and gave her usual nod of acknowledgment and approval to the poster that dominated the reception area:

An attractive woman of at least 80 years languished against a palm tree, wearing a string bikini. The caption declared:

I *AM* Acting My Age!

Myra flipped the switch on the automatic coffeemaker. Nothing happened—no red light, no sputtering of water. She looked down behind the stand. As she suspected, the plug had been pulled out.

"Now who did that?" she asked, lowering herself painfully to one arthritic knee so she could reach the plug. When she straightened, the coffeepot was still silent.

"Power must have gone off last night," she grumbled. "Or a breaker tripped off again."

She went first to the circuit box, opened it, tested the main line, then pushed the individual on-off rockers. She heard the refrigerator go off and come back on, which meant the office at least had electricity. Back at the coffee table, she still couldn't get the coffeemaker to respond. Frustrated, she tried the wall switch next to the table.

The coffeepot corner exploded and a thundering blast rocked the entire building. Water flew everywhere. Slivers of glass sliced into her face, arms, and legs. Her desk shattered and jagged fragments of wood and metal catapulted in every direction.

She gasped, slapped her hands to her chest and looked down—a large stake of wood protruded from between her breasts.

"Help!" she cried softly as an icy numbness took away her breath. She crumpled to the floor while the explosions echoed all around her.

Chapter 2

Ted Yost heard the faint click inside the bedside alarm that told him he had only seconds before the small speakers would vibrate with raucous music, a babble of voices, or jarring static. He pulled one hand from beneath the covers, ran his fingers across the top of the clock/radio and pushed the *off* button.

He enjoyed the moment of victory at having outwitted the alarm, then turned slightly to see if he had awakened Mel. For several seconds he watched a wayward strand of his wife's hair rise and fall across her face with each soft breath, then he gently eased out of bed.

Ted had no desire to get up at 6 a.m., but he'd agreed to meet Nathan Sorkin at CORPS headquarters around eight. He hoped he'd allowed enough time since he had no idea how long it would take him to drive from Sonoma to San Francisco during the morning commute hours. But he was damned if he was going to get up any earlier than six. He'd just have to hurry along with his morning routine.

In the short time since he'd given up being a full-time newsman, he'd gotten used to sleeping in, having a leisurely breakfast, and taking a walk with Mel before settling down to write at his home computer.

Well, not really. Ever so often he would get an itch, an itch to be out in the world chasing stories, reporting the news. But there was little work for freelancers anymore—national and international news-gathering organizations had cut back or were closed down. And those that remained were mostly tainted by the political bent of the corporate owners.

He'd tried to reassure himself that going into retirement had been the right thing to do. He'd been fed up, decided it was time to write the novel he'd been thinking about since the Vietnam War ended.

Then one day after surfing the web and reading a dozen or so unsatisfying blogs, he tried writing one himself.

He'd started with a weekly blog. And much to his surprise, he'd picked up a readership. Then a couple of months ago he'd struck a resounding note when he'd narrowed his focus, primarily commenting on and citing examples of how the public was affected by dirty political practices.

Now he was not only being read, he was being quoted.

Caught a lucky break, that's all, he told himself as he shuffled into the bathroom.

Things were going smoothly until a couple of weeks ago when he got a call from Bill Tana, a friend and "reliable source" in D.C.

"It's sketchy," Bill said, "but it seemed the kind of thing you might want to run with."

"Not another of your nutball conspiracy theories, I hope," Ted said, laughing. "Or maybe you're pulling my leg?"

"There's always a reason for my paranoia, old man. Something's floating in the air and it has to do with that healthcare stuff you're always bugging me about."

"Healthcare *stuff.*"

"That's what I said. Don't tell me you're going deaf, too."

"Smart ass!"

"Do you want to hear it or not?"

"Go."

"The word around the circuit is there may be a big push to ditch Medicare, or at least significantly undercut the funding."

That put the novel back on hold.

Again.

He'd dropped Tana's rumor into his blog as a gossip item and was surprised by angry reader response: If he knew something specific about the future of Medicare, he should put up or shut up.

* * *

"No more credit, Della. That's final!"

"Come on. Please give me a break."

Della Paoli paced in tight circles in the pre-dawn darkness as she talked. A gust of cool early morning air made her pull her sweater tighter around her shoulders. She hated having to plead with the grower at the San Francisco Flower Mart.

"It's the new Winter Festival Celebration this weekend," she continued. "I'll sell every flower I can stock. After that, I'll catch up … we'll be even. Please!"

"Della, it's been three weeks. I got bills to pay, too, you know."

"This is the last time. I promise!"

There were murmurs in the neighboring stalls. The grower looked around, saw the glares of other sellers. "All right, already. But this is it. From now on, cash only."

With a broad smile, Della squeezed his hand and moved from one display of cut flowers to another, smelling and gathering the blossoms to her face as she went.

As usual after completing her order, she stopped at a nearby cafe for coffee, an English muffin, and conversation with other flower vendors. Della kept checking her purse to make certain her social security check was still there. A quick mental rundown of expenses reassured her—by the end of next month she would be debt-free for the first time since her husband died six months ago.

Her spirits soared as she walked to her ancient, faded red Volvo station wagon.

She turned on the radio while waiting for two large trucks to lumber onto the street ahead of her. The early morning traffic was light; she could divide her attention between the few cars and trucks on the road and the city's skyscape.

Della crossed the Golden Gate Bridge, smiling when she passed truck-mounted workers in the center lanes shifting yellow pylons from right to left with circus-like dexterity to create more lanes for commuters headed into the city.

The coastal hills were still just an outline, with a hint of the dawn light beginning to show itself. She glanced across at the lights of the East Bay just before she drove under the painted rainbow surrounding the opening arc of the Waldo Grade tunnel. The pastel colors made her laugh out loud, as they always did. Soon she was on the long, coasting stretch leading into the outskirts of Mill Valley and on to her downtown flower stall.

She flipped on her turn signal, moved into the exit lane, and was suddenly cut off by a bread van driver, apparently in a hurry to keep to his early morning delivery schedule for fresh, hot sourdough. He passed too closely on her left and cut in front of her. She gasped and stomped on the brake pedal, tossing the Volvo into a skid.

The small station wagon struck the guardrail, spun back across the road, and rolled into the ditch separating the exit road from the freeway.

Della's head spun, mingling the real and the unreal. Her world became a confused blur of white and red lights. She was catapulted into space, flowers tumbling over and around her in a kaleidoscope of color. She was lifted, carried through a soft, ethereal spectrum. Everything went black.

* * *

Della tried to turn her head to one side, then the other.
Nothing.
What happened? Was she awake or dreaming?
She willed her eyes to open. The lids remained clamped shut.
A dream?
No, there were voices. Real voices. Loud voices.
She strained to hear, caught only a jumble of meaningless sounds.
She tried to move again, tried to force her lids open.
But she was trapped, wrapped in an opaque cocoon.
She needed some kind of physical response. Anything!
Not a sound escaped her lips.
Icy panic crushed her.
Scream! She had to scream.
Nothing.

12

She wanted to reach for her constricted throat. But some powerful force held her wrists, arms, legs.

A coffin! They were carrying her to the cemetery.

The vision was clear—an open grave. Grim men with shovels would lower her into a deep hole; toss heavy, black dirt on top of her; smother her.

Stop! My God! Stop!

Her mind exploded into a wild confusion of reds and oranges that stabbed her brain and pushed her through a universe of exploding stars racing to engulf her.

Silent screams grew louder and louder.

I'm alive! I'm alive! I'm alive!

* * *

An image of Nathan Sorkin flashed through Ted Yost's head as he drove toward San Francisco. Sorkin was a knockoff of Albert Einstein: white hair flying in all directions, sad eyes that had seen too much despair.

Ted tilted the rearview mirror to look at his own hair.

What happened to that carrot mop I never paid attention to? Turned fifty-five and it started coming out in clumps. Shit! Now it's starting to fade to gray—like an old cat.

He pushed at the mirror, shoved so hard he thought it might crack the windshield.

Turning fifty hadn't bothered him, but when he hit sixty he started expecting to find pieces of his body—a toe here, an earlobe there—left behind in the bed when he got up of a morning. The sands in the hourglass were in free-fall.

He glanced down and stared hard at the official *Press Pass* still clipped to the car's sun visor.

Used, torn, old.

He shifted in his seat and changed the radio station. Clifford Alden's jazz rendition of *Angel Eyes* filled the car; for a moment the music made the five-mile-per-hour, bumper-to-bumper traffic almost tolerable.

What an idiot. Didn't even try to change Nathan's mind about an early morning meeting.

"Sure," he muttered.

As if I could get that man to do anything he didn't want to do.

Some fool in a Porsche forced his way into Ted's lane, almost shearing off the front fender of his new Prius.

"Happy now that you've moved up one whole car length?" he yelled inside the closed car.

Off to the left, on the other side of the median, red and blue lights were blinking, slowing traffic even more. Ted could see emergency vehicles on the berm of the Mill Valley exit, along with an overturned red Volvo station wagon.

A guy rubbernecking in a car to Ted's left turned to look at him, shrugged, and continued on. The car behind honked and Ted picked up his speed.

Forcing himself to settle down, he changed the radio station to NPR. But after a couple of minutes he found he couldn't concentrate or even comprehend a panel of experts discussing the dissolution of the U.S. infrastructure. He changed the station again, this time to classical music. Mendelssohn was much easier on the psyche.

When did our world become so unmanageable?

He used to follow in-depth newscasts like a bloodhound, aware of every nuance, hip to all the catch-phrases. Now, after forty years as an active journalist, he'd begun to believe that chasing the answers was not as damn important as he'd once thought.

He was distracted for a moment by a young woman singing and pounding on her steering wheel, head bobbing up and down like a banshee, oblivious to everything around her. He inched forward, hit the brakes, and resisted the temptation to tap the back bumper of the Porsche, now trying to wedge back over into the lane it had come from.

Ted looked at the press pass again.

Yeah, over*used, old.*

Breaking news: An explosion and devastating fire have hit the offices of the Coalition of Older and Retired Persons in San Francisco. Authorities are already questioning whether it was an accident or arson. The organization, often called the talking corpse by its enemies, is an outspoken critic of the administration's management of healthcare and the Medicare financial crisis.

Ted fumbled with the radio's volume, turned it up.

The fire department's arson unit has released a statement that a bomb is the likely cause. We have also just learned a seventy-eight-year-old employee of the organization was in the building at the time and is in critical condition.

Bette Golden Lamb & J. J. Lamb

Chapter 3

When Ted Yost approached CORPS headquarters a sudden chill left him shaking.

He circled a yellow-caution-tape police perimeter before finally parking three blocks away from the CORPS offices. He took off on foot, excused and pardoned his way through the clots of spectators along Franklin.

Gusts of acrid air stung his nostrils and mouth. When he reached the storefront entrance, he stopped—about all that was left of the building were the charred remains of the outer walls and window frames edged with fangs of glass.

The firemen were finishing up—snake-like hoses were gathered and rolled, axes stowed; one fire truck was already leaving the scene. A cop, using a bullhorn, tried to scatter the crowd while a pair of yellow-slickered firemen poked in the ruins.

As Ted debated whether or not to try entering the burnt-out building, a hand came down, rested lightly on his shoulder. He turned, looked into the sad eyes of Nathan Sorkin, and wrapped an arm across the director's shoulders.

"I was on my way when I heard the news report on the radio," he said.

"Glad you're here, Ted."

They stood, both silent, watching the last of the fire trucks drive away.

"We've had lowlifes threaten us over the years," Nathan finally said, "but this is the first time they actually did anything." Tears streamed down his cheeks. Nathan blew his nose into a large paisley handkerchief. "I should have listened. This whole thing was set up to get me."

"Any idea who it is?"

"Just a voice. Another telephone schmuck whispering that they were going to kill me if I didn't stop taking potshots at the Administration's Medicare policies."

"And you just let it go?"

"What's to do? It could have been the skinhead I had the police throw out last week. Or it might have been a loose cannon from a Tea Bagger group. Maybe it was one of our sister organizations." Nathan immediately shook his head. "No, they wouldn't have the *chutzpah* to pull off something like this. That's why we started this group in the first place. Got tired of watching big organizations made up of old farts sitting on their *tuchis* doing nothing."

"When you raise a ruckus, you create enemies," Ted said. "Some more powerful and vindictive than others."

Nathan nodded, took a deep breath, pulled a hand down across his face. "Suppose it could have been one of the pharmaceutical companies."

"Pharmaceutical?"

"Yeah, they're the money behind a trio of advocacy groups for seniors. It's nothing more than a way to funnel funds into the campaigns of friendly politicians."

"It's worth looking into."

"For God's sakes, don't you get it? There's no *one* person or group. We've pissed off a lot of people. They would all breathe a lot easier if we were out of the way."

"When was the last threatening call?"

"That first day we met, when you came down here to talk about your Medicare blog item." Nathan bowed his head. "What really hurts ... they got Myra instead of me." His voice caught and he could barely get the words out. "I watched the paramedics take her...they said she was critical." He clutched Ted's arm. "She was so pale."

Ted's insides were raw; he balled his hands into tight knots. "Myra's a real fighter, Nathan.

"Yeah," Nathan said in a quavering voice. "

"Didn't think she'd let me in that first time I came to see you. But she's a woman who grows on you."

"Myra runs the *gantse megillah*. And it wasn't love at first sight when it came to you."

"You weren't all that friendly yourself," Ted said. "Man, was that only a few weeks ago? I feel like I've known you for years."

A cop tried to shoo away a bunch of spectators. When they didn't budge, he yelled, "Move on! Move on! There's nothin' here for you to see!"

"You didn't seem like much of a *mensch* at the time."

"Hiring me is not a like dangling a carrot in front of the mule. People don't get to tell me what to write."

When Nathan was silent, Ted said, "And you really pissed me off when you stopped talking about Medicare and started ranting about Galen Hospital and Hygea Corporation."

"I've been after that bunch ever since Hygea became *the* big deal on the healthcare scene."

"And you dragged me into it."

"I needed your help. They're a clever bunch of *nudniks*."

"Not nearly as clever as you."

Nathan lowered his head for a fight. "If you're so smart, Mr. Big Shot Newsman, tell me why tiny Marin County is now the national corporate headquarters for Hygea? We both know those guys like to shout their name from the rooftops. Why a fancy-schmancy bedroom community instead of San Francisco?"

They stood at the edge of the building, Nathan stared absently at the cluster of people milling around the yellow police tape. The cop was still ragging on the crowd, but the bystanders still ignored him, kept staring at the totaled building as though they expected it to reconstruct itself.

"They're the ones behind this *dreck*," Nathan said. "I know it!"

"Who?"

"Hygea!" Nathan said, driving a fist into his palm. "We both know corporations will do anything to get what they want."

Ted stared at the charred mess where the CORPS offices once stood. "Then I'll need everything you've got on Hygea," he said. "And I want to know who's been feeding you your background info ... and the sooner the better."

"A Congressional source," Nathan said. "And that's all you're getting."

"Not good enough."

"*Oy*, you're like a blind man," Nathan said. "Hygea's using a Galen Hospital ethics committee to introduce and push a national agenda to under-fund Medicare. Maybe get rid of it all together."

"And all you're offering up to me is an ethics committee? Hell, they've been on the scene for years."

"Not this one. Galen's added a new one, a different kind, six months ago. This one's supposedly about economics. And the only person that isn't new in the bunch is the administrator, Robert Holt."

"And CORPS' interest?"

"Isn't it obvious?"

Ted pulled out a small notebook and scribbled in it. When he finished, he turned back to Nathan: "If a national healthcare company like Hygea is really trying to bring down Medicare, then there must be a Washington connection." He tapped Nathan lightly on the chest. "Don't hold back on me. I'll need that Washington source of information."

"I can't give it to you."

"You mean you won't," Ted said. "What else do you want to happen before you change your mind?"

Nathan's shoulders sank lower as he stared hard at the destroyed entrance, then stepped forward. A policeman stopped them, checked their IDs, and logged in their names before allowing them to pass.

Broken glass crunched under their feet as they walked through the doorway. "Can you believe this?" Nathan said. "Look what the bastards have done!"

"Maybe it would be best if we didn't go in," Ted said.

"No, I've got to see for myself." As they stepped through what was left of the doorway, he stopped and put a hand on Ted's arm. "Tell me at least you were bringing me some good news this morning."

"If you want to call it that. I wiggled my way into an appointment with Hygea's CEO."

A fresh stream of tears flooded down Sorkin's cheeks. "You know what I hate most about getting old?"

Ted pulled at an earlobe, shook his head.

"I spritz at the drop of a hat." The director took a large paisley handkerchief from his back pocket and scrubbed the tears from his cheeks.

"Bet you were always a crybaby."

It was a few seconds before Nathan spoke. He'd turned into a small man, his face drawn into despair.

"Maybe Myra didn't like you in the beginning, but I always knew you were a *mensch*."

Ted clapped a hand on Nathan's shoulder and laughed. "That's not what you said a few minutes ago."

They moved on through the rooms of the devastated offices. Nathan stopped near the former volunteers' workroom, kicked at the rubble with the toe of his shoe, and bent to pick up a singed poster that miraculously had survived the blast and fire.

He held it up for Ted to see the large photo of a group of people standing in front of a huge CORPS banner. Everyone was smiling and hailing the photographer with a digital salute.

Nathan turned his sad, wistful eyes to Ted. "We begin again."

Bette Golden Lamb & J. J. Lamb

Chapter 4

Ted stepped through the automated doors of Hygea's Galen Hospital. He couldn't believe his eyes. What he remembered was a small local medical facility surrounded by lush lawns and massive flowerbeds. It had all been swallowed up and reincarnated into a corporate campus of steel and concrete.

The vast complex spread out like a huge wagon wheel—a hub with spokes that led to every possible service related to healthcare: Emergency, Trauma, ICU, Surgery, Medical Specialties, Ancillary Services; even a Nursing and Medical school. If it weren't for the detailed array of color-coded directional signs, he would have gone nuts circling through the maze of satellites.

He leaned on the chrome railing of the airport-style walkway. As it carried him toward Administration, he studied a list he'd printed off the internet of Galen's new Bioethical Review Committee members. Only one was familiar: Rev. John F. Bradberry.

The walkway nearly up-ended Ted as he reached his destination. He cursed his inattention when he noticed someone staring at him outside of the brushed metal entry doors to the administration offices.

"John Bradberry?"

The man tilted his head and nodded.

"Ted. Ted Yost." He stepped forward, hand extended. "I thought it was you."

"Good to see you," Bradberry said.

"How have you been?"

Bradberry was silent.

"Well, you look prosperous. I hope everything's good for you."

Bradberry nodded.

"Anyway, what luck running into you. I was just on my way to see Garrett Rudge."

"I doubt he'll see you now. There's a meeting scheduled at ten o'clock."

"The Bioethical Review Committee?"

Bradberry's eyes narrowed. "That's right."

"Seemed logical since you're a member," Ted held up the list he'd been studying. "If you have a moment, maybe you could fill me in on what you guys have been doing the past six months."

Bradberry went through an exaggerated routine of looking at his watch. "I'm almost late now." He half turned to enter the satellite. "Perhaps another time."

Ted touched the minister's shoulder. "I'd appreciate that, John."

He watched Bradberry enter the reception area where he was buzzed through to the inner offices.

Ted stopped at the desk. "I have an appointment to see Garrett Rudge."

The receptionist gave him a questioning look, tapped a few keys on her computer keyboard, studied the monitor, and said, "You're not due until late this afternoon, Mr. Yost."

"I know, but it's very important that I see him as soon as possible."

The woman was dressed in a no-nonsense plain brown suit; two pink spots of blush highlighted her cheeks. Ted wanted to reach out and smooth them away. He jammed his hands into his pants pocket.

"He's truly unavailable until after lunch."

"I'll wait."

He plopped in a chair and tried to focus on a *New Yorker* he found in a stack of outdated magazines on a side table, but his thoughts drifted. He slumped down and thought about his first encounter with Rev. John Bradberry.

* * *

The minute Ted stepped off the plane in Saigon, the humid air became a hot blanket that smothered his skin and made it difficult for him to breathe.

What am I doing in this hellhole?

But rookie reporters do as they're told. That's what. He needed the experience and at least it was a real assignment: Why did the U.S. continue to be in the middle of a war that was destroying our nation's young?

It was that or the obits page.

He spent fourteen exhausting months with a Marine detachment composed mostly of nineteen-year-olds. They climbed in and out of helicopters, ran through heavy jungle undergrowth filled with deadly snakes and roamed through burned-out villages where the people's eyes glowed with hatred.

The decay of the sharp, proud unit into a group of drug-wasted zombies gave him all the ugly answers. The U.S. had turned its "boys" into bitter men who would never quite fit into the American mainstream again.

He'd had it. He planned to return to the States after one final helicopter assault and he didn't give a rat's ass if the *Chronicle* dumped him.

He'd been under heavy fire on most of these runs and managed to keep it together. But today, he knew the damn chopper was going down. He was going to die.

The pilot dropped them on the exposed shore of a muddy river and he forced himself to jump out with the others. The deafening jet engine, the thumping rotor blades, flying dirt, and the clatter of automatic weapons sent him dashing up an embankment. He burrowed into dense underbrush, shaking.

Then silence.

He looked around for some sign of the others.

He was alone—only the sound of his pounding heart thumped in his ears.

He slapped hard at a cloud of bugs eating his face and crawled through the thick undergrowth. One hand after another, he shoved ahead. The only thing that kept him moving was sheer panic and the hope he was going in the direction given at the pre-mission briefing. Right now he couldn't remember any of it.

After 20 minutes in the sopping undergrowth, an explosion startled him—scores of birds flapped skyward.

Ted jammed a hand into his pocket and withdrew his only weapon—a Swiss army knife. After unfolding the largest blade, he pushed himself up into a crouch, knife extended.

The dense vegetation slit open and an American in blood-spattered fatigues stumbled forward cradling the nude corpse of a small Vietnamese girl. The child was ripped apart, bowels bounced against the bloodied man's thigh.

Transfixed by the image, Ted clamped his jaw down against a scream clawing at his throat. He almost didn't see the second blood-drenched girl clinging to the man's leg.

He forced himself upright, stood tall on rubbery legs. The child stared at him with solemn eyes, but the man looked right through him. Ted stepped into their path. The stench of the over-ripe corpse made him gag. He reached out and grabbed the man's dog tags, read the name.

"Chaplain Bradberry!" Ted shouted. "Put her down!"

"I can't," Bradberry whispered. "If I do, she'll die. I *have* to get her to a field hospital. Now!"

"She's dead, Chaplain. There's nothing anyone can do for her."

In a sudden lunge, Bradberry grabbed a fistful of the girl's intestines. "They can! They can! They can put them back. I've seen them! They can do it!"

Ted swallowed hard, positioned his arms under the body, and started to lift her away. The chaplain watched for a moment, then yanked at the corpse, thrusting the two of them into a grotesque tug-of-war.

Only when the tiny girl at Bradberry's side began to cry did they stop. The chaplain tried to soothe the little girl, but held tight onto the dead body.

Ted let go of the corpse and picked up the wailing child. He hugged her close to him, rocked her back and forth, but she still continued to cry.

Loud rustling in the underbrush sent Ted into a panic. He swallowed hard, knew they were surrounded. He pulled the child closer to him, wrapped a protective arm around the chaplain. A figure jumped up through the brush.

"Goddam it, Yost, where the hell have you been?"

"Here! Right here!" he choked out.

"Friggin' civilians!" the Marine sergeant yelled, shaking his head in disbelief. He gave a hand signal to his platoon, then shouted at Ted and the chaplain:

"Get your ass in gear. We're gettin' the hell out of here."

It was only when they got back to the base that Bradberry surrendered the tiny corpse to the medics and became so physically violent, so out of control, he had to be restrained.

The scuttlebutt was that Bradberry had been living with the murdered mother of the girls and had "gone native."

Before leaving Vietnam, Ted visited Bradberry at the military hospital in Saigon. He wanted to know more about the man, more about what had happened in those hills. But the chaplain would talk to no one.

Back in the States, unable to block the visions of the chaplain and the two young girls. Ted searched until he found Bradberry in a California VA hospital.

For six months he visited Bradberry, but the chaplain would sit in silence, stare straight ahead as though Ted wasn't there.

He stopped going.

Now, sitting in Galen Hospital, Ted shivered.

Chapter 5

"Hey, Garr? How's it hangin'? That California sunshine still holding—"

"Someone bombed CORPS yesterday." Rudge blurted it out into the disposable cell. It cut right through the Mickey Mouse gibberish Wade Wilson liked to toss around. "Nailed an old woman. She's close to death."

"CORPS, you say?" Wilson spoke without missing a beat. "Those the left wing bastards who marched on our fair capital last year? "

"The same."

"Them and every other nut group in the good old U S of A. You'd think they owned Washington." Wilson chuckled, obviously amused by his own cleverness.

Rudge held his breath, then let out a long sigh. "You know damn well who they are."

"Why on earth would anyone want to burn out a bunch of old geezers like that?"

Rudge remained silent. He reached across the desk and pushed a chrome ricochet ball, starting the series bouncing one against the other. The rhythm of the sharp clicks calmed him, kept him focused.

"Someone hurt, you say? Well, that'll teach those people to behave with more gentility. Most unbecoming for senior citizens to act like a bunch of teenage hooligans."

"I don't seem to find it as amusing as you do."

"Uh, huh. Uh, huh! Well, lighten up. You got to know they had it coming." A soft snort emphasized the next words. "Can't make an omelet without breaking eggs." Then his voice turned sour. "That old bird was there at the wrong time. That's all. Just some old lady, anyway."

Rudge envied Wade Wilson's power base, but he disliked the way the man made him feel like a sun-dulled lizard.

"Easy for you to say, sitting in your comfortable office three thousand miles away."

"Boy," Wilson's voice turned brittle, "there's nothing comfortable about sitting in D.C. You certainly won't climb that ladder by being comfortable either." A long meaningful pause set Rudge on edge. "You get what I'm saying?"

"What makes you think this will keep CORPS out of our hair?"

"I think it'll slow them down for a spell, and that's all we're buying. Time."

"I suppose you're right."

"Do the police have any suspects?"

"Not yet."

"Too bad."

Rudge could visualize the man leaning back in his chair, feet on his desk, mouthing that phony Southern accent.

"It's going to make it tougher dealing with Ted Yost, though. I haven't been able to wiggle out of meeting with him later today."

"Yost? Now where have I heard that name before?"

Rudge brushed some imaginary lint from his pants. "He's a retired hotshot newsman turned blogger. My informants say he's somehow hooked into CORPS."

"Garr, you worry too much. Who cares about some old newsman? Pretty soon all those newspaper pricks will be dead anyway."

"And your point?"

"Open your eyes, man. Newspapers are like senior citizens." Wilson chuckled. "They're on the way out."

He tapped a pencil on his desk and said nothing.

"Just see what the old fart has to say."

Rudge rolled his eyes to the ceiling. "Again, easy for you to say."

"For cryin'-out-loud! Be respectful, then get rid of him." Wilson's voice had turned to ice. "Listen, I've got to go. Just wanted you to know everything's fine and dandy." He paused for an instant. "I trust there's no trouble with our time frame at your end?"

"Everything's under control."

"That's what I like to hear, Garr. That's what I like to hear."

With a click, Wade Wilson was gone. A mental replay of the terse conversation echoed in his head. It left behind an uneasiness that made him shift in his chair.

That phony southern gentility of Wilson's never camouflaged the deadly snake in the grass. Rudge refused to think about what would happen if he failed to hold up his end.

Deliver ... or cut himself a real piece of trouble.

Bette Golden Lamb & J. J. Lamb

Chapter 6

The Bioethics Committee members were due any minute. Garrett Rudge needed to pull himself together, to forget about the D.C. call. But he was troubled. Partnering with a man like W. Wade Wilson kept you dangling, and as much as Rudge hated it, Wilson owned him...for now.

He sat down and studied the oversized conference table that extended to almost the full length of the small room.

Give them a place to spread their arms and legs or they become inattentive and restless.

But this morning, he was the restless one.

He pushed a finger between his shirt collar and neck, toyed with the knot of his rep silk tie. He sat up tall, shoulders thrown back—slouching wasn't an option when you were shorter than everyone else in the room.

He doodled a scraggly looking five-pointed star, then wadded up the paper and tossed it across the room, smiled as it landed in the wastebasket.

It had been a roller coaster ride since he joined Hygea on his forty-fifth birthday. But in two years he'd accomplished what he'd set out to do: Galen Hospital was now a total healthcare facility, Hygea was a national star, and he was the reason why.

If he could only bring this Wade Wilson project off, and do what else that had to be done, the career payoff would be huge.

"Morning, Garrett." Robert Holt, the hospital's administrator smiled at Rudge and pulled up a chair at the opposite end of the table.

Rudge said nothing, raised a hand, not ready to give up his reverie.

"Helluva week, huh?" Holt said. When Rudge still refused to respond, the man busied himself scribbling notes, probably some useless piece of information.

He stared at Holt. He detested the 63-year-old, couldn't help it. He was a constant reminder of what Rudge couldn't allow himself to become—a burnt-out shell, barely hanging on to his job until retirement. It was hard to believe that this man spent twenty years guiding Galen through some of the most cataclysmic changes in the healthcare industry.

All Rudge saw was someone who didn't contribute much of anything, and had the energy of a slug. Each meeting the drone planted himself in a chair and uttered barely a word when Rudge really needed his support, his voice, his vote.

From day one, he'd wanted to fire Holt, had bitten back the final words any number of times. But the man's twenty years as administrator gave him important alliances, and he had the medical staff in his hip pocket.

It seemed everyone liked Bob Holt—except Rudge.

The other committee members started to file in one by one.

Sarah Silver, the ICU nurse, and Zach Wolfe, the gerontologist, edged into their chairs, and continued to hold hands, even after seating themselves.

If he'd known they were bed partners six months ago when this special committee was created, they would never have been seated at this table. Pillow talk could literally fuck things up

Wolfe had a good reputation with patients but he wasn't one to toe the line. And both he and Silver's smiling faces and easy going manners were deceiving. They had sharp tongues and were aggressive patient advocates. Hard to shut them up at times.

Typical woman—talk an issue to death and come up empty. And the doctor/boyfriend was a smart-ass. Could do without him, too.

The CEO briefly eyed Clifford Michaels, an engineer and the committee's token black. His 6'4'' frame barely fit into his chair.

Word is that you're a fiscal conservative, Mr. African-American. That's why you're here. But I'm still waiting for useful feedback.

Rudge's secretary slipped past the seated committee members and handed Rudge a note. He scanned it and looked up at her.

"He's here? Now? He wasn't supposed to come in until later this afternoon."

She nodded.

"Did you tell him I'm not available?"

"He insisted on waiting."

Rudge waved her away, but knowing that Ted Yost was early made him even edgier.

The other committee members were all in their places when the last member, Rev. John Bradberry, finally slid into his seat.

Like an oversized chessboard, they sat ready to play the game. But could Rudge manipulate the moves of the various pieces scattered around this table or would he find himself with five rogue knights?

* * *

Good morning," Rudge said after Holt called the meeting to order. He paused to pull a small sheaf of papers from his briefcase and placed them carefully on the table in front of him. For a moment he pretended to search for the appropriate words to begin.

"It's been six months since this special committee was formed. Six whole months of weekly meetings. And where are we in the process of altering patient care?" He looked slowly around the room. "Let me enlighten all of you: we are right where we started."

The CEO studied each member again—an actor into his soliloquy. "We need to get down to brass tacks. Effective solutions!"

He picked up the papers in front of him and tossed them into the middle of the table. "We have nothing of substance here. Talk, talk, talk. Do nothing." He smiled stiffly at each person. "Time to take the initiative. That's what you're here for."

"And what's wrong with talking?" Sarah Silver said. "How else can we absorb the mountain of information we've been buried under?"

"What's the bloody hurry, anyway?" Zach Wolfe said, shifting in his seat.

"The number of hospitals throughout the country is decreasing drastically every year," Rudge said. "It doesn't stop while we sit here and shoot the breeze."

"Is that what we're doing?" Wolfe asked.

"I wouldn't call these get-togethers shooting the breeze," Silver snapped. "At least it's not my idea of fun and games,"

"Galen's under the hammer, Sarah."

"Brass tacks! Hammers!" Bradberry blurted. "Hype. Industry hype. That's all it is."

"We need to take action. Now! That's not hype, Reverend."

"We all know the state of healthcare in this country. We didn't need to invest six months of meetings to find that out."

"Your point, Reverend?"

"Excuse me." Wolfe held up a restraining palm to the minister. "Let *him* cut to the chase, Reverend." He turned to the CEO. "What *do* Galen and Hygea have planned, Garrett?"

"I have—"

"—specifically," Bradberry said, "what does Hygea have planned to assist old people, poor people?"

"More questions? We all know the questions," Rudge said. "It's the answers we're looking for."

"And *your* answers?" Bradberry said, pointing a finger at Rudge.

"Look at our older population, Reverend. Their numbers have increased at a staggering rate. And then we have the baby boomers. They're further complicating the whole scenario." He tossed out a hand. "Basic facts you seem to keep sliding over."

"Me slide? You're the one who still refuses to answer direct questions. Where are the healthcare standards planned for Medicare patients and people with no money?"

"We all know that funds subsidizing that kind of care have melted faster than the Arctic ice. This is a for-profit hospital." Rudge glared at the minister. "Bottom line: Galen can no longer afford to treat everyone who comes through our doors."

"Galen will *not* treat certain patients?" Michaels asked.

"People still die. We all die. Ultimately, there are no miracles."

"Don't patronize me," Michaels said. "You haven't answered my question ... you haven't answered *any* of our questions. We're talking about those who will never get a shot at Galen's state-of-the-art technology."

Rudge pointed at the black man. "Are you accusing Hygea or Galen Hospital of discrimination?"

"Can you guarantee it doesn't exist?" Michaels shot back.

Rudge took a deep breath. He needed to slow down the pace. "Let's do what this committee was designed to do: focus on the seriously ill and dying elderly population. These are the patients who can run up astronomical costs for a single hospital admission."

Bradberry shot up out of his seat. "Garrett, you want us to underwrite a policy that allows selected patients to die without the hospital making any effort to save them ... because of the expense?"

"We need new guidelines, Reverend. That's why we're here in the first place." Rudge lowered his voice. "If a patient's prognosis is poor, and he or she is elderly, then we should seriously consider termination of care."

"Shut down life support systems?" Silver's eyes went wide, her mouth dropped.

Rudge cringed. The nurse's soft malleable face had turned to stone.

"Cut medical care when the cost-to-benefit ratio doesn't meet corporate goals?" Bradberry said.

"You all know," Rudge said, "that we've been turning off life support systems for a long, long time."

"I'm not interested in yesterday," Michaels said. "We're talking about tomorrow." The black man was composed but his eyes probed Rudge.

"What I'm suggesting," Rudge said, "is that we take the next logical step."

Bradberry slammed a fist down on the table. "Selective euthanasia of the elderly? That's your next logical step? That's your solution to the high cost of healthcare?"

"We need a policy that allows us to devote the appropriate time, care, and resources to patients whose prognoses are more favorable."

"And can afford them?" Silver said.

"You're asking us to condone murder!" Bradberry shouted at Rudge.

Rudge jumped up. "That word is not acceptable. We're here to find medical solutions within the law." He glared at the reverend. "What did you think these meetings were about?"

"What I may have thought in the beginning," Bradberry said, "or even until a few minutes ago, doesn't matter."

"Solutions! That's what we need. Drastic solutions. Humane, yes. But still drastic."

"Am I the only naïve one here," Bradberry said, "the only one who thinks there must be a better way?"

"Wake up! You've seen all the projections. How did you think we were going to lower our costs?" "I thought this was about bioethics," Silver interrupted. "Now we're talking about budgets."

"Ethics, budgets, cost containment. That's the whole picture," Rudge said, as if explaining it to a nitwit. "And if any of you doubt that, then you don't understand the problem.

Chapter 7

Dick Abrams visualized the scatter of important papers covering his desk, and smack in the middle was a long list of things that *had* to get done today.

But he realized thoughts like that were only a distraction; he'd damn well better focus on President John Armistead Tyler who was waiting for him in the Oval Office.

He glanced at his freshly shined shoes and made sure any stray bits of dandruff were absent from his dark suit. Of course he'd already checked all of that before leaving for his appointment, but he knew the President was strangely obsessive about the grooming of everyone who came to see him. With all the things on a President's agenda, Abrams never could never understand his rabid obsession with how people should present themselves.

Like anyone was going to go into the Oval office looking like a slob?

Maybe the President was worried about offending the Great Seal of the United States woven in the middle of the rug in that cloistered room, or maybe he thought the portrait of Abraham Lincoln gave his long dead hero a viewing site from the grave.

That tickled his funny bone.

He nodded to several of the Secret Service personnel and checked his watch to make sure he was on time for his appointment.

"Hi, Josi," he said to a new intern he'd been introduced to only the day before.

"Hi, Mr. Abrams."

"Call me Dick," he said, slowing for a half a second before picking up the pace. He waved as he continued on, returning her wide smile. It took all his concentration to keep his eyes on her face instead of traveling to where her huge breasts were barely contained in a conservative blouse and suit. His wife would kill him if she knew what was going on in his head.

Hell, she doesn't know the half of it.

It was probably juvenile but even after three years as Chief of Staff he still got a rise out of strolling down the West Wing of the White House. He allowed himself that bit of vanity. After all, he was a part of the Executive Branch, and at the operative core of John Armistead Tyler's administration.

As he walked into the Oval office, his eyes rested on the President, backlit by a wintry sun coming in through three large spotless windows. He looked at ease and unexplainably comfortable for someone who'd had a very rough three years in office. War, pollution, global warming, energy problems, and healthcare costs were not issues the President liked to focus on and his poll numbers reflected his lack of involvement.

Plainly put, his stats were in the toilet.

There was no denying it—he was a lightweight in the accomplishment column and the voters knew it. If Tyler had any hope of winning again, or propping those size thirteens on the ornate desk for another four years, he needed to show his stuff.

And he would need something awesome.

Abrams thought about three years earlier when he'd been asked to serve as the President's Chief Of Staff. Like an idiot, he'd simply walked away from his Senate seat.

Actually, it wasn't quite that simple.

Becoming Chief lost him the opportunity to chair the Senate Banking, Housing and Urban Affairs Committee. At the time he'd been blinded by the President's declaration that there was no one with a better handle on the nation's pulse ... and his country needed him.

Ego. Every politician's undoing.

"I'm still not convinced about this Desisto thing," the President said. "I don't even want to think about what the opposition would do to me if it gets out. Hell, even a whisper before we're ready and I'm toast."

"No worse than what they'll do to you when Medicare goes dry," said Abrams.

"I gotta tell you, Dick, the whole concept scares the poop out of me."

It pissed Abrams off when the president's diction slipped into his back hills Southern roots, especially when he got caught up in complex situations.

"No doubt we'll have to play down the fact the program will be of greater benefit to budgetary problems than to actual healthcare," Abrams said.

"That's the least of my worries," Tyler said "The public hates government no matter what government does." The chief executive's frown deepened. "I still don't think that I can get away with putting my stamp of approval on a program of selective euthanasia. No matter what kind of fancy words the spin doctors use to describe it." The President picked up a carafe of water, filled a glass, and took a sip as if he was trying to get a bad taste out of his mouth.

"Who does Maurice Seldon have ram-rodding this thing?"

"Wilson," Abrams said.

"W. Wade Wilson?" The President leaned forward across his desktop. When he received a quick nod of assent from Abrams, he added, "What's he doing mucking around with Desisto? And why wasn't I told.?"

"It's what's happening, sir." Abrams said. He raised his palms upward and shrugged.

"I don't like being kept in the dark. You know that." Tyler picked up a solid silver casino chip, a gift from a Nevada delegation that had paid a visit earlier in the day. He drummed his fingers on the desk. "I thought our esteemed HHS Secretary was going to find someone inconspicuous to carry the ball on Desisto. Hell, that's why I put that idiot in Health and Human Services in the first place—to follow orders." He manipulated the chip through the fingers of one hand like a seasoned gambler.

"That was the plan. But Hygea and Wilson didn't think Seldon was moving fast enough, so they sort of did an end run around him and stepped up the pace."

"Damn that Wilson! He'll be the death of me yet." The President flipped the chip in the air, caught it with one hand, and slapped it down on the back of his other hand. He gently rolled back the covering hand as if revealing something momentous. "How do you tell heads from tails on a casino chip?" he asked, squinting at Abrams with one eye closed.

"What?"

"Never mind." He placed the chip in the center of his desk, pushed it slowly this way and that with his index finger. "That Wilson plays politics like it was a game of roulette. Moves his bet around until he finds a hot spot, then rides with it."

"He did help you get elected, Mr. President."

"Yeah, and in between he helped finance a couple of reelection campaigns that allowed the opposition to gain control of the Senate."

"So why don't you tell Seldon to get rid of him?" Abrams didn't bother to hide his distaste for Wilson.

The President cocked his head to one side and gave Abrams a do-I-need-to-answer-that look, then said, "The man sits on a mountain of money, and he gets things done."

Abrams grinned. "Just making sure we're both still working from the same get-elected-at-any-cost script."

"I suppose it doesn't really surprise me that a controlling son-of-bitch like Wilson would take to Desisto like a fish to water." Tyler was getting agitated. "But getting into bed with Wilson could leave me standing bare-assed on the White House lawn. That man would rent out his mother for medical experiments, if the price was right."

"Well, Seldon thinks you should take another shot at assisted euthanasia."

"And that from a man who's dumb as a post. Dick, I'm leaving that pile of crap alone. Everyone who's ever tampered with that has gone down in flames. Mess with it again and I might as well concede the election here and now. No, thank you!" He spun around and stared out the window for a moment, then whipped back around to face Abrams. "Wasn't Seldon the one who brought us the Desisto Project in the first place?"

"I believe you're right, sir."

"So what's going on? Am I missing something? Why isn't Seldon here to explain any of this?"

The President picked up the telephone. "Katie? See if Maurice Seldon's around the Capitol anywhere. If he is, I'd like to see him. Now! Thanks."

"So?" Abrams queried.

"So, the next time I start talking about appointing someone from the opposition to a cabinet post, it's going to be your responsibility to start chanting: Seldon, Seldon, Seldon."

* * *

"Mr. President," Maurice Seldon said. "As I've said before…we can't tamper with the existing healthcare package this late in the term. It's my recommendation that Desisto be initialed immediately."

The staff had tracked the HHS Secretary down in the White House exercise room and made it clear the President was waiting.

John Tyler never got tired of having people at his beck and call. He was known for pulling people from any department on a "right now" basis for the slimmest of reasons. At the moment, he was enjoying Seldon's discomfort at standing in gym clothes in the Oval Office.

Tyler stared at the HHS Secretary and Dick Abrams, who shared a leather couch on the other side of a glass coffee table.

"We've had meeting after meeting about this, Maurice," the President said. "And frankly, my attitude hasn't changed one iota: I don't want fingers pointing at me."

"Mr. President," continued Seldon, "please believe me when I tell you that we all share that concern."

"Don't patronize me! And those grass roots bioethical committees Hygea created across the country? I can't believe anyone with their wits about them would approve something like Desisto."

"Nothing's finalized, Mr. President. Everyone knows nothing happens without your final signature."

"And what makes you think I want any part of it?"

"Because we're giving the people what they need with Desisto," Seldon said. "After all, isn't it our moral obligation to preserve the financial integrity of the nation?"

"What's your point?" The man irritated him. Always stating the obvious.

Seldon stared at his scuffed cross-trainers for a moment before answering. "You've been trying to push through your Middle East program for three years now, right?"

"Yes, and if we'd held control of the Congress at mid-term—"

"But you didn't, and you won't this next time, either, unless you come up with a dazzler that puts you back in the running. Right now, Desisto appears to offer what your Administration needs. Unless, of course, you want to be remembered as the president who wiped out Social Security and Medicare in a single term of office."

"You know, Mr. Secretary...uh, Maurice, I sometimes wonder just whose side you're on."

"I'm here only at your pleasure, Mr. President."

The President looked from Seldon to Abrams. "I don't like moving in the open like this," he said, giving them both a stony stare. "Is it really Desisto or lose the election?"

They both nodded.

The President rose and paced back and forth between the chair and his desk. "Who ever dreamed up this ridiculous cloak and dagger name—Desisto Project? Was that you, Maurice? Because it looks more like a conspiracy than a project."

"I really can't remember, Mr. President," answered the HHS secretary. "Probably came from the same think tank that created the scenario in the first place."

"They call that *thinking*?" He roughly spun the antique globe that stood behind his desk. "I'll bet that idea came out of some healthcare company's fertile, twisted imagination. Either way, I still don't like it."

"No one *likes* it," Seldon said.

"But you're proposing it, nevertheless."

"If we're going to save Medicare," Seldon said, "it's an absolute necessity."

"Don't lecture me," the President snapped. He sat back down behind his desk and nodded at Seldon. "I still want to know how W. Wade Wilson is mixed up in this Desisto thing."

"Wade came in, looked down from the top of a huge pile of Hygea money, offered a few suggestions, and I let him run with them."

"He's a lobbyist, damn it. And now I'm told he's considered the lead dog."

"What difference does that make, Mr. President? We need him … and his connections."

It wasn't the kind of answer Tyler wanted to hear, but he didn't pursue it. "Thank you for coming over on such short notice, Mr. Secretary," he said, eyeing the sodden exercise clothes.

"I'm always at your disposal, Mr. President," Seldon said.

"Yes, well, remember, I don't want this thing blowing up in my face. It's me, John Armistead Tyler, the historians will roast, not you."

"That's always foremost in my mind, Mr. President. Perhaps we can find a way to hang the whole thing on Congress."

"Now wouldn't that be nice, especially considering the lack of cooperation they've given this term." He spun around and took in the panoramic window view. "See what you can do to

accomplish that. See what that fucking W. Wade Wilson can do."
He raised a hand, dismissing Seldon.

Once the HHS secretary was out of the room, the President
got up, walked around his desk, and sat down next to Abrams on
the couch. "What do you think?"

"About what?"

"Don't play coy with me, Dick. How sincere is Seldon about
Desisto?"

"Maybe you should talk to W.W. about that," Abrams said.

"No, just give me a reading."

"Seldon's a political animal, Mr. President. Not only that, a
member of the opposition party. I'll keep an eye on him."

"If you so much as look like you're going to say 'I told you
so,' I'll personally put you on a bus back to Seattle."

"We're all always at your disposal, Mr. President."

"Asshole!"

"Like I said, I'll keep an eye on Seldon."

"Good! I don't want him resigning before the election."

"You mean you'll need someone to blame if Desisto goes
sour, and who better than a semi-loyal member of the opposition,
along with Congress?"

"Screw you, Dick Abrams."

"What about W. Wade Wilson?" Abrams said.

"Yeah, well screw him, too." He took ion a deep breath and
sighed. "But not before this whole mess is settled."

Chapter 8

"Today's census report," Garrett Rudge's assistant said, handing him a computer-generated printout. Rudge placed the papers in the center of his desk without looking up.

"Thanks."

"Don't forget Mr. Yost. He's still in the waiting room." She turned and left the office.

Rudge hadn't forgotten. He just didn't want that man in his waiting room, now or ever. He'd even used the rear entrance to his office coming from the committee meeting to keep from seeing him until it was absolutely necessary.

He frowned as he scanned the 24-hour readout of the hospital's patient population and their medical status, focusing on recent admissions.

At first glance, the report was mostly the expected hospital entries. Then he zeroed in on two patients listed as critical:

Myra Jackson—78 years. Trauma patient. Multi-system injuries.

To OR for surgical removal of foreign object in the mediastinum.

Massive blood loss. Extremely critical.

Della Paoli—66 years. Stroke vs. automobile trauma -ICU.

Unresponsive. Critical.

He took his gold Cross pen from the inside pocket of his jacket and slowly circled both names.

Gathering the papers from the desktop, he slipped them into the thin glove-leather portfolio and pulled out his notebook computer.

Things were looking up.

47

He punched in Jackson's name and searched for a status update, then did the same for Paoli. Nothing new on either of them. He tapped the keyboard then brought up the women's demographics and personal insurance records.

Myra Jackson

Next of Kin: Stanley Jackson, nephew; #7 Boardwalk Plaza, Tiburon CA. (415) 555-8832.
Medicare: Part A & B. Active
Address: 4022 Geary, 2C, San Francisco CA

Rudge tapped both the Medicare double coverage and the upscale address with his pen, then checked the other critical care patient on the list.

Della Paoli:

Next of kin: None
Medicare: Part A. Part B—Not Active.
Address: 4555 Grove St. San Rafael.

He looked again at the "Next of kin" entry for Paoli, and the Marin County address, which he knew was in a rundown part of San Rafael. He leaned back in his chair, smiled, and took a deep breath. The serene moment passed quickly when the intercom buzzed on his desk.

"Yes?"

"Sorry to interrupt, Mr. Rudge, but Mr. Yost is still in the reception area. He won't leave, no matter what I tell him."

"Okay, okay. I'll just be a moment."

He reached into his portfolio and pulled out a disposable cell phone, punched in a long string of numbers, waited for the caller-protecting circuitry to connect him to Wade Wilson's office. He stood and paced in a tight figure eight behind his desk.

"Government Relations," a female voice said. He knew it was Wilson's young assistant, Calli Morin.

"George Desisto calling," he said.

"If you'll hold, please, Mr. Desisto, I'll check to see if Mr. Wilson's available." In a few seconds she was back on the line. "I'm sorry, sir, but Mr. Wilson is out of the office."

Rudge replaced the receiver and again started pacing, this time the length of the office, his memory flipping through the earlier committee meeting. But that only silenced his restlessness for a brief time. He waited for Wilson to return his coded call and when the phone finally rang, he jumped and grabbed at it.

* * *

"Hey," Wilson said, "what's the emergency? I was going to call you after lunch."

"Are you on a safe line?"

"Gawl darn, this constant paranoia doesn't suit you, son. And it's starting to get under my skin."

Rudge ignored the exasperation in Wilson's voice. "I'm worried"

"Oh? Anything that would delay our plans?"

"No, not that. In fact, I may have some good news."

"So, let's have the good news first," Wilson said.

"We have two candidates. The preliminaries indicate one in particular has the potential to match the optimum profile."

"When will you know for certain?"

"Possibly late today—"

"Halleluiah! That's great news. And I just got the word that Desisto is a definite go. We are officially on count-down."

Rudge dropped into his chair, dizzy from a rush of adrenaline. His hands began to shake; he couldn't speak.

"Did you hear me, Garr?"

"Yes, of course. Sorry. I was just looking for an update on the candidate." He reached for a handkerchief and dabbed at his forehead.

"Anything?"

"Not yet."

"I want up-to-the-minute reports, Garr. If it works out, we'll hit the target date right on the nail."

"I'll keep an hourly tab on the patient's progress."

"There you go. So what's the bad news?"

"Ted Yost."

"We already discussed that snoopy bastard."

"Well, talking about him and having to deal with him in person are two different matters."

"Garrett, don't cry on my shoulder about piddling nothings."

"Yeah, well, if Yost and CORPS have joined forces, you won't be able to toss them off as a piddling."

"Monkeywrenchers! Just like that damn environmental bunch of losers. And of course the ACLU will find a way to step in, too. And God knows who else." A harsh blast of laughter made Rudge's ear tingle. "Who the hell is going to listen to any of them—until it's too late?"

"Maybe, but it feels dicey to me."

Wilson laughed. "Yost's just a retired, old fart."

"I've been checking into the old fart's background."

"So have I, Garr. So have I."

"Then you know he's always been a troublemaker. And since he's started blogging, he goes right for the balls on any subject that attracts his left-leaning attention. He may be old, but that doesn't mean he's not dangerous."

"Let *me* worry about that tiny pimple on your ass."

There was a long uncomfortable silence before Rudge responded. "My butt isn't the only one that's hanging out in the breeze."

"Whoa, man. Before you get your bowels in an uproar, let's think the situation through."

"*You* think it through! I'm the one dangling at the end of this trial balloon. If anything goes wrong, you and your Washington friends are going to crash with me."

"Calm down, boy. There are other ways to deal with this troublemaker."

"Such as?"

Long pause. "Let's find out more about the man. For instance, does Yost have marital problems?"

"What kind of sleezy crap is that, Wade? Bringing his family into—"

"I said this was a secure line, but it's still not the best place to discuss this kind of thing. Get me?"

A sharp pain stabbed Rudge's eye, the flashing lights of a migraine washed out his vision. "It's just that Yost seems pretty damn chancy to me."

"Geez, you send me up a tree. For Christ's sake, relax." Wilson's ease with words belied a will laced with steel. "We have the full backing and support of the Executive Branch of the U. S. of A. What more do you want?"

"I don't want to feel like the fall guy in this project," Rudge said. "Politicians' alliances change on a whim."

"For a bright man you're pretty stupid at times."

"Asking questions doesn't make me stupid."

"Get with it, Garr. The Administration has a critical national problem on its hands. No, make that a national disaster." Wilson's voice turned soothing. "Believe me, they need this Desisto balloon to fly."

Rudge fought with the pain that tore at his head. "And if it flies away, I'm still the one dangling."

"Hell, no one said it was going to be easy. But you bring this off, and there'll be no stopping you. Probably be running Health and Human Services before the year is out." Wilson chuckled. "We know how to take care of our own."

"Listen to me, Wade! Yost is trouble. He's made a career out of hacking his way through red tape and bullshit. And right now, he's sitting outside my office, not yours."

The pause was so long this time that he almost asked whether Wilson was still there. But then he spoke again. "Two calls in one day about the same guy. Maybe you aren't the right man for this project after all."

He wiped at the beads of sweat that bubbled up on his forehead. "I need reassurance and I'm not getting from you."

"Uh-huh, uh-huh. So tell me about the committee," Wilson said, ignoring the jibe. "What's the current status? Will we get the votes we need?"

"I think so, but it's not in the bag yet."

"I thought you told me they...understood?"

"They understand all right."

"So, will they bite the bullet?"

"They're wearing down. It's turning into just another problem to solve so they can get the hell out of that conference room. Euthanasia? What's for dinner? Selective euthanasia? Who's fixing the damn toilet? Drone on, drone on. "

"So you're going to give them the easy solution, so they can go home and get on with their lives?"

"That's the plan."

"You're a wily varmint, Garr. Probably why we like you."

"I still don't like this head-to-head with Yost. The man's a doer."

"Oh, for Christ's sake, I'm up to my neck with this bellyaching. You have a committee of five reputable people, unlimited resources—social workers, federal and state studies, legislative study committees, academic studies, etcetera, etcetera. By the time Yost's able to wade through that moat of shit, we'll have skedaddled into green pastures."

"I don't know, Wade—"

"Now wait a minute." There was a long pause before Wilson spoke again. "I'd hate to think you're having doubts about our project."

"Don't be ridiculous!" he said, his voice taking a condescending bent. "I'm fully committed to the concept. But it would be stupid to ignore someone like Yost rallying the troops; it could be one hell of a battle."

"There's no time for a battle. I just put you on the fast track."

"Yeah, and I'm running as fast as I can. But I don't want this guy to trip me or slow me down before I get to the finish line." He started the chrome balls on his desk ricocheting into each other. Click. Click.

"So when's your next committee meeting?"

"Monday morning at ten." Click. Click.

"And we do have a candidate?"

"Like I said, it's looking good." Click. Click. Click. "Hell, if we're lucky, maybe by then we'll have a couple of people to choose from."

Silence

"Listen carefully. Giving that committee a choice could blow the whole thing."

"I don't understand—" Wade Wilson always had an ace up his sleeve. Rudge had been smart to record all their conversations, stash them in a safety deposit box.

"Give them one person, one human being they can relate to," Wilson said. "They'll need to feel they've done something positive, something worthwhile. We don't want them thinking Holocaust."

"I hadn't thought about it that way."

There was another stretch of silence.

"Wade, are you there?"

"I'll tell you, Garr, sometimes when I hear myself talking like this, when I bully, step on, push people around, I *know* I've become a cold bastard. But that's neither here nor there. We have to think of the greater good."

"I know."

"Man, the country's drowning in old, poor, sick people. Medicare is dying. We've got to start changing the numbers."

"I believe that," Rudge said, his headache starting to ebb.

"You handle the grass roots situation, I'll handle the politics and anything else that needs fixin'. And I assure you, I don't envy your end one little bit. But when you bring this off, you're going to have a lot of high-placed people in your pocket."

Silence.

Wilson finally spoke again. "Remember, by next week it will be all be over."

Rudge swiveled in his chair to look out the window. He restarted the metal balls, ricocheting one against the other.

Chapter 9

Wade Wilson hopped a little two-step around his desk, then pulled out a disposable cell and used the same protocol Rudge had used to reach him.

While he waited for Maurice Seldon to return his call, he did a mental playback of his conversation with Hygea's top man in California.

Rudge had shown real alpha aggression during their conversation—a nasty warning to Wilson. The Hygea CEO was a key player, the linchpin in the whole equation. If he couldn't bring *all* of Hygea's regional committees on board, the entire project was lost before they were in the ball park. W.W. had depended on Rudge's raw ambition to keep him in line, but maybe he'd underestimated the man.

And the journalist?

No matter what he'd said to Rudge, Yost was a real fly in the ointment. A snooping newsman in cahoots with CORPS was the last thing he needed at this point.

He would have to handle it.

When the Secretary of Health and Human Services called back, Wilson jumped in without preliminaries, "Desisto is on schedule and should be up and running next week."

"Great news!" Seldon said. "I knew Hygea would come through for us."

"Rudge is carrying the ball like a real pro."

"I assume then that I can relay this to the Chief of Staff and the President?"

"Of course."

"Excellent! Excellent!" Seldon sounded more relieved than elated.

When Wilson hung up, he frowned, then congratulated himself for not mentioning the budding partnership between CORPS and Ted Yost.

* * *

Maurice Seldon enjoyed all the perks that being Secretary of HHS brought his way. For instance he couldn't recall the last time he'd found it necessary to buy a disposable cell phone, leave his office, and hide out in the open to make a private call.

He didn't like it.

He observed the walkway's foot traffic; no one seemed interested in him nor was anyone close enough to hear what he had to say. Satisfied, his gaze rose, rested on the towering Washington Monument as he made his call.

"He'll run with it?" The voice was demanding, harsh in his ear.

"Damn well better if he wants to get re-elected." Seldon had not wanted to make this call, but he'd had no choice: this was the man who'd convinced him to accept when Tyler held the cabinet post out to him; this was the man who controlled the contributions that could send him back to Congress. A tough old bird, he was not afraid to step on toes, to alienate friend and foe alike; far right of any Blue Dog Democrat, but still the man who controlled the Democratic purse strings in Seldon's home state.

Seldon was suddenly distracted by walker coming toward him, a man almost too perfect in appearance—thirties, buzz cut, a *Washington News-Sentinel* clamped under one arm, a large Starbucks cup clutched in the other hand.

"Everyone wants to get re-elected," the politico snapped. "The point is, does Tyler have the courage, the guts to do what needs to get done to keep the nation from being sucked into a fucking bottomless pit?"

"Is he a true American patriot? If that's what you're asking, the answer is no," Seldon said. "Bottom line, he's running scared and wants to stay in the White House."

"Obviously! But Medicare is a financial albatross. If Tyler doesn't take positive action to solve the problem, he won't survive, you won't survive, and the country won't survive. You do understand that don't you ... he will not survive ... you will not survive ... the country will not survive?"

Seldon held back a response, waited for the person closing in to pass, move out of hearing range. Their eyes never met, the other man's movements were stiff and unnatural.

Probably some damn low-level Fibby tailing me. Wouldn't be the first time my opponents tried to turn my ass into a dart board.

"Are you there?" the phone voice demanded.

Seldon waited.

"Do you hear me? We're talking about survival. Everyone's survival. Do you understand that or not? Are you ready to sacrifice your career for the good of our country?" There was a brief pause. "Seldon?"

The man with the newspaper was still on the perimeter. Seldon turned his back on him and stared up at the 500-foot obelisk again.

The voice screamed in his ear. "For God's sake, Seldon, tell me: do you think the President will do what needs to be done?"

"It'll be touch and go."

* * *.

"Sorry to bother you," Seldon said when Dick Abrams picked up at the other end.

"No problem other than you almost missed me."

"Things are moving fast," Seldon said. "We're running with Desisto."

"Great news! Then everything's in place? What about the senator? Still damn hard to put my trust in a liberal."

Seldon laughed so hard it took him a second or two to stop. "Not this one—this one will jump up and down like a puppet."

"You seem pretty sure about that."

"Listen, you may not like old W. W., but you've got to give the man his due. He plays those senators like a Stradivarius." Seldon laughed again. "This particular liberal has been placed in the catbird seat, but it's W. W.'s claws that'll do the snaring."

"Must be a good sound bite in there somewhere, Maurice. But are you sure the Senator will do it?"

"Oh, I'm sure Wade Wilson will take care of that end very nicely."

Chapter 10

Ted Yost was into a slow boil. He shifted back and forth in his seat, even thought about having a cigarette. He stared hard at a plaque on the reception desk that screamed at him in bold black letters:

THIS IS A NON-SMOKING FACILITY

Twenty years since he'd had a cigarette and no corporate ghoul like Garrett Rudge was going to make him take on that filthy habit again.

But bad habits die hard. He could almost feel the pleasure of the smoke curling in his lungs. He took a couple of deep breaths to wipe away the nicotine memory.

Today's reality: the receptionist was totally ignoring him and he'd been sitting in this uncomfortable seat for more than two hours.

He uncrossed, re-crossed his legs again and again and thought about the beginning of his career. Fresh out of journalism school, it had been pure stubbornness, combined with the ambition to be top-notch, that got him one-on-one interviews with those who lived in the upper stratospheres.

It was heady stuff. And he missed it.

He rubbed at his neck, then leaned over to stare at the dark brown industrial grade carpet. Ugly.

Blogging was a new and different experience—he was out there on his own without the official backing or protection of a metropolitan daily newspaper, international wire service, or national weekly news magazine. It was liberating in a way—strange and scary. But it kept him in the game, kept semi-retirement from hampering his need to dig out the truth, no matter who got caught in the crosshairs.

Truth, his elusive adversary. Always demanding, heavier than any albatross.

Ted slumped down in the uncomfortable chair, wondering if working with CORPS would accomplish anything. He still wasn't comfortable with the association—when did any of these organizations really get anything done?

He rubbed his knee, looked at the exit and thought about his novel again. Instead of hanging around Garrett Rudge's office, he should be home pounding out that great American novel—a cloaked autobiography, of course. What else was there left to tell?

The beginning would be about as interesting as watching paint dry—nothing fascinating about the small Ohio town where he grew up. The fact that family hardships forced him to shoulder adult responsibilities at an early age was not only deadly dull, but pretty much a cliché for many families.

He was the eldest of five and an only son, so his father, a cobbler, had no choice but to rely on him to help make and repair shoes even before Ted turned nine.

He worked in his father's shop, delivered newspapers, picked up odd jobs when and where he could while his younger sisters handled all of the household chores. It was hard work. Ted remembered going to bed most nights, not only exhausted, but hungry. The family barely survived.

His mother spent her days doing little more than praying, whether at home or in the nearby church.

When Ted got up in the morning, she was praying; while his sisters fixed breakfast and got everything ready, she was praying. When he came home from school, she was praying; when he left for the shop, or returned from his paper route, she was praying.

At some point he accepted that praying what she did—her contribution to the family.

But one day he overheard his mother and father arguing and he found out that the money he worked so hard for was not helping to buy food or pay the rent, but was given to the church by his mother. Almost over-night, he changed from a dutiful son to a loud-mouthed brat.

His mother added screaming at him to her daily ritual of praying. The more she warned about the loss of his immortal soul, the more his exhausted father tried to smooth things over, the more Ted hated both his mother and father.

Then the nightmares started.

At first, they happened only occasionally, but as the tension grew, waking in the night became routine. He would cry out, then, drenched in sweat, he would yell until the neighbors banged on the walls.

His father bartered an appointment with a doctor who said Ted was physically fit, but run down, overworked, and needed rest. Over his mother's objections, Ted was sent away to his grandmother's farm.

Ted picked up an outdated magazine from a low table in the reception room and flipped through the pages, stopped at a Gucci ad and wondered what his father would have said if someone ordered a shoe like that.

He closed the magazine and glanced up at the generic art work that decorated the reception room walls. The paintings were all pretty much alike in their nothingness, but in one corner was a child's sketch of a red barn. It was beautifully framed and stood out—a kid's statement about something simple, yet grand. It was almost a duplicate of his grandma's barn on the small farm off a back road in Ohio.

Ted stood to stretch his stiffening legs, then walked a couple of circles around the reception area, thinking about that long summer when he was eleven years old.

* * *

Ted stepped off the stuffy bus in the tiny, under-populated town of Oler, a few miles from where his grandmother lived. His extra clothes were packed in an old sheet, which he'd knotted closed and hoisted over one shoulder.

There was no one there to greet him when he arrived and he had to ask several people for directions to get to the farm. He hitched rides and walked and when he got there, he found his grandmother on her knees in the front yard, attacking a green and yellow carpet-like spread of dandelions.

"Grandma!" he called out as he ran up the path.

She smiled, stabbed the weeding tool into the ground, and used the handle to push herself to her feet. She flicked her hands with disgust at the yard full of weeds before opening her arms to him and pulling him into a big hug.

Ted didn't know his grandmother very well, had only seen her a few times at large family gatherings. But at that moment, it was as if they'd always been together.

"Little Teddy Yost.," she said. "Humph, and not so little anymore." She took a step back and studied him; he was almost as tall as she was.

What ever worries he'd had about coming to the farm for the summer were suddenly gone.

"You get on into the house this instant and change out of those city clothes," she said. "Then we'll get some good honest farm dirt on you."

They spent the rest of the day strolling, looking at the buildings, animals, and crops. Wherever he turned, there was lots of space, room for him to fit into. And the amazing taste of the air—it remained on the tip of his tongue to this day.

That first night, his nightmare returned. The same one he always had—blood-thirsty demons chasing him, catching him, and ripping out his tongue.

He awoke, gagging, battling with the sheets, his face burning with tears. His grandmother came rushing into the room.

"What is it, Teddy?" She hugged him in her arms, rocked him back and forth.

He groaned, but couldn't speak.

"It's all right; boy. It's all right."

After a while, she asked again, "What is it?"

"Demons!" he gasped. "Demons from hell, Grandma. They were everywhere. I couldn't get away from them." He clasped his hand to his mouth, felt his lips, then his tongue. "They cut it out!" he cried. "My tongue, Grandma, it was gone."

She planted a big kiss on his cheek, squeezed him tighter. "Too much excitement for one day. It's only a dream, Teddy. A bad dream. I can assure you, there are no demons in this house. I mean, not that there aren't such things, it's just that they've never been able to put up with me."

And then he was smiling.

"That's better! Now, what's this all about?"

He wanted to tell her how he felt, but he couldn't find the right words.

By the time summer was almost gone, Ted had fewer and fewer nightmares. He also began to understand more about himself.

He explored the farm, fed the animals, and watched how his grandmother improvised, made things work without any real effort. Everything was so much easier, simpler. He felt better; and finally understood that he was safe.

On one of their last afternoons, the two of them sat on the rickety porch swing and snapped beans and sipped fresh lemonade.

"Do you believe in God, Grandma?"

Without losing the rhythm of swinging, stringing, and snapping, she said: "Oh, yes, Teddy, I certainly do believe in God."

"Why?" he asked and wiped at his brow. The slim glass tube of red mercury on a large "Coca Cola" thermometer on a nearby shed showed 96°.

Estelle Yost leaned back in the swing, smiled, and took a sip of lemonade. "An intelligent question, Teddy," she said after awhile. "Kind of thing we all get to wondering about now and then—who are we; why do we exist. That sort of thing, right?"

He nodded.

"I'm not a learned woman, Teddy. Barely got through high school, having to always take care of my younger brothers and sisters. But I can tell you, even in my darkest hours, I've always believed in God. The thing is, though, my idea of just who or what God is has changed more than a mite over the years. I'm not sure why, but I seem to have a little better handle on things. Either I just got older, or I've become a little tetched from having lived alone for so many years."

"Aw, there's nothing wrong with you, Grandma." He gave her a big smile.

"Huh!" she'd grunted. "We may be the only ones who subscribe to that notion, Teddy." She took another sip of lemonade. "Anyway, as I've grown older, I've come to feel a kinship with every living thing, animal, and plant alike."

She paused and bent forward so her head was very close to his. "Tell you something else, Teddy, if you promise not to ever tell anyone else."

There was no way he was going to jeopardize the most intimate adult conversation of his life. He shook his head.

"Well," she said, "I believe that everything in this world is a part of God, and He's a part of everything."

"Everything?"

"Yes, everything," she said, leaning back again. "For instance, you see that rock over there?"

He nodded.

"Well, I bet you don't think that old rock has life in it. But it does, you know. And the trees, and the animals, they're all part of God. But they don't worry about any of that; they just live and accept things as they are, as they're supposed to be."

"I don't understand."

"Just because you can't see something, doesn't mean it doesn't exist. For instance, do you believe in the truth?"

"Yes," he said, not really certain what she meant.

"So, how many times have you told the truth and someone, maybe everyone, didn't believe you? Maybe even called you a liar?"

"Lots of times."

"Are you a liar, Teddy?"

"No, Grandma."

"Then why'd people call you one?"

"I don't know."

She started the swing moving again and gave him a wide smile. "And you never will. I mean, that sort of thing used to bother me a lot, particularly when I was about your age. But I'll tell you, I did find the answer."

"You did?"

She picked up a bean, pulled the string, and snapped it into three pieces. "I believe that the truth, like God, really does exist. It lives and it is written down in a big book that floats in the universe; a book that contains every action, every thought that's ever been. And it's written and preserved for eternity. No matter what anyone says, the truth is always alive. 'And ye shall know the truth and the truth shall make you free'," she said with a smile.

"I remember that from church," he said gruffly.

"It doesn't matter where you heard it. The truth is the truth and nothing can ever change that."

"Yeah, well, maybe."

She sighed, reached out and placed a hand on his shoulder. "Listen, Teddy: If you're a good person and believe in the truth, you'll be an important part of things, a part of God. It doesn't matter what anyone else thinks. As long as *you* know, it doesn't matter whether people accept it or not, it's still the truth; it exists."

He thought for several seconds. "But what if I'm wrong about something?"

"Well, that can be a problem sometimes. You can't let it discourage you, though. You just have to keep digging until you find what you're looking for; sort of like that yard out there— we've been digging all summer and still haven't gotten rid of all those darn dandelions. But it can be done."

The summer of his eleventh year, Ted Yost put his demons to rest and took on the shackles of the truth-seeker.

* * *

Ted Yost could feel his skin crawling. He tapped his foot while glancing at his watch until his antics annoyed the receptionist. She buzzed Rudge and spoke softly. When she hung up, she clicked the computer keys with her long red nails for several seconds without pausing. Then, without looking up, she said, "Mr. Rudge will see you now." She nodded toward the door behind her.

Ted laughed to himself and said: "Thank you." He'd learned long ago not to make enemies of the guardians and the sentinels.

* * *

"Sorry to barge in like this," Ted Yost said as he entered the CEO's office.

"A later appointment would have been much more convenient." Rudge took in the man with a wild mop of hair and disheveled clothes "For both of us." He returned Yost's handshake, then indicated a chair.

'What can I do for you, Mr. Yost?"

"I'm here to represent not only myself as an interested party, but the Coalition of Retired Persons. Specifically, we want to know about the proceedings in your Bioethical Review Committee."

Rudge smiled at him, wondering why he'd been so afraid of this ordinary-looking person. "I'm sure you're aware that I'm under no obligation to provide you, CORPS, or anyone else with that information."

"In other words, it's nobody's business?"

"I didn't say that. I only said I'm under no obligation to open up the proceedings of that committee to anyone on the outside."

"You must report to someone."

"Of course, but that's beside the point."

"Under the Brown Act—"

"Bluffing won't get you anywhere, Mr. Yost. The Brown act doesn't apply and you know it." He sat back in his high-backed leather chair and said, "When the hospital board voted to reorganize and become a private corporation, that took us out from under the state's open meeting law."

Yost nodded. "So now you're not responsible to anyone other than Hygea Incorporated, is that it?"

"Don't try to bait me, Mr. Yost. Galen is first and foremost responsible to the people of the community, whether it's here or anywhere else in the country."

Rudge could feel his stomach grinding, bile rising.

"Then what can you tell me about your bioethical committee?" Yost asked. "I think the community is entitled to know about any new policies being contemplated at Galen Hospital."

Rudge scooted back into the protection of his tall, over-padded swivel chair and made a steeple of fingertips beneath his chin. "New? Our committee has been in existence since the early 1980s."

He watched Yost take a small spiral notebook out of his inside jacket pocket, flip over several pages. The fact that Yost was tall was one strike against him, and his messy clothes didn't sit well, either—it made him want to look in a mirror to recheck his own appearance.

"But there have been some recent changes."

"Yes?"

"My understanding is that Galen's original ethics committee was started by a group of physicians concerned about turning off life-support machines for terminally ill patients."

"And that concept," Rudge said, "hasn't changed."

"But why a second committee? One with all new members, and just within the past several months."

"What's wrong with that?" Rudge found himself holding his breath, waiting for an answer.

Yost shrugged.

"The committee is composed of members of this community. How on earth could you fault that?"

"I know their names and affiliations. On the surface, they seem to be a somewhat small, but well-balanced group." He paused, then added: "With one exception."

"Oh?"

"Patient representation."

"Is that why you're here?"

Yost's eyes bored into him. "I'm here because there are rumors, Mr. Rudge," the man scribbled a few notes," that you are in the process of changing end of life protocols, something to do with selective euthanasia."

Before he could stop himself, Rudge slapped both hands on the top of the desk. "I'm not going to discuss that with you."

"Is that a yes or a no?" Yost said with his pencil poised over his spiral notebook.

"Euthanasia remains an explosive subject, whether Oregon or any other state has legalized assisted suicide or not. Why on earth would I want to discuss anything that controversial with you?" The man was poking at him, like Wade Wilson. It made his nerves stand on edge.

"You still haven't answered my question."

"Nor do I intend to. If there's something else, then let's get on with it. Otherwise, it'd time for you to leave. Unlike you, Mr. Yost, I'm not retired. I still have to work for a living; and there are a number of important matters—"

"I don't see that my being retired has anything to do with this discussion."

"As I said before, I don't *have* to provide you with an explanation, or anything else.'

"Maybe not, but I *will* get to the bottom of this, with or without your cooperation."

"Is that a threat?" Rudge moved to the edge of his chair. He was furious; furious that Wade Wilson had wedged him into this tight corner; furious this man was still sitting there.

"Take it any way you like." Yost returned his notebook to his pocket. "Retirement isn't a dirty word—one you seem to throw out like garbage. But prior to my retirement I spent more than forty years digging for information, from this country's involvement in Vietnam to questionable campaign practices. Make no mistake, Mr. Rudge, I always got what I went after."

Rudge glared. "You're no longer a newsman, Mr. Yost, nor is this a war. Take your accusations and threats elsewhere."

"Sir, that wasn't a threat. It was a simple statement of fact. I *can* and *will* find out what you're up to."

Rudge tapped his fingers on the desk, thought about his earlier discussion with W.W. He had to do this right.

Damn it! Look at the man: As useful as yesterday's newspaper. Wilson knew what he was talking about. What do I have to worry about from this has-been? The Desisto Project's not only on firm ground, it's backed all the way to the White House

He leaned forward. "I have nothing else to say to you, Mr. Yost. You've already taken up way too much of my day."

Rudge stood and stepped around the side of his desk, walked to the office door, and opened it. He didn't offer his hand, only jerked his head toward the reception area.

The interview was over.

Chapter 11

Rev. John F. Bradberry left the hospital committee meeting, hurried home, and stormed into his study. When he slammed the door behind him he was trembling. He felt like he had a raging fever that would soon bring him down.

He stared out the window into the garden, eyed the soft, soothing greenery he had planted many years ago. Out there was a peaceful place where all the rules were simple. His world was complicated and unyielding.

His wife opened the door without knocking and came into the room. "John, is there something wrong?" Her voice was quiet, concerned.

Bradberry turned and without a word crossed the room, grabbed her by an elbow, and ushered her out. He slammed the door behind her and locked it.

She slapped at the wood. "John, open the door! Please! Tell me, what's the matter?"

Her voice pierced his brain like hot pokers. He shouted, "Audrey, if you say one more word I swear to God I'll come out there and wring your neck!"

It wasn't the first time he'd raised his voice to her, but he'd never talked to her with such hatred, such violence. The words shocked him into silence.

Bradberry collapsed into his reading chair, slumped over, held his head in his hands. "My God, what's happening to me?"

But he knew. It was that committee. Over the last six months, each session had become more and more stressful until a fiery rage he thought he'd buried years ago returned to torment him.

"John!" his wife said, knocking on the door. "There's someone here to see you."

A rush of relief made him sit up.

I can apologize now.

"Who is it?" He opened the door and his heart sank as he watched her walking away from his office.

Ted Yost was waiting in the living room. He hesitated, then stepped forward, offered his hand.

"I hope it's not presumptuous of me to stop by without calling first," Ted said, "but there's a lot of information—"

"It's all right," Bradberry said. "Don't worry about it." He started to offer him a seat, then invited him to his study.

When they were settled side-by-side on the leather couch, Ted said, "I thought this might be the right time to discuss Galen's Bioethical—"

"Ted—" Bradberry interrupted, his head down. The words refused to budge, trapped in his throat.

What could he say to this man who had carried him out of the raging fires of hell; the man who had saved him from death in the jungles of Vietnam?

Bradberry finally stared into his eyes. "I've never thanked you."

"Thanked me?"

"Yes. For getting me out of that hellhole."

Ted was silent, his eyes soft, understanding. "You would've done the same for me."

Bradberry shook his head. "All that insanity—fresh out of seminary. I was so idealistic, should never have gone there."

"None of us should have been there." Ted placed a hand on Bradberry's shoulder. "That war's been over for a long time."

"Not for me." Bradberry clutched his side, squeezed his thighs. "It's never been over for me. How can I forget that child? She's with me awake or sleeping."

"It was a horrible way to die."

"No!" he said. "*That* poor little girl found eternal peace. It's her sister who haunts me. They took her from me, don't you understand? I was so insane—it was months before I even knew who I was. When I tried to find her, she was swallowed up with all the other refugees. Vanished."

"You did what you could—you saved her life."

"You still don't understand. When her mother was dying, I promised I would take care of her babies I swore by all that was holy that those children would live." He pulled himself away from Ted, slumped into the far corner of the couch.

"There was nothing else to do, John."

"I'm damned ... the best of what I was, what I could have been, died in that place."

"You had the capacity to love, to reach out to help others; I doubt if you've ever lost it." Bradberry looked up, searched Ted's eyes. "Look, maybe I'd better leave."

"No! Stay ... tell me why you're here."

"I'm working with CORPS ... we're interested in the Galen bioethical committee."

"I see."

Bradberry stood, crossed the room and sat down behind his desk. He placed a hand on his Bible for a moment, but felt no comfort from the connection. He looked at Ted again. The reported seemed small against the backdrop of book shelves that stretched from floor to ceiling.

"Any problem with that?"

"They're a militant group."

"John, they get things done."

"And what exactly are *you* doing for that organization?"

"Background investigative work."

He continued to study the journalist. "What do you need to know?"

Ted scooted to the edge of the couch. "Rumor has it your committee is putting together a pilot program for selective euthanasia."

Bradberry shuffled papers on his desk. "Ted, I owe you a tremendous debt, but please don't ask me to break an oath of confidentiality."

"I appreciate your situation. But if somebody doesn't speak up, we could be looking at deaths justified only by corporate

73

expediency and economics. I need information. Will you help me?"

Bradberry tapped a pencil from end to end on his desk. "It's Rudge you should be talking to, not me."

"Tried that."

"And—"

"He talked in circles, put me off."

"I could give you background on the committee members. I would be comfortable helping you with that."

"That's a start."

Bradberry related in detail what he knew about each member of the Galen ethics committee.

"Nothing to criticize, at least on the surface," Ted said. "Were they all hand picked by Rudge?"

"In one way or another. But he may have made some errors in judgment."

"How's that?"

"People aren't as predictable as the corporate mind might like to think; they may not go along with what he wants.

"What do you think his goal is?" Yost asked.

Bradberry suddenly stood and hurried to a sliding glass door that opened into the garden. "Legalized murder!" And without another word he stepped outside.

The interview was over.

* * *

Audrey Bradberry sat at her piano, closed her eyes as the Slavic sadness of Chopin mirrored her unhappiness. Silent sobs shook her slender body until she threw her arms across the Steinway, rested her head, then rushed to the sofa. The overpowering sense that her husband no longer loved her, may never have loved her, was overwhelming.

She lay with tears streaming down her cheeks and stared at their wedding picture sitting on a mahogany tabletop across the room. She wiped her face and studied the tall, skinny man with large melancholy eyes; he'd looked more like a boy than a Vietnam veteran.

Her father had forced her to attend the church dance where she met Rev. John Bradberry. But any chance of fun was crushed when he reminded her that she was an old maid and couldn't afford to waste time sitting at home reading books.

"Find a husband, for God's sake. Don't make me ashamed of you."

"How many of these church dances and socials do I have to go to before you understand that no man will ever want me with you always hovering over me?"

"It's not my fault you're a spinster; not my fault you're plain, have no talent, and can't attract a man."

She said nothing more. Her mother had passed on the family tradition of silence. No one stood up to her wealthy father. No one.

That night she'd entered the stark church assembly hall unhappy, defeated. Then she saw John Bradberry, and he saw her. Their eyes locked and when the band started to play, she watched him float across the room, and before he reached her, she held her arms out to him.

In the beginning they danced with hesitant steps. "My name's Audrey."

"I know."

She liked to relive that night, but she still couldn't explain the animal heat that fired them, turned them into people they never were before.

They left the church together, not touching, but both talking, telling everything. She was lost in his voice, his face. His hand, like hers, was sweaty, but neither would let go. It wasn't until several blocks out that she said, "My car is in the church parking lot."

"I'll walk you back," he said. "I don't live too far from here."

She offered to drive him home, but once inside her convertible, they turned silent. She drove aimlessly. He turned on the car radio, but remained on the far side of the seat, close to the door. After a few miles, she pulled over and stopped.

"It's closed," he said.

"What?"

"The zoo." He smiled, pointed out the window to a pair of stone pillars and an iron gate.

The streets were deserted, but there was a full moon that washed the landscape and left behind an eerie silence, interrupted only by the cries of the zoo's nocturnal creatures. They sat for a long time, neither speaking.

She shivered. He reached out and drew her close to him. "Is that better?"

She couldn't speak.

His fingers slid down her cheek, her neck; lips found her mouth. She unpinned her hair, let it cascade down to surround them in its softness. "Undo your dress, Audrey. I want to touch you." Her hands shook as she tore loose the buttons of her blouse. The rest of their clothes melted away and they were left feverish and lost in each other's arms.

Now, Audrey cried for that lost passion.

* * *

As the late afternoon sun dipped below the housetops, John Bradberry left the safety of the garden and returned to his study.

He paced back and forth, seeking relief from the pool of emotions that were usually kept under tight control. After several minutes, he sat down at his desk and began to write his Sunday sermon:

Make haste, O God, to deliver me; make haste to help me, O Lord.

How many times have we had those thoughts?

How many times have we surrendered our despair to God, then returned to Him again, and again, with more anguish?

Our quest is voiced in different words each time, but the meaning remains constant.

Help me, O Lord. Help me!

A new century was to bring a new time, the dawn of a new age.

We would learn to be gentle, to love, to care for one another; then, we would begin to respect other creatures that share this planet; we would stop annihilating them, taking what they have, whether we truly need it or not.

The killing of fellow beings is wrong. And while we say we kill in order to survive, I say that is a lie.

Help us, O Lord. Help us!

If we are at the threshold of rebirth, why am I so fearful; why am I afraid of the future?

Are we not all basically good people? Are we not all God's children?

Make haste, O God, to deliver me; make haste to help me.

O Lord, I look around me day-after-day, I see the wealthy growing richer, while the poor are desperately poorer.

Why do we still have nations where people continue to die of starvation?

Are these people not our brothers and sisters?

O Lord, help me to understand.

Are we not all one in Your eyes? Are we not all individuals of infinite value in Your heart?

Help me to understand, O Lord!

We beseech Thee, O Lord: tell us why You have allowed us to kill one another in war after war ... the bombings, the holocausts—

John Bradberry threw his head back in despair, clamped a hand across his mouth to stifle a gathering scream.

Chapter 12

Nathan Sorkin wondered, as he had so many times over the years, what had prompted him to bring together the initial group of dissident, shit-kicking senior citizens under the banner of CORPS.

He no longer had time to visit his grandchildren, or even take a day off and go to the movies, something he and his wife had always loved to do. Maybe it was her death, the death of his beloved Dora, his loneliness.

But he wouldn't kid himself. It wasn't about her—it was about him. When he walked down the street, or listened to the news, or talked to friends, he heard it over and over, the basic lack of justice throughout the nation. Human beings were cruel to one another.

People over fifty? Well, that was the start of it, but it only became worse the older they got. It wasn't only that they got screwed out of jobs. That was bad enough. But it was the lack of dignity, of basic respect, that was disappearing, never to return.

Nathan believed everyone, from the youngest to the oldest member of society, deserved to live with dignity. And that was it. Plain and simple.

He looked around the temporary CORPS offices. He'd hastily rented and thrown the place together to keep the organization viable. It was little more than a cluster of cramped rooms separated by paper-thin walls. He could hear the volunteers grumbling about having no equipment or supplies to work with, and he felt bad. No matter how hard he tried to block out their voices, they came through as if they were standing in the room next to him.

He was a born workaholic and he could usually function under any conditions, but today he was distracted not only by the buzz of the CORPS workers, but also by the void Myra left behind. All he could think about was Myra Jackson, dedicated worker, friend, and victim of the vicious explosion that had sent her limp, wounded body to the hospital.

His mind replayed the image of the brutal stake driven into her chest by the blast, of the blood pouring from her wounds, and of the wrenching scene as the EMTs loaded her motionless form into the ambulance.

He knew she would die, that he would never see or talk to her again. How could *anyone* live through that?

If only he could have been with her at the hospital, been there to offer words of comfort and encouragement. But he was told him only family was allowed in ICU.

Wasn't he her family, too?

When Ted walked in and gave him a thumbs down, Nathan was pacing around his desk. He was relieved to have the distraction.

"I was really counting on you. You were supposed to talk your way into that bioethical committee meeting, even though my gut told me that wasn't going to happen."

"Sorry."

"Did you at least ask the schmuck about sitting in?"

"Considering the warm welcome the 'schmuck' gave me, asking would have only given him another opportunity to verbally slap me around."

"You're disappointing me, Teddy."

"Don't give up yet. At least I know John Bradberry, one of the committee members. That gets me a foot in the door. Sometimes that's all you need."

"Good! Because we need to know exactly what's going on in there."

"I couldn't agree more."

"My sources were correct, then, they're into end-of-life treatment changes?"

"Rudge never said yes, but I hit a raw nerve when I slapped him with selective euthanasia.

"So now we go to Plan B."

"What's that?"

Nathan stopped pacing, scratched his head, and said, "I'll be damned if I know."

* * *

Ted spent a couple of hours in the business library before going home, reading up on Hygea Corporation, Galen Hospital, and all the other healthcare operations under its corporate umbrella.

He was sitting in the breakfast alcove, his head buried in research material, when Mel came in from the supermarket. She gave him a perfunctory greeting and proceeded to put away the groceries.

"Cat got your tongue, Mel?" he asked, using one of her favorite expressions. "Haven't seen you this quiet for a long time."

"You were up pretty late last night, Theodore," she said.

"Theodore? Well, I guess I was. I had a lot to read."

"Until four a.m. or so."

"Hell, why didn't you say something if it was bothering you? You usually don't mind."

She ignored the question. "Did you forget we had a date for nine holes at McInnis today?"

"Oh, no!" He looked at her across the top of his half-frames. "I did forget...obviously. I owe you a rematch."

"Where were you?"

"I got involved with a CORPS project."

"Up to your old tricks again, huh?" They stared at each other, Mel biting her lower lip, her back against the kitchen counter. She looked down at him.

"What tricks?" A pinched whiteness circled her lips; her eyes were dark and angry. "What tricks?" he repeated.

"The Crusades."

"You know how I hate when you say that. Every time my work interferes with something we were going to do, you hit me with that same put down. I don't like it, and I don't think I deserve it. This is something that has to get done. It's important, not just to me, but for the whole damn country. It looks like there's a nasty conspiracy at work here, some kind of cover-up."

"When hasn't it been important?" she said.

"What do you mean?"

She turned away, faced the kitchen cabinets, and started to put away the rest of the groceries. "Why can't it be light and fun for us, or just plain frivolous sometimes?"

He put down a sheaf of papers. "You're really pissed, aren't you?" He got up and went to her, turned her around to face him. He tried to hold her but she moved out of his reach.

"Damn it, Ted, we've been married forty-three years. That's a long time by anyone's standards. But we've spent precious little of that time enjoying the world together or even something as simple as a round of golf."

"Hey, that's not true." This time he grabbed her and swung her around in a circle. "We've had plenty of good times."

"All I remember is reading books and magazines and watching a lot of television. Alone."

He was silent as she moved away from him along the edge of the counter. She stood there, staring long and hard at him.

"This was supposed to be our time," she screamed. "Our time!"

The words hit him like bullets.

"Don't look at me like a wounded lion." She took a ragged breath. "When you retired, we were going to be together. To find each other again. Go to all those places you talked about. Places I never got to see." She leveled a finger at him. "You promised me, Ted Yost. You promised me."

He felt himself slipping away. He couldn't get back to her. She seemed so far away. "I know I promised," he said softly, "but this CORPS thing came up. It's important."

"And I'm not?"

"Why are you doing this? "He sat down again, looked at her? "Are you trying to say you don't love me anymore?"

Her mouth dropped, her eyes opened wide. "Not love you?"

"That's what I said."

She looked at him with wide eyes. "I know you're not stupid, so you must be blind as a bat." Her hands rested firmly on her hips and she thrust her jaw out. "Have you ever stopped to think about what it's been like being married to you?"

Ted blinked and shrugged.

"Well let me tell you. *You* had to go to Viet Nam right after our honeymoon so you could write about that war."

"You know I—"

"What I know, is that you left me alone," she said.

"Mel—"

"When you came home, I got pregnant. When our first-born was delivered, no Ted Yost; *you* had to be in Algeria to record another French defeat."

"Mel, I wish—"

"No, Ted, it's *I* who wish; wish you'd been here, with me."

Warming to the subject, she paraded back and forth across the room, glaring at him.

"Oh, yes," she continued, "then there were the Mau Maus in Africa. After all, you were already in the neighborhood, so why not drop in and cover that? Home would still be there when you got around to it."

"It's what I did," he said.

"What you *did* was stay away as much as possible," she shouted.

"Someone had to report the truth about what was happening."

"Oh, yes. The truth! Who said it always had to be *your* truth?"

He started to speak, but she waved away his protest. "It was my fault, too. I remember when you finally came back from the jungles, the deserts—all my resolve about not having any more children melted away. You were alive, and I swore to myself that

83

was all that mattered. So we had a second son, and I'll be damned if you weren't back in Algeria when *he* was born."

She dropped into a chair opposite him and rested her head on her arm. "Didn't you ever realize how lonely my life was while you were chasing around all over the world?"

"Yes, but—"

"Raising two kids by myself. Taking any half-assed job so I could quit at the drop of a hat to spend time with you when you finally came home. I think you forget my major was journalism, too, before we even got involved with each other."

"I didn't forget. That's why I thought you'd understand how important all of this was. Without newspapers there's no national focus on any one issue. The electronic media isn't hacking it yet, and they may never."

"My God, you were in and out of Viet Nam for fifteen years. And who cared? Who gave a good goddamn? Sometimes I think I was the only person who read, or even believed what you wrote."

"You're probably right about that." He said the words without an ounce of humor.

She looked across at him for several silent seconds, tears welled in her eyes. "That's not true! Lots of people read what you wrote. If it's truth you want, I think those stories were a big part of why the U. S. finally left that hellhole."

"I'd like to believe that."

Melissa got up, rushed around the table to her husband, and wrapped her arms around him. "I'm sorry. But I need you *now*."

"Don't be sorry. Everything you said is true." She squeezed him tighter; he took a deep breath, felt like he could breathe again. "Mel, I can't lie to you—given the same circumstances, I'd do it all again."

"I know."

Chapter 13

"Tana residence."

"Are you the maid?" Ted asked.

"Who wants to know?" The young girl giggled.

"A dirty old man from California."

"Hi, Uncle Ted. It's me, Patty." She covered the phone, but he could still hear her yell, "It's for you, Dad. Uncle Ted."

"So you're not going to talk to your godfather, just toss me away like an old shoe?"

"Never! But Tommy's picking me up in a few secs, Teddy bear. We'll talk next time." He winced as the receiver cracked loudly when she dropped it, and was gone.

"Thought I'd changed this to an unlisted number," Bill Tana said when he picked up.

"You can't hide from the press."

"Unfortunately, that's all too true." A long suffering sigh followed.

"Sounds like that daughter of yours has turned into a real teenager. What happened to that sweet little thing who used to play Chinese checkers with me?"

"Tommy-the-boyfriend happened. That and hormones." Another heavy sigh. "Spit it out, Yost. What's up?"

"No how-are-you, how's Mel? Where's all that charm everyone always talks about?"

"Fuck you, man. I've had a helluva day. No, make that a helluva week. Not in the mood for small talk from pseudo friends."

"Pseudo? Hey, it's me, your old buddy Ted. Remember?"

"Yeah, yeah. Get to the point."

"I need a nose job."

"No way, man. Last time I snooped around for you I almost lost my ass."

"Big corporate shenanigans warping that brain of yours?"

"What the hell are you talking about?"

"The way I hear it, you're up for executive VP at that stuffy PR firm you've hunkered down into. Pretty high up on the corporate ladder, if you ask me. And to think you used to be a pot head, among other things."

"Enough of my sordid past. Just tell me why you called, because I really am beat."

"That little plum about ditching Medicare you tossed my way?"

"Gotcha."

"It's more like ditching Medicare patients."

"So it was worth looking into?"

"Yes. And now I'm up to my ears in it and need a solid, discrete D.C. connection. You!"

Bill's breathing pattern noticeably changed. Ted realized his friend was walking through his house, phone in hand, probably looking for an out-of-the-way quiet spot.

"Poor timing, Ted. At least as far as I'm concerned. This new job is all-consuming. Don't have time to wipe my ass or pull up my pants before I'm running again. Maybe I could get someone—"

"Don't try to palm me off, Tana. I know you thought you were doing me a favor, but you know as well as I do that favors can be very expensive, no matter how well intentioned. Besides, you're the only reliable D.C. denizen I trust."

"Retirement must be getting to that Twinkie brain of yours. You used to do all your own fucking leg work."

"Sure, when I had someone footing the expenses. I don't have that kind of budget anymore."

"Yeah, I suppose not. Maybe you could get a grant."

"Turning fifty hasn't changed you from being the smart-ass you've always been."

"Yeah, and moving through the sixties hasn't morphed you into anything brighter than you ever were. Still looking for some fucking windmill to tilt. Only this one's already been toppled by others."

"You keep forgetting that it was you who put the fucking windmill in my path; I didn't go looking for it."

There was a long pause. "Got to admit, it was sort of a knee-jerk reaction on my part—secret political shenanigans, call Yost. But the more I think about it, what the hell, you know? Euthanasia isn't something new. There're already laws in some states that condone it."

"But that's assisted euthanasia ... for people who request it."

"So?"

"So, this is *selective* euthanasia. You know, the kind based strictly on economics—if you're too old, die; if you're too sick, die."

There was an even longer pause. "Okay, okay. So you're right." Bill's voice dropped to a whisper. "The rumors are growing, coming from more quarters. But so far no one's talking about the epicenter, who or what's at the core."

"Exactly. So how about following through with this and start chasing down some of those rumors? And a good place to start might be to find out who Hygea Corporation has its hooks into back there."

"Hygea?"

"That's the best I can do right now. I need to know what you can come up with. And no, it can't wait until Monday."

"You've got this saving a life shtick all fucked up, Ted. When you saved *my* life, it means *you're* responsible for me, not the other way around."

"Whoever thought of that didn't know squat about gratitude, and knew damn little about human nature."

"Fuck you very much, Ted Yost."

Chapter 14

Garrett Rudge stepped from his office into the hallway of the Administrative Satellite and headed for the rear exit that led to the employee parking lot.

There were few people in the hallways and, as he'd hope, no one stopped him along the way. Once outside, he took a deep breath and admired the clear bright sky as he waited for the keyless lock to click open.

He'd had the sleek, black AMG E-Class Mercedes for only three months; but he'd fallen in love with it from the moment he saw it on the dealership showroom floor and was still learning new things about it.

He slid into driver's seat and allowed himself a moment to breathe in the luxurious new-leather aroma. Eyes closed, he again mentally ticked off the items on the checklist he'd covered prior to leaving his office—the status of Della Paoli, Hygea corporate affairs, and routine hospital matters.

Nothing could be left to chance.

Satisfied, he tapped the button that brought the powerful engine to life, then drove out of the parking lot for the first leg of his trip to Sacramento. Once on I-80, he removed his tie, shifted into a comfortable position, tuned in KCSM-FM, the local jazz station, and reviewed the day's events:

The face-off with Ted Yost dominated his thoughts.

Wilson had sent over a full bio on Yost, who was not only a respected journalist, but a Pulitzer Prize winner for a series of hard-hitting articles that exposed much of what had gone wrong in Vietnam. The old hack's nose had been into just about every conflict around the globe.

Rudge didn't like the man. There was a looseness about him that he coupled with unpredictability. And it was the worst possible time for veteran newsman like Yost to show up as the Desisto Project was nearing completion.

His Friday evening glow was fading. Doubts were creeping in.

Maybe he should have steered clear of Wilson and his D.C. pack—the lobbyist could definitely bring him down.

I won't go down alone, W. W. I know how to become a fucking canary.

But, there were real advantages working with a pro like Wilson. The lobbyist had been able to investigate every member on the ethical committee, from their diaper years to the present. He probably knew more about them than they knew about themselves.

He forced Yost and Wilson out of his head only to replace them with the sharp exchange he'd had with John Bradberry during at the Bioethics Committee meeting.

The Reverend's holier than thou façade about the poor populations seemed empty under close scrutiny. He headed the largest and richest church in the West—politicians screamed for his endorsement. He was never denied a permit to do anything he desired for any of his properties.

None of it looked kosher to Rudge. Especially when the redevelopment of the condemned areas drove the minister's wealth way over the top.

Turns out the good reverend was no different than any other fat cat.

I suppose kicking those poor people around doesn't count when you do it, Reverend, Fucking hypocrite. That must be how it works when you marry a mousey little heiress and become rich.

Rudge rubbed at the stiffness in his neck, then clutched the leather-covered steering wheel a little tighter

They tell me you're a Vietnam vet? Yeah, well, careful, Reverend! You could end up in another bloody fiasco

* * *

Robert Holt stood at his office window, looking down into the hospital parking lot. He should have been at his desk working, but he'd stepped away from his computer, dizzy from the rush of endless information, endless requests, endless streams of words demanding some kind of action. All he could think about were the lovely days he and his wife had spent at the ocean—how the tides would ebb and flow around them.

He yearned to lay in those waters again, yearned to float away to nowhere.

He was jolted from his reverie. Garrett Rudge was leaving early.

Holt watched the CEO stride towards his Mercedes in the reserved section of the parking lot.

Like he doesn't have a care in the world.

Holt smiled. Now he could sneak out early, too. He snatched up a pile of professional magazines and stuffed them into his portfolio until it bulged. He had no intention of reading them, but a heavy load of homework was the mark of a productive administrator.

He hated the façade.

Galen had been his life for more than twenty years. And as its Hospital Administrator, he'd taken great pride in his management style and accomplishments. But the hospital he'd had so much pride in had become a factory that "processed units" instead of treating people.

His whole world was turned upside down. The buyout by Hygea brought Garrett Rudge into his life. Since that day, he'd become a powerless, ineffectual automaton, nothing but a high-priced paper pusher. A puppet. A yes-man. An employee who had to stuff his portfolio with piles of nothing in order to look as though he was really something.

Even thinking about it made him feel more useless.

Maybe if Rudge went down?

Some other SOB would only take his place—maybe someone worse. And he knew he was through, no matter what happened.

Right from the start he'd known Hygea wanted to reduce the length of hospital stays for elderly patients, cut back on the number of elderly sick patients they admitted. Was it strictly money?

He didn't think so. Rudge and Hygea were up to something. But he just didn't care what it was.

Before leaving, he glanced back at his neat, organized desk; his hand shook as he reached to open the office door.

* * *

Holt left the hospital, cut across the large parking lot, and continued down the street to the bus stop, hardly noticing his surroundings. The wooden passenger bench was empty--he sighed as he collapsed into it and stared at the departing rear end of the bus he had just missed. He tilted his head back and stared at the sky.

Joan had been dead for almost a year. He tried to visualize her, but lately it was getting harder to do—as each day passed, he was losing more of her essence. Now she only appeared to him in his dreams

Within a few minutes another bus arrived.

By leaving early he'd avoided the start of the rush hour and he was able to slip into a window seat for the 20-mile ride home. The bus carried him away from the congested area surrounding the hospital grounds. Soon he was on the freeway, staring out at vistas of rolling hills and the blue waters of Richardson Bay. He nodded off into a light sleep, Joan's face floated above him.

The hiss of the bus brakes jolted him awake. He looked out the window at the sky—the sun was melting away, leaving behind traces of pink haze. It was his stop.

He walked home through the suburban neighborhood loosening his tie as he entered the front door; he dumped keys and briefcase on the sofa before kicking off his shoes and padding through the house. Without really caring, he inspected the job performed by the cleaning lady.

The mindless routine reassured him, allowed him time to anticipate, to savor, the scenario that was to follow.

He turned the radio to a station with bland pop music, set the volume so the sound would follow him to the bathroom. He stripped off his clothes and took a hot shower, washed his body carefully and systematically. As he dried, he avoided the large mirror over the twin sinks. His sagging white flesh would only make him sadder. In the shortest possible time he'd become a person his wife would not have recognized.

Holt thought about his dream of Joan while he was on the bus. Her eyes were soft and inviting and she was mouthing his name.

But it was only a dream. Joan was gone—really gone. He'd scattered her ashes on a pine-shaded hilltop overlooking the ocean in the exact spot where they'd made love on their last anniversary,

It was still early in the day but he pulled on a pair of clean pajamas and drifted into the kitchen. He wasn't hungry, yet he reached for a thick chunk of cheese and wrapped a piece of week-old bread around it. He took a small bite, chewed without tasting.

Returning to the living room, he sank into the same chair where he sat every evening. He glanced at the television, then turned away with a heavy sigh, reached over to a wheeled serving cart next to his chair and picked up an unopened bottle of Chivas Regal. Now and then he considered buying a less expensive Scotch but he always rejected the idea—there wasn't much else he wanted to buy.

He cut through the plastic wrap-around seal, pulled the cork, and carefully filled an old-fashion glass. He took a long swallow, and then a second, before closing his eyes to more fully experience the sharp, almost searing sensation in his throat. Warmth radiated down, spread into his chest. Without opening his eyes, he took another long swallow. Then his head fell back against the upholstered headrest.

Chapter 15

On the outskirts of Sacramento, Garrett Rudge slowed to the speed limit after spotting a California Highway Patrol cruiser. He'd made the near-90-mile trip in good time for a Friday afternoon. At the next exit, he took the off-ramp and drove a short distance to Capital West Lodge and checked in.

Rudge's oversized room had a panoramic view of the Capitol's manicured lawns and lush gardens. He was partial to this hotel, where he ran into senators, congressmen, governors, state politicians. And he knew he would see many of them tonight.

After unpacking, he ordered a bottle of single malt Scotch from room service, then took a long, hot shower. Stepping out into the large room, he forced the day's events out of his mind and focused on the feel of the plush carpeting under foot as he dried himself. He stood in front of the double closet's full-length mirrors and slapped his hard, flat abs. A near-religious program of bodywork since his late teens had paid off with a physique few men in their late forties could claim

He turned to view his backside in the mirror, snorting as he remembered overhearing some female's snide comment about how men's asses tended to flatten out as they grew older.

"Not yet, sweetheart," he told his image, "Not yet!"

A tap at the door interrupted his thoughts. He wrapped the bath sheet around his middle, and opened the door for room service.

The waiter gave him a quick up-and-down look before asking, "Will there be anything else, sir?"

The twenty-something was hitting on him, but he was in no mood to play. Instead, he signed for the Scotch and added an overly generous tip before sending the sex hustler on his way.

He poured a couple fingers of the liquor and downed most of it in a single gulp. The buzz hit him, reminding him of the many days in his past that were lost to drinking in order to forget.

He stared again at the mirror. "You're still there, aren't you, Evie?"

Almost thirty years since the death of his twin sister, Evelyn, but it was *her* eyes that stared back at him when he looked into a mirror, any mirror.

The momentary alcohol high disappeared. He remembered Evelyn when she was diagnosed with muscular dystrophy.

Twelve years old.

By fifteen, the weakness had progressed to the point that she seldom left the house for anything other than medical appointments. She made it through one desperate year of attending high school, then had to quit. But she never stopped studying, learning; going through one tutor after another until they had nothing left to teach her.

Rudge's decision not to go away to college had been an easy one—they lived in Davis, home to a University of California campus. He could attend and still remain close to his sister.

Over the years he'd watched her grow weaker. His mother and father accepted her fate, but he never could.

Was there a God? He didn't think so.

Rudge thought about pouring another drink. Instead, he sprawled naked on the king-size bed and closed his eyes, drifted back to that last weekend with Evelyn.

* * *

For their twentieth wedding anniversary, Rudge's parents left the house late Friday afternoon to spend a long weekend alone at a friend's beach-front house in Carmel.

Almost from the moment the door closed, Evelyn demanded that her brother join her for a "hush-hush"—their term from childhood for a secret twins' talk.

Stretched out on the living room sofa, she motioned for him to sit on the floor next to her. He plopped down and made their secret sign, assuring her that he was sworn to secrecy—it was the kind of kid stuff she held onto. He took her hand and noticed how pale her skin had become.

As he looked into her faded grey eyes, he knew ... knew his sister would be gone soon.

"Garr," she said softly, squeezing his hand, than added in a rush, "I want someone to make love to me." A long moment passed. She cleared her throat, whispered, "I want to have sex ."

He leaned back, pulled his hand away. "Geez, Evie! What the hell are you talking about?"

"I'm talking about an intimate relationship, Garr," she said, chin held high. "I need you to understand, help me." She reached out, made him take her hand again. "You've been on dates, lots of them, right?" she asked.

"Yes."

"Have you ever gone all the way."

"I ... uh ... well..."

"Of course you have. I can feel it. I'm your twin and we know everything about each other. S o don't lie, not now."

"Okay ... okay. Maybe a few times."

"Well, no one has ever made love to me, Garr. I'm nineteen years old and I've never even kissed anyone except you and Mom and Dad."

He started to object, but she shushed him.

"I'm going to die soon; we all know that." When he tried to object again, she squeezed his hand harder. "Mom and Dad won't talk about it, but I have to have someone to share my thoughts with. So, like when we were little and played play tag, you're it."

He hesitated, then nodded.

She turned her head, stared out the window. "For a long time I was afraid of death, but that's gone now. What I feel is ... cheated. No, make that pissed. I'm pissed about all the things I haven't been able to do, things I'll never get to do."

She ran fingers through her limp hair, hair that was dull and lifeless.

"I knew almost from the start I'd have to give up my dreams of climbing mountains, chasing rainbows." She laughed. "For a long time I fooled myself into believing I would get to do at least a few ordinary things, like go to school dances, attend parties in funky clothes ... have a boyfriend."

She turned back to him.

"I've even fantasized about running away all by myself, backpacking, eating and sleeping under the stars. But, Garr, I would have been happy just to ride a bicycle, or go to a movie with other girls and act silly."

She doubled a fist and pressed it hard against her mouth to keep from crying.

"Lately, my thoughts have been stuck on just one thing—I need to know what it would be like to have someone hold me, kiss me, want me. I ... I—"

"Evie! We couldn't. *I* couldn't."

She looked at him, shook her head slowly from side to side. "I didn't mean you and me!" Tears spilled softly at first, then in torrents.

"Don't cry, Evie." He got up, sat on the edge of the couch and wrapped his arms around her. "Please don't cry."

"I don't want you to feel sorry for me, Garr." She hugged him to her and whispered in his ear, "You can understand what I want, can't you?"

Rudge held her for a long time, confused, uncertain. He whispered, "I love you, Evie, You know that. I'd do anything for you."

"I love you, too," she whispered. "And I need you to do this ... find me a lover."

* * *

Evelyn created the mood for the rest of the weekend.

Under her direction, Rudge used Saturday morning to turn the upstairs into an intimate retreat, complete with incense and scented candles in every room. He found a black, lacy nightgown and negligee for Evelyn in their mother's wardrobe.

A little past noon, they shared a joint. It was a habit they'd gotten into of late, whenever their parents were not around. There had been some parental sniffs and frowns, but no comments, no questioning.

Self- conscious at first, they avoided each other's eyes, but the marijuana relaxed them and they began to giggle.

"Have you thought of someone?" she asked.

"Are you sure you want to do this, Evie? With a complete stranger?"

"If it's someone you know, someone you vouch for, then he won't be a total stranger, will he?"

"I suppose not." He took a drag from the joint, held it, and let it out slowly. "This isn't going to be easy."

"Sorry."

"I have been giving some thought to one of my fraternity brothers, Nolan Rhodes."

"Oh!"

It was the first time he'd seen even a tinge of sparkle in her eyes in a long, long time. "Yeah ... nice guy ... a bit shy. Don't think he dates much, though."

"Ugly, huh?"

Rudge laughed and handed the one-drag-left joint to Evie. "No, not ugly. Not at all."

"And?"

"If you're thinking of tonight, there's not that much time left to get hold of him."

She nodded.

"Okay! He's a townie so maybe it won't be all that difficult to chase him down."

It only took two phone calls.

"I'm going out to meet with him, Evie. I should be back within an hour or so."

* * *

"We agreed on eight o'clock," Rudge said when he returned home. "Is that okay?"

She blushed. "You ... you didn't have to ... to pay him, did you?"

"If he'd asked for money, he wouldn't have been the right guy." He took a deep breath. "My God, Evie, I would never, never embarrass you like that."

She blushed again and gave him a soft smile.

"So what's next?" he asked.

"Would you think me terrible if I asked you to help me with a bubble bath?"

* * *

About 6:30, Rudge filled the sunken tub in the master bath with mounds of scented bubbles. Evelyn was light as a feather as he carried her to the tub and lowered her into the steamy water. There was no embarrassment between them –he'd seen her nude many times since she became ill, more saddened each time as he watched her body waste away.

Heady aromas swirled around her; bubbles caressed her now hidden body.

She flicked the fingers of one hand at him. "Out, Garr! Allow me to soak and dream for awhile."

* * *

When Rudge's fraternity brother arrived–right on time–the two of them, both nervous, exchanged a few pleasantries before Rudge led Nolan up the stairs. The soft beat of erotic African music came from the master bedroom.

When the two of them entered, Evelyn was sitting on the edge of the king-size bed, smiling. She had draped the black nightgown and negligee around her to cover as much of her as possible.. Rudge couldn't remember the last time he'd seen his sister wearing makeup, and even now she'd used only light trace of color for her lips and eyes. Her hair was a delicate frame around her face.

"Nolan, Evelyn; Evelyn, Nolan."

Rudge turned and left the room, closing the door softly behind him.

* * *

Rudge awakened, startled. Someone was poking him in the ribs. His parents! They'd come home early!

He twisted around on the couch, saw the family room TV was on, playing some unrecognizable movie. He looked up and saw Evie standing over him, wrapped in an old flannel robe, a silly grin on her face.

"What time is it?" he mumbled.

"After two," Evie said.

"Oh ... oh! Nolan! Is he still here?"

"No, silly, he's gone."

"And?"

"And what?"

"You know ... the two of you. What happened?"

She squatted down, wrapped her arms around his neck, and kissed each cheek several times.

"Garrett Rudge, you are the most wonderful brother of all time."

He gently pushed her out to arm's length and said, "So tell me all about it."

She sat back on her haunches and gave him her evilest Evie scowl. "You've got to be kidding.

"The only thing I'm going to say is that at the start, it was kind of awkward, for both of us. And then it became the most wonderful thing that's ever happened to me."

Rudge could breathe freely again; the worry, the strain were suddenly gone. "That's all you've got to say?"

"No, I want you to fix me some scrambled eggs, toast, and hot chocolate." She stretched up onto her toes, arms spread wide. "I don't know why, but I'm famished!"

* * *

Rudge, dressed in a custom-tailored black cashmere sport coat, sharply creased dark gray wool slacks, and a soft, silvery silk shirt, sipped champagne from a tall crystal flute. He moved casually through the large room, from person to person, engaging in brief conversations, mostly with people he'd been introduced to at similar gatherings during the past couple of years at "The Residence."

It was an exclusive club, admission by invitation only. Most of the people in the room held positions of great influence, either in business or government.

There were no women present.

Rudge settled into a sofa covered in rich brocade, one of many scattered throughout the salon. A young pianist fingered Bach on a Steinway concert grand, illuminated by the flickering light of a ceiling-high fieldstone fireplace. A sweep of original Georgia O'Keefe tumescent flowers decorated the expansive walls.

Rudge, like the others, paid little attention to the décor, more captivated by a portable stage set at the far end of the long room. Most of the platform was concealed by black silk curtains. But with each passing minute, there was a growing sense of anticipation until the atmosphere became charged with unbearable excitement. The men talked louder, telling ribald jokes with champagne-relaxed tongues. Eyes darted back and forth between the stage and a huge grandfather's clock set off to one side.

Seconds before the hour, the hubbub tailed off to near silence. Tension gripped the room as a deep, resonant chime sent everyone searching for a seat. On the tenth gong, a woman entered at the back of the room and glided majestically toward the stage. Everyone stood to watch her slow, sensuous promenade.

She was tall, more than six feet. Coal black hair cascaded across her shoulders in stark contrast to her milky white skin. She glowed with a silvery luminescence; her thin, sharply crested lips glistened in dark pinot noir red.

Rudge, like many others, was captivated by her angular face—chiseled high cheekbones melded into deep facial caverns, bisected by a prominent nose with flaring nostrils. He felt small as he looked across the room at her dark turquoise eyes.

As she cut a path through the audience, every movement was accented by the flick of a black velvet cape wrapped around her body. The dominatrix stepped onto the small stage.

No! Not tonight!

Rudge turned, and without a single *excuse me* or *sorry*, or *pardon me*, he wedged and bumped his way toward the now-closed double entry doors.

Once in the lounge area, he made his way to a dark corner of the room and collapsed into a burgundy, overstuffed, leather chair, and closed his eyes. Never before had he shied away from The Residence's sadistic program of chastisement, punishment, and humiliation in this grandiose room filled with influential men, men he admired and attempted to emulate.

The audience did not know what he had done in his life to willingly subject himself to such exposure and pain, nor did they care. Like him, they were there of their own free will to endure excruciating physical and mental pain that would drive out debilitating memories that interfered with moving forward with their lives.

Unlike other visits to The Residence, this time the image would not go away ... an image of Evie, sitting on a kitchen stool, happily licking butter from her fingertips, a tan moustache of melted marshmallows decorating her upper lip, and jibber-jabbering about everything and nothing.

The scene always segued to Evie's funeral. She had died two days after her date with Nolan Rhodes.

The less-than-confident medical diagnosis was that she had died from over-exertion. The doctor's words were seared into Rudge's brain forever.

Rudge believed then, and continued to believe, that he was responsible for his twin sister's death.

Bette Golden Lamb & J. J. Lamb

Chapter 16

Sarah Silva was signing off on Della Paoli's nurse's notes when an end-of-shift lassitude hit her hard and kept her from concentrating, Words blurred as she tried to read what she'd written. She finally turned away from the computer.

"Better hurry, it's almost time for report," her team cohort said, "That is unless you plan on clocking in for the next shift. Our adorable Supe would love you for it."

"No thanks." Sarah crossed her eyes and gave her a goofy smile. "I'll get it together in a minute."

It was a silly act. She was worried. Thinking about the committee meeting earlier in the day was slowing her down. The heated discussion continued to run through her head, leaving her troubled and undecided.

She leaned back into her chair and looked at the patients scattered among a maze of equipment that crawled in, out, and around the room: Monitors reported cardiac, pulmonary, arterial, chemical functions. And there were IV tubes, feeding tubes, tubes that probed and poked like a moving jungle of hungry snakes, burrowing into noses, throats, chests, arms, legs. And over it all was the constant rasp of suction that was loud and constant, like a demanding animal requiring constant feeding.

Sarah wondered what it would be like to wake up enclosed in all of this equipment that winked and blinked at you as it sent out alarms and buzzers that meant someone's life, maybe your life, was in danger.

She looked over at one of the other patients, Myra Jackson. The woman had gone through six hours of surgery. It was as though some freak must have thought she was a blood-thirsty vampire and tried to drive a stake through her heart.

Crazy world.

"How's Jackson doing?"

The other nurse looked up and frowned at Sarah. She didn't like anything that distracted her from her notes.

"Hey, I'm trying to wind up here. I've got plans for later on." But she shrugged, pulled up her computer notes and looked at the screen. "We keep pumping the blood in, she keeps leaking it out. A nicked lung, stomach, and a bruised heart, to say nothing of the crap that's still hanging around from that chunk of wood. None of it's doing her any good. She's lucky to still be with us. Things don't look too great."

"Poor woman," Sarah said.

"She's lived to almost 80. Be grateful and call it a day."

Sarah thought about the committee again. "Do you really feel that way?"

"Hell, yes. We all have to go sometime. Why should she lie there and suffer?"

"Maybe Myra Jackson doesn't feel that way," Sarah said.

"Yeah, well, those are the breaks. Someone upstairs ..." she pointed at the ceiling "... said it was time." She went back to finishing her notes.

Sarah turned back to the computer screen and looked at her entries. She was almost finished.

The ICU unit was equipped to handle up to fifteen patients, but Galen didn't have the staff for that kind of census, and hadn't in the three years she'd been there. Most of the time, she was forced to float from unit to unit. Lesser skilled personnel picked up the slack, but the responsibility always fell back on the nurses' shoulders.

Sarah stood and stretched before making her final rounds. Then she was up and moving among her three patients.

Standing next to Della Paoli's bed, she looked at the sweat-drenched hair cemented to the patient's skull. Tears rolled down the woman's cheeks.

"It's all right." Sarah squeezed Della's hand. "I know you're frightened, But you're safe with us now." Della's respirations slowed. Several seconds passed and Sarah pulled a syringe from her pocket.

"I'm going to give you medication to help you sleep." She injected the med slowly into one of IV ports and continued to observe the woman. Her breathing became slower and deeper.

When Sarah returned to the nurses' station, she greeted the first arrivals of the swing shift before signing off on her notes. Now she was ready for the evening report.

* * *

Della tried to fight the sedative. But she was rising, drawn into a vortex of swirling colors, The brilliance undulated through a rainbow, swelling into an array of blues that danced before her eyes. The colors changed, turning into tinted wisps of pink that doubled back, evolving into puffs of purple.

In the distance, a shimmering form emerged, morphed into an enormous butterfly that swooped her up and carried her above the clouds where she was surrounded by a swarm of golden butterflies.

Far below, she could see herself walking hand-in-hand with her father, laughing as they strolled through the park. She was happy as they rolled in the grass and stared at the puffy clouds riding across the sky; to Della they looked like heavenly flowers scattered far and wide.

Daddy was calling her, "Della, stop chasing the butterflies, Leave them alone!"

Glass jar in hand, with the warm sun beating down on her, she looked at all the yellow butterflies floating near her. And the most perfect one hovered over her head. She studied the velvety body, the delicate wings.

The lid seemed to float away from her glass jar and she stared at the fresh grass inside. Cat-like, she shifted to hands and knees, then trapped the creature inside the jar. She squealed with delight.

"Della! Della! Let the poor creature go!"

She shook her head, watched how it beat its wings against the hard glass. Each flap left a residue of lemon-colored powder. It fought hard and with its last strength, flew upward, Della crashed the lid home—a prison door slammed shut.

At first she was engrossed with her captive. But soon it became lethargic. Worried that her nesting grass had become stale, she replaced it with fresh blades, adding even more. But the creature perched on the end of one thin spear, its wings barely pulsating.

Della cried. Her beautiful friend was shrinking into nothing. She removed the cap, up-ended the jar, and dumped it onto the lawn.

As she stared at the dying butterfly, a toddler came bounding up and grabbed the insect before she could stop him. The boy clenched the creature in his grubby little hand, then tossed it aloft, trying to get it to take wing again. It dropped to the ground, dead.

Della wanted to bring back it back, make the butterfly life its wins again. But she was floating away, far away from her childhood. It was gone and she was climbing higher and higher and higher, then falling down, down, down and crashing into nothingness.

Chapter 17

"Friggin' scare job?"

"Those are my orders," Al said, easing out of the black Chevy Malibu. "And don't let that Jason-Does-Dallas thing of yours flip us into nightmare alley. Got it?!"

Denny fell into step. "Can't find a jazzier ride to heist?" he said, ignoring the order. "Jeez, an old Malibu." He barked out a laugh. "Bet there's even a kid seat in the back. What are you, some kind of soccer mom?"

An arm whipped out, snatched Denny by the collar. "Listen, you turd. If you can't keep your mouth shut, I'll find a way to shut you up—permanently." He glared at Denny under the streetlight then roughly shoved him away. "Don't know why the hell the boss always sticks me with your sorry ass. I've about had it with this arrangement."

"Okay, for crissakes." Denny rubbed at his throat. "Keep your goddam paws off me."

Al glared into his partner's eyes a moment longer, then reached out and shoved him away. "Keep your big trap shut until we're back in the car and out of here."

They walked silently down the tree-lined street; most of the houses were protected by tall hedges on all sides. It was long past sunset and the word was that the Yosts rarely missed a Friday night out at the movies.

The two of them tucked in against the scraggily hedge of the Yosts' home. Through a small gateway they could see the dim glow of a porch light over the front entrance, but there were no lights on inside and the nearest street light was too far away to expose them. Al made a circling sign. They split up to cover the full perimeter and met again at the back of the house.

Creeping up the stairs of a large redwood deck, Denny tripped on a loose board; the sound stopped them mid-step. When everything remained silent they moved on. Al turned on a small, thin-beamed flashlight, tested the screen door, found it unlocked, and slowly slid it open. He used a shim to release the latch of the sliding glass door, and they were in.

"Friggin' kid's play," Denny said as if he'd been the one to get it done. Al ignored him and played the flashlight beam across the room, stopping briefly at a spinet piano and a sofa positioned flat against an opposite wall. The rest of the space was filled with bookcases.

"You do the sofa," he said to Denny. "And keep it quiet."

"Why? Ain't nobody here."

"Just *do* it!"

"Hate this kind of thing, Give me something to blow up--."

"Shut your mouth and do as you're told."

Al drew a pair of wire cutters from a back pocket, pulled away the top of the upright piano, placed it on the floor, and pressed one boot into the middle of it until it cracked. He then cut through each piano string, nodding slightly at the twang following each snip.

Across the room, Denny grabbed a planter and dropped it into the middle of a glass coffee table.

"You're so damned stupid!" Al growled. "What is it you don't understand about being quiet?"

Denny ignored the comment, stepped into the middle of the plant, and crunched his way through the broken glass to the bookcases. He started with the top shelf and flung books in every direction across the living room.

"Is that quiet enough for you, boss man?" He didn't wait for an answer, and got none. He pulled out a switchblade and stabbed it into the sofa. The air became heavy, difficult to breathe as particles of dusty fiber filled the room.

Al moved down the hallway, Denny close on his heels. Together they tore the bedroom apart, slashing mattress and sheets, dumping dresser drawer contents onto the polished oak floor.

As Denny moved to the walk-in closet, Al used the flashlight to check his watch. "That's enough. Let's get the hell out of here." Denny ignored him and reached into the closet. Al grabbed his arm. "You don't hear too good, do you, asshole?"

"Let's at least make it interesting."

"You want me to haul ass out of here without you?" He aimed the flashlight straight into his partner's eyes.

Holding a palm up between his face and the bright beam, Denny said, "All right, already. I got it, man."

* * *

Ted pulled into the driveway, pushed the park and ignition buttons on the Prius dashboard, and pulled Mel into his arms. "Pretty romantic stuff. That couple in the movie reminded me of us."

Mel laughed. "Chop off thirty years, thirty pounds, get two different personalities, and they fit us to a tee."

"This is more what I had in mind." He held her face in his hands and gave her a long, lingering kiss.

"Mmm … I like that … let's go inside instead of necking in the car."

"And what's wrong with necking in the car?" He nibbled at her earlobe.

"Right now I'm in the mood to dance." She swayed in the seat and gave him a seductive smile.

"We'll make it a Frank Sinatra night."

They walked hand-in-hand to the front porch. Ted unlocked the door and let them in.

Mel reached for the light switch. "How about a brandy before—"

They both gasped at the shambles in their living room—books, plant soil, and broken glass covered floor; curtains and drapes were pulled from their rods; and the smell of spilled booze permeated the air.

"Jesus Christ!" Ted said. "What the hell happened here?" He bent over, picked up two framed pictures; shattered glass dropped to the rug and crunched under his shoes as he followed Mel to the piano. The top lay splintered on the floor; then they saw the tangled mess of cut strings.

Mel stood with a hand over her mouth, touched the silenced piano keys. "Why would anyone do this?" Tears rolled down her cheeks.

He drew her to him. "I'm sorry, Mel. I know how much you love your piano."

"Such a waste. So … so mean." She looked from the piano to the emptied book shelves. "And all our books. Why?"

He bent down to pick up a book, its spine broken, and tried to put it back on a shelf. It slipped from his hand and splayed open at his feet.

"First the CORPS building, now this." He looked into his wife's teary eyes. "My fault," he said. "Has to be connected to what's going on at Galen Hospital."

"Is this supposed to scare you off?" she asked.

"Can't think of any other reason. It sure as hell wasn't a random break-in." He pulled her to him, kept squeezing her tighter. "Can't put you in this kind of danger. What would I do without you?"

She looked away from the mess, her piano. "If they wanted to frighten me—it worked."

He nodded.

"But, we can't let some anonymous creeps push us around. To hell with them and whoever sent them."

"What are we going to do?"

"First, we don't kto9uch the phone or any light switches," he said. "They think that's what triggered the explosion at CORPS headquarters. He pulled out his cell, called the police and the fire department, then made a reservation at a local motel.

"Helluva way to end a movie night out," Mel said and slumped down on the floor.

Chapter 18

W. Wade Wilson, settled into his high-rise condo for the weekend, swirled a double shot of single-malt Scotch in a heavy crystal tumbler. He liked his liquor neat when he drank, which was no longer as often or as much as most people thought. He knew the debilitating effects of booze, had seen its insidious power destroy too many careers, men and women alike. It tended to make them loud, obnoxious, and loose with information around people who weren't to be trusted. Liquor and wine—good liquor and wine—were there to be savored, not misused to turn your life into one big fuck-up.

He put his feet up on the sofa and held the tumbler up to the light. The amber liquid was hypnotic, could put him into a trance if he allowed it to. Getting involved with any kind of booze was dangerous for a man like him. Tori had told him that, that night five years ago.

He rubbed a finger lightly against his fleshy lips, could still imagine her mouth on his.

Pretty Tori; beautiful Tori.

Tori, with the long blond hair that brushed against his face, swept across his body, tantalized his him when they made love. He'd called her his trophy wife. But although she was young, she didn't dance to his or anyone else's tune.

A sudden flush of heat aroused him as he remembered her naked body. He took a swallow of the Scotch, ran a finger around the rim of the tumbler.

Smooth, silky skin.

His eyes tracked to the black and white 8x10 portrait he still kept of her. Those probing eyes followed him no matter where he stood or sat.

Sapphire eyes. Dangerous eyes.

She was the one who pushed him into dumping his PR firm to become a political gun for hire. "Hide behind the walls, look out from the cracks, conquer the world."

That was how she described what he did.

He held his glass up in a toast to her. "Would have been second-rate without you, little lady."

But he was without her now, without her because he'd been drunk that last night they were together. Not falling down drunk, but carelessly inebriated.

* * *

"You're an old fool to let some dumb-ass senator outsmart you," Tori said.

"These environmental issues are sensitive—can't just go hog-wild bullying politicians for votes. Not if you want to stay in the lobbying business, not if want to keep from having your ass nailed to the barn wall."

Tori sat at her dressing table, applying makeup, combing her hair, getting ready for one of the frequent functions they were obligated to attend. As always, she'd shopped for days to find just the right dress for the event. Tonight's outfit was carefully spread out on the bed, waiting for her to slip into it. Stunning as always.

She shifted her gaze away from the eyeliner brush, and looked at him. "Seems to me that's exactly what happened to you last time out, got your hide hung out to dry."

Then her eyes took in the three fingers of Scotch he was carrying around as he paced and waited for her. "W.W., darling, you've been drinking too much lately."

He looked at his glass, started to take a sip, then sat it down on his dresser. "And why should that matter to you? You still seem to have enough money to spend on clothes and jewels."

She put down the eyeliner, stood—naked as a blue jay—walked slowly and provocatively over to him, and with just the hint of a smile, she slapped him hard across the face.

His drunken response was to grab her slender neck with both hands, twist and shake her head. A loud snap made him stop, release her. He watched in horror as she crumpled to the floor in a heap at his feet, her head resting at a distorted angle.

Surprised sapphire eyes stared up at him.

He reacted in a frenzy of activity—tried to breathe life into her mouth; pumped at her chest; pleaded for her to move, to react. He pulled at his hair, shouted, cried.

All the while her eyes watched him; she seemed to be waiting for him to finish all of his frantic foolishness so she could scream at him, make him own up to his weakness, his cruelty.

But all he heard was his own heavy breathing, then the shattering crash as he threw his glass against the bedroom wall.

* * *

Wilson had gone over that moment endless times, trying to change the scenario, like redecorating a hideous room.

What if he'd slapped her back?

What if he'd screamed at her?

What if he'd just walked away?

What if he hadn't fucked up?

His cell phone rang, turning the past into the present. He stared blankly at the small lighted screen, ran the back of his hand across the tears running down his cheek.

He finally made out the caller ID—Levi Black.

The coincidence was almost too much for him—here was the same the person who had taken care of everything that terrible night. Only the two of them knew what really happened, knew how Tori had gone from being a wife to becoming a missing person, a statistic, a memory.

Levi Black, his faithful friend since kindergarten, who hung with the east side gangs and later became a made man; Levi Black, who had saved his life when he'd stupidly mouthed off to one of the Dead Eyes, a gang from The Projects. The lowlife had wanted to use W.W. for target practice, had put one .38 round into his leg before Levi arrived in a stolen Caddie, scooped him up off the street, and sped away as more slugs kerplunked into the side of the sedan.

In the back office of a gang-connected doctor, Wade had said he and Levi were now blood brothers, responsible for each other's lives. Levi hadn't answered, but ever since he'd always been there to protect Wade, to save him from himself.

W.W. patted his right leg, the leg that might have been amputated, wouldn't be there, if it weren't for Levi, then reached for the phone:

"Speak to me," Wilson said.

"Had a couple of rubes take care of it. It's a done deal."

"No interruptions, no problems?"

"No way."

"Let's hope Yost gets the message."

"Whatever."

Chapter 19

Ted plowed through the crowds in San Francisco's Union Square. It was packed with shoppers. Just about everyone was carrying one or more large shopping bags, each boldly imprinted with the name of a department store or an exclusive shop.

He studied the faces and actions of the shoppers—attractive, vibrant, involved. They sent text messages as they walked, talked on cells, watched and manipulated the screens of smartphones, carried on conversations with each other while laughing and pausing to glance in store windows.

This crowd seemed so much more independent than he'd been at their age.

Was that really true?

He'd been a father in his mid twenties, and while covering the Vietnam War, all around him kids in their late teens were being brutalized and killed. And back home? Mel was working at low-paying jobs struggling to raise their first child.

Different world.

He looked around at these pretty people. War? Americans dying in Afghanistan and Iraq? None of that seemed to have a place in this carefree environment.

Ted found the café where Nathan Sorkin liked to meet and took a window booth so he could watch the Market Street scene and keep an eye out for the CORPS director. They'd picked a time in between the breakfast rush and the surge that would come at lunchtime, but the popular eating spot was still busy.

He expected Nathan at any minute and was dreading the meeting. He'd spent the night tossing and turning, unable to sleep as he asked himself over and over whether the Hygea-Galen business was something he really needed in his life.

The answer, in the wee hours of the morning, had been no. He was going to drop the investigation, his whole investigation.

He'd almost called Nathan to tell him on the phone, cancel their meeting. But he had too much respect for the man to not tell him face to face. Nathan would have to understand that he couldn't put Mel's life on the line.

Even now he was uneasy about her. They'd moved into a motel room and a friend was with her. He wanted her here with him, but she'd made it clear that she wasn't about to be smothered by his fears.

And he knew she was right. But dammit, it was Mel!

Being in dangerous situations wasn't a new thing for him, but having his home trashed was something he'd never considered a possibility.

Naïveté.

Well that could get them both killed. He was willing to take the risk for himself, but not for Mel.

He took in a deep breath, looked out, and tried to relax. It was a great people-watching spot. Off in one direction was the cable car terminus, where the operators and conductors labored to manually turn the cars around before starting the journey back up the Powell Street hill; throngs of tourists, and a few locals, stood in long lines waiting to grab a seat, or stand on a step to hang free off the sides of the cable car. He smiled as he saw a hustler trying to sell bogus tickets to unsuspecting out-of-towners, promising front-of-the-line spots to board.

He became so wrapped up in the street opera that it surprised him when he heard Nathan Sorkin's voice.

"Hi," Nathan said. "Just saw you yesterday." He slid into the booth opposite Ted and pulled a napkin from the dispenser. As usual, he began tearing the soft, folded paper into smaller and smaller pieces. He leaned forward, gave Ted a closer look. "You're looking kind of peaked, my friend. You okay?"

"Not really, but before we get into that, how's Myra?"

"Stull critical, unfortunately. Came her straight from the hospital. Wanted to see her, but they wouldn't let me in."

"If there's anything—"

Nathan raised a hand. "I know. I know. We can only wait." He took a deep breath. "Now, why the special meeting? What's going on?"

Before Ted could answer, the waitress arrived with water and took their orders—toasted English muffins and coffee for both of them.

"I didn't want to do this on the phone," Ted said. "But I thought you should know that last night, while Mel and I were out to dinner and a movie, our house was broken into and torn apart from end to end."

Nathan's face collapsed into his doleful Einstein persona— eyes leaking tears, white hair flying everywhere as he tried to rake the unruly strands with gnarled fingers.

"Thank God the two of you were out. You could have been killed."

"No, I don't think that was the intent. The investigators didn't find any explosives, like at your offices. And there was no attempt to burn down the house."

"Trying to scare you off?"

"I think so. A warning."

Nathan started on another napkin. "Maybe we quit all of this. I never thought—"

When Nathan said it, *quit,* it slapped him right in the face. Quit? He'd never been a quitter, and he wasn't going to start now. And when it got down to it, Mel probably wouldn't want him to quit either.

"No, we don't quit. We're just getting started."

"But this really worries me, Ted."

"Me, too." He took a sip of water. "We just have to be more careful, more alert. I've already made arrangements to have a security system installed at the house while we're staying at the motel. Probably a closing-the-barn door-after-the-horse-is-gone kind of thing, but I'll sleep better ... I hope."

"Did they do a lot of damage?"

119

"Yeah, but the worse part, the really sad part, is that they trashed Mel's piano—cut every string. They also smashed our family pictures, destroyed our books, and generally made a mess of everything they could get their hands on. But from what I could tell, they didn't search the house. Wouldn't have found anything even if they had."

The waitress set their orders on the table. Ted immediately took a long sip of the hot coffee, grabbed for a glass of water to cool his mouth.

"And you think it's connected to your digging into Galen and Hygea for us?"

"What else? I mean, I suppose it could have been kids out tearing things up just for kicks. But it didn't look or feel that way—no beer taken, no food eaten. And cutting the piano strings? I don't see kids taking the time to do something like that."

"There may be more going on with Hygea than we originally thought." Nathan started ripping up another napkin.

"The evidence is piling up that *someone* doesn't want us digging around in Galen Hospital's internal affairs." Ted poured water into his coffee. "And you can be sure Garrett Rudge has probably ferreted out the fact that I know John Bradberry, which certainly is going to make him feel even more nervous about me."

Nathan was silent as he sipped his coffee, oblivious to the fact the hot brew had almost burned Ted's tongue off. "I'm sorry I dragged you into this mess," he said, almost whispering the words. "First they almost kill poor Myra, and now they're after you."

"*I'm* okay with it. But Mel? I 'm not about to have her end up like Myra. I have to keep her safe."

Nathan was quiet for a long moment; when he finally spoke, he emphasized each word. "You know there's no way to do that." He stared out the window, looking at the passing crowd. "Life is short and the older you get, the more you want to hang onto it." His face relaxed into a sad smile. "But we both know you can't."

He carefully opened a small plastic cup of strawberry jam, smothered half of his muffin, took a big bite, and chewed slowly. "We have to do what's important to us at any cost. Otherwise we might as well be dead anyway."

* * *

Ted drove over to the main branch of the San Francisco library on Larkin to do more research on euthanasia and Hygea Corporation. He knew it might be faster to hit the Internet, but he felt the need to get away from electronics and work with actual newspapers, magazines, and books.

After an hour or so, he started shifting in his seat to relieve a stabbing back pain. Ancient injuries? Growing tension? Or it could be something as simple as sitting too long in a straight-back, unpadded, oak chair. He didn't know and it didn't matter. He intended to keep digging in the library files—he needed as much information as he could find, and as quickly as possible. But there was still time to walk away, no matter what he'd said to Nathan. Run with the investigation, or turn his back on the whole thing?

Finally he closed his notebook, stuffed it into his leather portfolio, and started walking back to the garage where he'd parked his car.

By the time he got to the garage, he'd accepted the fact that he was in too deep to drop out. He would continue his investigation with Sorkin and CORPS. But there had to be a strong D.C. connection. Asking Bill to birddog the thing wasn't going to be enough. Telephones weren't going to be enough. *He* needed to go to Washington.

Cruising along Van Ness, he used one hand to massage his lower back, then shifted to his neck. He wasn't really against assisted suicide. At least he didn't think so. But legalizing it, as some states already had, made him uncomfortable.

It was that old slippery slope thing; once you started down, there was no turning back

But it's a giant step from assisted to selective euthanasia.

Deliberately withholding care? Putting people to death based on economics?

He wondered whether the public would go for it. Or was he being cynical when he thought Americans seemed less sensitive to the right and wrong of things? Wasn't Holocaust more and more becoming just another word?

Making selective euthanasia would take a real selling job. But then, with sugar-coating and a few good sound bites you can make almost anything fly.

Ted glanced in the rearview mirror as he drove down Lombard on his way to the Golden Gate Bridge. Then took a second, longer look. Something was off. He was almost certain the gray Chevy Malibu had been on his tail ever since he pulled out of the downtown parking garage.

Uneasiness tweaked his awareness; he waited until the last minute to make a sharp right turn onto Scott, then accelerated until he was doing more than 40 by the time he reached Marina Blvd. He barely slowed as he careened left and dodged back and forth across the two westbound lanes leading to the bridge. A quick glance in the mirror told him that it wasn't his imagination working overtime. That damn Chevy changed lanes, sped up, slowed down every time he did.

He thought he'd lost the tail by the time he was on Doyle Drive, but when he looked in the mirror, the gray car was not only there, it was catching up to him.

The idea of being followed made him shift in his seat. First, his house had been trashed. Now, someone was on his tail. They, whoever *they* were, had serious intentions.

None of this was new to him—he'd been shot at, but always outside the U.S. Everything had been staged to scare him off from some story, otherwise they would have nailed him and walked away clean.

Hell, maybe he had a death wish. None of the attempts stopped whatever he was doing.

He squinted, tried to catch a good look at the face of the driver, but all he got was a breadth of shoulders—an outline that made him think it was a man. No, there were two of them.

Two of them!

He sped across the Golden Gate Bridge, hoping he'd get caught by the cops and stopped. Maybe he could call to…no, no. He visualized his cell phone sitting on the dresser in the motel.

Calm down, Yost, you're losing it!

But the hairs on his neck prickled and a knot was growing inside his stomach.

He stretched and moved closer to the inside mirror, tried to read the Chevy's license plate as they plunged into the murkiness of the Waldo Tunnel. Then he felt a sharp jolt; his head jerked back and forward, spit flew everywhere.

The asshole rear-ended me!

Ted swallowed hard, sped up, and at the last possible moment veered off the freeway at Mill Valley. The Malibu's grille remained only inches away from his rear bumper. As he got closer to the Tam Junction intersection, he started blasting his horn. Other drivers pulled out of his way as he roared through every red light, veering right into town rather than taking the left toward the Coastal Highway.

The Malibu lost a little ground as he sped through the village streets, was never more than a half-block behind. By now, Ted's hands were shaking so badly he could hardly hold onto the wheel.

A rolling stop and a sharp left put the Prius on the winding, hilly route to Panoramic Highway. The Chevy was falling behind on the curves. Ted pushed the little hybrid hard, hoping someone didn't back out of a driveway or drift across the center line coming from the other direction.

Three roads at the crest—Muir Woods, Stinson Beach, and the back route to Tam Junction. He ran the stop sign, held his breath, and kept going on Panoramic.

After about a half-mile, he pulled off onto a side street, turned the car around, and waited.

His chest felt like someone was pounding on it. He looked down at his shaking hands and barked a small laugh—he'd crossed his fingers.

He sat and waited, but there was nothing. He reached for a tissue to blot at the sweat on his forehead and cheeks, and laughed out loud.

When he arrived at the motel, the gray Chevy Malibu was waiting for him across the street.

His heart started racing again—he reached behind the front seat, scrabbled around until he found the three-cell Maglite that was tucked under the driver's seat. He slapped it against his palm, opened the car door. From the corner of his eye he saw the motel room curtain move. He knew Mel was there.

He stepped out of the Prius, looked across the street at the Chevy, then glanced back at the window. He saw his wife's worried face and the slow, negative shake of her head.

He couldn't stop now.

He turned and started across the street, tapping the end of the big flashlight rhythmically into the palm of his hand. Before he was halfway there, the gray sedan accelerated away from the curb, turned left at the first corner, and was quickly out of sight.

When he turned around, Mel was no longer standing at the window.

Chapter 20

"You promised you were going to stick to blogging," Mel said after Ted when Ted brought her up to date on Nathan Sorkin and told her a trip to Washington was necessary.

"We'll only be gone for a few days."

"We? Are you out of your mind? What about the house? We can't go away and leave it in that God-awful mess. At least, *I* can't."

"I've arranged for an alarm system to be installed while we're gone and—"

"Good! I'll stay and supervise."

"After what's happened, there's no way I'm going to leave you in California by yourself."

* * *

By the time the Saturday night redeye landed at Dulles International in Washington, Ted and Mel were exhausted.

On the ground, they boarded the aerotrain to the main terminal where they immediately spotted Bill Tana at the gate— the tall, dark-haired man would stand out in any crowd with his rugged, handsome features. Mel dropped her carry-on and ran straight into his arms..

"Couldn't you have left the old goat behind so you and I could do some real visiting?" He lifted her off the floor and spun her around in a circle.

"It's been way too long. I miss you and Kelli," she said with a laugh. "Where is that beautiful wife of yours?"

"Home, keeping an eye on the beastly teenager."

Tana turned and reached out to shake hands with Ted, but instead, they threw their arms around each other and squeezed out a tight bear hug.

"For God's sake. You still look like a kid.," Ted said.

"Save the phony flattery. You had me hooked with the phone call last night. I'm here only to serve."

"And we appreciate it."

They walked to the luggage carousel, got there just as it started to turn. Bags began dropping from the delivery chute.

"Hey, Mel, would you call and see if you can get us reservations at the Best Western in either Falls Church or Arlington while I watch for our luggage?"

"No, no, no!" Bill interrupted. "You guys are coming home with me. Kelli has the guest room ready and waiting."

"I don't think so." Ted glanced around the area, wondering if someone was watching them. "Thing is, I don't want you getting caught in the cross-fire. Things have been heating up fast in San Francisco."

"You come to D.C., I'm here."

"Look, you two, work out whatever needs to be worked out, I'm off to find the restroom," Mel started walking away. "And that's not open to debate."

Ted pulled Bill away from the crowd huddling around the carousel. "Someone sent a wrecking crew to our house. Messed up the place pretty bad."

"Maybe it was a simple B&E?"

"Nope. Nothing was taken. I mean, when we went through the place with the cops, we couldn't find anything missing. A diamond broach that belonged to Mel's grandmother was right there in her jewelry box on top of the dresser."

"That's strange."

"Then yesterday, some guys rear-ended me. Lost them, but when I got back to Sonoma they were parked across the street from the motel where we were staying."

"Any ideas?"

"My money's on Hygea Corporation and their head honcho on the West Coast, Garrett Rudge."

Ted spotted their luggage and pulled it off the carousel.

"Here, let me take that." Bill reached for the suitcase. "Can't let an old guy like you get a hernia."

"This old guy can still flatten you, you pissant." He started to lift one bag off the floor and hold it out straight out at shoulder height. It didn't work. "Long flight," he said

Mel returned, cell phone in hand. "Do I call for a rez, or not?"

"Not! You're coming with me; Kelli would kill me if I didn't bring you guys home. Besides, there's no way you're staying at a Best Western if they're looking for you. Why make it that easy for them?"

"We're not staying at your place," Ted said. "Probably even have your bathroom bugged already. Wouldn't surprise me if they had eyes on us right now."

"Sure you're not going paranoid on me?" Bill held up a hand as Ted started to punch his arm.

* * *

They tried to lay a false trail by changing cabs three times and wandering into two overcrowded malls filled with weekend shoppers. After checking out all four of the out-of-the-way hotels Bill had suggested, they went back to the first one and checked in. Ted thought they'd probably ditched anyone following them, but the hairs on the back of his neck continued to prickle.

The seedy dive they chose was nothing but an overpriced flea bag on the outskirts of D.C. Their room wasn't much larger than their walk-in closet at home and the shower stall had spots of mold here and there, and the water stopped for long stretches when they tried to shower. Between them they used most of the worst anatomical curse words known to western civilization. And when they finally collapsed into the bed, they could hear both the shower *and* wash basin faucets dripping in counterpoint.

Rather than getting the three or four hours of sleep they'd planned on, they spent most of the time on the soft, lumpy, and less-than-standard-size double mattress, reading background material.

Melissa scrolled through a stack of papers on Hygea's background, plus a condensed history of the current healthcare situation in United States. Ted used the time to catch up on who the healthcare powerbrokers were in the Washington name-game.

"Kind of dumb to arrive in D.C. on a Sunday and expect to immediately track down or get in touch with anyone," Ted said sheepishly.

"No comment."

* * *

"What do you mean you lost them?" Wade Wilson said in a low, menacing voice. I thought you had them at the airport."

"They got away," said the hoarse voice at the other end.

"I can't have that man running around loose. Did you say he had a woman with him?"

"Yeah, his wife."

"Are you sure it was his wife? It could have been a niece or some doxie."

"Listen, man, just because we botched up the tail doesn't mean we don't know who's who. It's his wife, damn it."

"I need you to fix this now. Trap and hold. You get my meaning?"

There was a long pause on the end of the line. "Not for the money you're paying us. Our deal with Levi Black doesn't cover kidnapping."

"I'm not talking about kidnapping, you fool. I'm talking about detaining."

"Same difference."

"How much?"

"Another hundred."

"Two hundred thousand dollars total? You've got to be out of your mind."

"It's your gig, man. You're calling the shots. If *detain* is what you want, then that's the cost. That, or we can shit-can the whole deal."

Wilson held the phone tightly, looked at the calendar. The next few days would either make or break them.

"Do it!"

Chapter 21

Ted Yost paced back and forth along the edge of the Potomac—the water was gray and looked forbidding; the breeze was icy cold. Lazy snowflakes settled on his navy-blue overcoat; every now and then he nervously brushed them away. It was hard to believe that the last time he stood at this very spot he was surrounded by blossoming Japanese cherry trees. Now, instead of soft, pink petals, a carpet of snow covered the ground.

He shook his head. How many years ago?

Too many.

The frigid weather made his joints stiff and sore; all he could think about was a glowing fireplace where he could warm his feet. He took in a deep breath that became a long sigh.

Yeah, he *was* getting old. His body pulled and tugged at him all the time; it sent distress and cautionary signals instead of the juice he needed to keep going at the pace he'd always gone. Last week he flew out of bed to answer the telephone and landed on his rump. It was the first time he'd forced himself to face up to it—things he took for granted throughout most of his life were changing.

He continued to pace.

Physical problems he could handle. But the restlessness and the awful feeling of being unsure of himself for the first time since he was just a kid? That was scary.

Maybe all this insecurity was just part of the normal aging process. And maybe he wasn't used to having to watch over anyone other than himself when he was on the hunt. But Melissa had to be in Washington with him; he couldn't leave her behind; she was in danger, too.

And maybe he was just plain scared and it was time to put all this conspiracy chasing behind him.

He looked across the water at the Lincoln Memorial. Melissa wanted to spend some time there; he hadn't wanted her to go, at least not alone. But she'd insisted. Wouldn't take no for an answer. He'd caved, decided she was probably safer by herself than she was with him, particularly if someone's goons were following him.

Still, his heart sank when she walked away and was too quickly out of sight. All his fears rose to the surface. Scenarios that repeated over and over in his head wouldn't turn off: their house trashed; his car being rammed; pursuers parked at the motel; wanting to fight back with only a flashlight; Mel standing in the window.

Vulnerable.

A chill that had nothing to do with the weather shook him hard. He pulled the fleece-lined coat collar up tight around his neck while his other hand balled inside his pocket.

He glanced at the sky for a moment, then back along the path he'd used. He could see little more than the fluttering snow, which was now coming down much harder than when he'd arrived.

A figure appeared in the distance, the snow kept him from seeing whether it was a man or woman. Even as the person got closer, he couldn't put a face on the bobbing head until only a few feet separated them.

"What took you so long?" he asked Bill Tana. Only then did he realize he'd been holding his breath; he exhaled a burst of pent-up air.

"You and your paranoia about bugged phones drives me bonkers. How am I supposed to remember where we had that last Easter Sunday rendezvous? What was it, five years ago? Man, it took a lot of thinking. And I've already been to two other possibilities."

"Did anyone follow you?"

"If they did, they're mighty confused about the where-and-why-fors of Bill Tana. Actually, I spotted the tails when I left my house. They didn't have a chance."

"Now maybe you'll believe me."

"I always believe you, Ted, especially since I'm more paranoid than you ever dreamed of being. And by the way, you were right—there is a bug on my land line at home. Found it outside in the junction box; left it in place for now. Maybe whoever's listening can make more sense out of my teenage daughter's rap then I can."

'They've been to your house? Now I know I should never have brought you into this."

"Now don't go soft on me, old man. They're not after me—they're after you."

"Still, I'm sorry for dumping this on you, even if you're the only person left in this town that I can trust."

"Well then, believe me when I tell you we'd better get moving. I don't like setting myself up for target practice, no matter how bad the visibility is."

They walked rapidly to a nearby gym, just a short distance from Bill's office, doing a look-both-ways-before-crossing at every intersection. They saw few cars and even fewer pedestrians. Once there, Ted was grateful to be inside a warm building. They checked in, got a guest pass and locker keys, and went to change.

Bill pulled out a well-worn t-shirt with a faded "Vat 69" logo on the front and a pair of red satin gym shorts and handed them to Ted.

"You expect me to wear these?" He dangled the shorts on one finger and looked around the locker room. "Be lucky if I'm not tagged as some congressman's gay locker room buddy."

Bill laughed. "Sorry, those are the only extras I have, at least clean ones. But don't worry about your rep; no one will come close to you with these on." He pulled a pair of ratty looking sneakers from the bottom of his locker.

Ted sighed and started to get undressed. "This is the only place you could think of to get us off the streets and out of sight?"

"To quote a friend of mine, 'gratitude is not your strong point.'"

Ted laughed. "Touché."

131

"If you think about it, this is an ideal place, and it sure as hell wouldn't hurt that gut of yours to lift a few bar bells. You look like you're starting to get soft on all that home cooking. Melissa must be spoiling the hell out of you."

Ted winced as he squeezed into the shorts. "This is what I get for saving your miserable ass. I should have thought twice before I yanked you out of San Francisco Bay, just left you there as fish food."

Bill's face flushed slightly, a faraway look came into his eyes. "Yeah, I sure did get in more than a little bit over my head that time. But you gotta admit, I'd have been all right if they hadn't cuffed my hands behind my back."

"Yeah, about as right as a duck on a rollercoaster." Ted threw an arm over Bill's shoulder. "Just a wayward flower child in the Haight."

"With a major in Asian poppies." Bill turned to look at Ted. "I guess enough time has passed that I can ask and maybe you'll give me an answer."

"You want to know how I got those loan sharks off your back?"

Bill nodded.

"Hell, no big secret—you could've asked me any time." Ted sucked his gut in even more. For a moment, the shorts didn't wrinkle and tug quite as much. "After I pulled you out of The Bay, I paid off the lousy ten grand you lost at those backroom Pai Gow tables in Chinatown."

"And they backed off just like that? Hard to believe; I thought Moco hated my guts, didn't care about the ten grand."

"All too true, but you gotta keep things in perspective. As far as your involvement went, Moco had an eye on the big picture and wasn't about to be sidetracked by some small fry like you. He wanted the ten grand, yes, but I convinced him that what he didn't want was a media spotlight on his gaming and dope operations. Not quite as dumb as he looked."

"I guess I owe you ten thousand."

"You don't owe me anything. Besides, I always figured it wouldn't hurt to have something to hold over your head for times like these."

Bill chuckled. "You really are a devious old fart, you know that?"

Ted winked and glanced at his watch. "Told Mel I'd pick her up in about an hour. Fill me in on what you've found out."

"We'd better move into the gym; people are starting to look at us kind of funny."

"Ha-ha funny, or weird funny?" Ted asked.

"With you, it could only be weird."

They left the locker room and moved into the gym. Ted said, "Don't know how to tell you this, buddy, but these sneakers smell pretty ripe."

"Why do you think they're on your feet instead of mine?"

They walked over to the weights section. It wasn't crowded, but most of the larger equipment was in use. Following Bill's lead, Ted picked up a pair of five-pound weights, straddled a bench, and initiated a series of swing-lift movements.

"From what little I've been able to find out, this is ugly stuff you've gotten yourself into," Bill whispered.

"How ugly?"

"You're dropping in on the tail end of a very fast-moving legislative ploy. Essentially, a healthcare biggie wants to legitimatize selective euthanasia as a way to cut Medicare costs."

"Who's behind it?"

Bill looked around, obviously to check on whether they were out of earshot of the nearest person. "Apparently it goes right to the top on the political side."

"And on the private side? Anyone other than Hygea."

"Haven't been able to pin that down … yet. But it's probably the whole healthcare industry."

"My experience is that this is a town that thrives on rumor, speculation, and leaked information."

"It hasn't changed," Bill said. "But I've been shut out of every place I've turned."

Rivulets of sweat raced down their faces, dripped onto the floor. Their exercise action was starting to slow.

"There must be a go-to person, a conduit between the corporate and political interests?"

Bill thought for a moment. "Ever heard of W. Wade Wilson?"

"W. Wade Wilson?" Ted finished a couple of reps. "Isn't he a big-time lobbyist?"

"Oh, yeah," Bill said. "He's big time all right."

"So what's his *schtick*."

"Power is his *schtick*. What else?"

"Do I detect a hint of respect in your voice?" Ted asked.

"This guy is at the very core of every healthcare plan that gets entered on any legislative docket. Or is even thought of being introduced in either house." Bill stopped, ran an arm across his forehead and flipped sweat off onto the floor. "He's an ultra-conservative—far right of Dick Cheney. So, if you're looking for a go-to guy on healthcare issues, he's the one."

"Yeah, yeah, I've heard that song before," Ted said. "He's not the first to hold those reins."

"You don't get it, do you?"

"Don't get what?"

"The word is that someone, or someones, at the top of the food chain has collared the President into believing selective euthanasia is the only way to keep Medicare from going down the tubes."

"Not this Wade Wilson?" Ted said.

"No. The guy is powerful, but he'd have to have an inner sanctum connection."

Ted stopped swinging his weights, stood, and stretched. "Hey, politicians for years have been claiming that Medicare is going to bankrupt the country. Suddenly, you and Sorkin think there's an imminent secret plan to reduce costs by bumping off people." He threw his arms up in the air. "And this going to happen without a huge public outcry?"

"So it would seem." Bill racked his weights and rubbed his head with a towel.

"And you can't find any links in pending legislation?"

"Not a one."

"So how is it going to reach the President's desk without any fanfare?"

"Laws get put on the books all the time without the public ever hearing anything about them—rammed though committees without hearings, attached to other legislation, Presidential executive order—"

"I know how the system works. This just seems too big for that. People aren't going to put up with it."

"Look at it from another way, Ted. Euthanasia has growing populist approval across most of the country."

"Voluntary, physician-assisted euthanasia, not *selective* euthanasia."

"Selective, smelective! You don't think anyone reads the fine print, do you?" Bill said with a snort. "Besides, the man in the street thinks anything that can go wrong only happens to the other guy, right?"

"No one is going to go for ending a person's life because it costs too much money to save selected individuals."

"You know, Teddy, my man, for an award-winning, highly respected journalist, you're damn naïve at times."

"Spare me the compliments."

"If people could get a committee to make the hard end-of-life decisions for them, don't you think it would fly?"

"No," Ted said.

"Think, again, buddy—no guilt because you haven't visited Aunt Edna at the nursing home, who by the way, you never liked in the first place; no further expense to take care of elderly family members."

"I still don't buy it, Bill."

"People could get back to the television, the internet, or whatever. And they could feel good about the situation because the system will do all the dirty work."

"You're way too cynical, kid."

"No, just realistic. Tell me the politicians and their healthcare industry backers can't make it fly."

Ted stared long and hard at his friend. "Let's get dressed and go pick up Mel. And on the way, tell me more about this W. Wade Wilson."

Chapter 22

Melissa climbed the steps of the Lincoln Memorial; her eyes searched beyond the columns that guarded the entry to the magnificent statue of the 16th President of the United States. It was a sight like no other.

Mr. Lincoln sat looking benignly at her.

Was there a hint of stoicism, or was it sadness that was etched on the face of this man of the people? Or was he simply a man weighed down with the resolve it took to meet a turbulent destiny?

She wondered how Lincoln would fare in the Washington circus today. What sound bite would they use to describe him? Man of the people? Too tame; it would never put him in office.

She'd been here many times in the past. But standing before the bearded figure inspired her all over again, made her even angrier at the overwhelming numbers of greedy Washington politicians dedicated to nothing but their own selfish careers.

A shiver caught her, ran from her toes to the top of her head. She placed a hand on her chest; it was tight from the frigid air forced into her lungs—the very same iciness that was cutting through the ski jacket she'd brought from home. She tightened her scarf around her neck, pulled upward on the cuffs of her sheepskin gloves.

She was calmer now that she was away from California, away from her devastated house, her shattered piano. She would be reluctant to admit it to anyone else, but there was an element of excitement in this cat-and-mouse thing, and for the first time, she could see why Ted was such an action junky. There was a price though—uneasiness rode high on her shoulders even though she tried to shrug it off.

Maybe she was just plain tired.

Melissa quickly looked around, tried to reassure herself that she wasn't alone. But most of the other visitors to the memorial were leaving or walking down the long, concrete steps. Somehow she had expected more of a crowd, even with the inclement weather.

She walked out toward the columns again, looked up at the sky—the snow was coming down harder and the day had turned an even darker, uglier gray.

Melissa clutched her jacket closer to her and tried to drive out the chill as she stood at the top of the steps, ready to head over to meet Ted and Bill at the Holocaust Museum.

Out of nowhere a voice blasted in her ear, low and mean. Her arms were pinned back with such force, bolts of pain shot up into her shoulders.

"Not a word or you're dead meat."

She went rigid with fear, but she tried to fight the vise-like grip, kick at the legs braced behind her. But the man grabbed her around the chest and squeezed until she could barely breathe.

"You're not listening, lady," the nasty voice said. "Cool it!" Then he punched her hard in the kidney.

Her mouth opened to scream but a pad of cloth smothered her, forcing her to inhale an acrid, sickly smelling chemical. She gagged as it burned her mouth and nostrils. She pushed at the steel-grip, but her body turned to mush and her legs buckled.

Soon she was falling away with only the darkness to catch her.

* * *

"She's not inside," Ted said, coming out of the Holocaust Museum.

"Was she planning to go someplace else after here?"

"If so, she didn't say anything about it."

"Have you tried her cell phone?"

"Can't. It was hooked up to the charger when those bastards broke into our house. Smashed it, along with everything else."

"Maybe you were supposed to meet her back at the hotel."

"No, no, no! We were perfectly clear about it—she was going to catch a cab from the Lincoln Memorial, then meet us here in the lobby of the museum at two." Ted looked at his watch and shook his head when he saw that they were more than a half-hour late. He collapsed onto a snow-covered step and looked around helplessly.

Bill rested a hand on his shoulder. "I still think she went back to the hotel. Probably mad as hell because she's worked up and worried."

Ted covered his face. "I should never have gotten involved with CORPS … should have stayed out of it … left it to others." He shook his head back and forth. "Sixty-five and still trying to stay in the game." He looked up. "Where the hell is she?"

"Want me to call the hotel, see if she's there?"

"No, I'll do that. Why don't you call your house? Maybe she went there?"

"I can try, but Kelli went off to a lecture at the Smithsonian. Won't be back until around dinner time."

"Dammit!" Ted pulled out his cell and a business card from the hotel, called, and then gave his room number after the operator answered.

The phone rang several times, then the clerk came back on the line. "Wanna leave a message?"

"Please tell Mrs. Yost to give her husband a call on his cell."

"Okay."

Ted clicked off, stared straight ahead. "Back to square one."

Bill tugged at his arm. "What say we take a swing by the hotel, just in case, and if she calls before we get to my house, we'll go pick her up."

Ted yanked away. "No, damn it! How many times do I have to tell you: this is where we agreed to meet. We should stay here."

"If she was going to wait for you, she'd be here. We need to get going."

"What the hell's the matter with you? I've got to find Mel."

"For God's sake, Yost, for once in your life will you listen to someone other than yourself?"

Ted brushed at the snow falling against his face, then spoke softly, almost in a whisper, "All right. We'll try it your way." He reached into his pocket, grabbed a handkerchief and blew his nose, then looked up at Bill. "What if someone snatched her?"

"Let's not go there, yet," Bill said.

"It would be one way to get me off their backs."

"It's probably worth considering, Were you followed when you left the hotel?"

"I don't think so, but in this weather, who could be sure?"

"So let's assume they found out where you're staying. Why not snatch one or both of you before this?"

Ted got up from the concrete step, brushed the snow off his coat. "Hell, I don't know."

"Yeah, well, we do know they followed you from California, or tried to. And they're onto our connection. So either they'll message you at the hotel, or call you at my house. Does that make sense?"

"As much as anything." They started down the steps. Moving away from the museum, Ted stopped. "Jesus, Bill, what if they kill her?"

"Cut it out, man."

Ted covered his face. "Does Kelli know about any of this?"

"None of the specifics."

"Please call her," Ted said, touching Bill's sleeve. "At least leave a message on her cell to let us know if she hears from Mel."

Bill nodded, made the call, "We'll find her, man."

"These people are powerful and not about to let anything stand in their way. They'll use Mel—you know that."

* * *

Sitting in front of the Tanas' fireplace, wondering if he would ever be warm again, Ted rubbed at the center of his chest where a gnawing pain had settled in.

"You don't look so good." Bill handed Ted a mug of hot, black coffee. "Why don't you eat something?"

"I'll be fine as soon as I see or hear from Mel." He got up and began to pace, taking sips of his coffee at the same time.

"Ted, sit down!"

"Dammit, don't tell me what to do. I've really gone over the hill when I start taking advice from an ex druggie."

"Never going to let me forget, always there to rub my nose in."

"I didn't draw the dirty pictures," Ted said, gulping down his coffee. "You did."

"When you get home you'll find a fucking ten-thousand dollar check waiting. As far as I'm concerned, you and I are water under the bridge."

"What makes you think I need you, you son-of-a-bitch?"

They were in each other's face, fists balled, when the phone rang. For an instant, neither moved. Then they both reached out at once. Bill backed away. "Get it!"

Ted yanked up the receiver

An electronically disguised voice said, "Listen closely, hot shot. I'm only going to say this once."

"Where's my wife, you bastard?"

"She's safe ... for now." The voice had an asthmatic, nasal twang. "The rest is up to you."

"I'm listening. What do you want?"

"We want you out of D.C. and back in California. Think you can do that. Like pronto?"

"Not without my wife."

"You need to pay good attention, Yost. You're booked on tonight's redeye back to San Francisco. Your tickets will be waiting for you at the United counter at Dulles, Got that?"

"I told you I'm not going anywhere without my wife."

"Pick up the tickets, stand by the gate, and the first time they call the flight, your little woman will be by your side. Do it! Or you're both dead. And that's a promise."

"Let me talk to her. How do I know she's still alive?"

"Man, you're not in the driver's seat here. You do like I tell you or—do I have to say it again?"

"If she's not there, I'll find you no matter what hole you hide in."

"Shut the fuck up! Pick up the tickets, take your wife's arm, get on the plane, and stay in California. There's nothing for you or CORPS in D.C."

Chapter 23

Senator Angelle Savage paced back and forth, ignoring the spectacular view of the National Gallery of
Art from her office window. She'd been jumping at the least little thing, and was bone weary from having had a bitch of a time sleeping for the past week.

At the moment, W. Wade Wilson, was holding on the line. She'd been expecting, and dreading, his call for more than a month, ever since she'd been seated on the Medicare select subcommittee. The supercilious bastard had to make contact sooner or later because he was the *de facto* lobbyist for the entire for-profit healthcare industry.

Now, he calls!

Still, a pleasant sense of new-found power made her smile as she picked up the phone.

"Mr. Wilson. What a surprise."

"Good morning, Senator Savage. I hope you'll do me the pleasure of having lunch with me today."

Before she could get her mouth in gear to decline, he jumped in. "Now, now, Senator. This is D.C., not Virginia City or Carson City." His southern drawl made her skin prickle. "When opportunities present themselves, action is the name of the game. And if you'll pardon the vernacular, Mrs. Harrington, uh, excuse me, no disrespect intended, *Senator Savage*, it could be a matter of sink or swim."

His choice of words made her smile. After all, there wasn't a hell of a lot of water in her home state of Nevada, and she would have bet her prize collection of silver dollars that he knew it was only outside the office and other political spheres that she used her married name, Harrington. She assumed that his little intended slip was meant as some kind of abstract dig. She wasn't taking the bait.

"Mr. Wilson—"

"I'll pick you up at noon, Senator. Got an interesting proposition for you."

His voice quavered with an undercurrent of excitement. No, more of an urgent you-better-come-or-else kind of energy that damn near fried the skinny telephone wires separating them.

She said yes, but was miffed at herself for not putting him off. Now she would need to have her secretary postpone an important brown-bag meeting about urgent Nevada-related matters that should have been taken care of yesterday.

Why had she agreed?

Was she playing the little girl again, afraid she'd make someone frown, chastise her? She checked her watch, moved to the mirror and finger-combed her short dark hair. As she looked for mascara smudges, she studied the serious brown eyes set amidst an inglorious patchwork of facial lines.

No, at forty-four, she'd given up trying to keep anyone from frowning, least of all men.

She shrugged away extraneous thoughts; she had a limited amount of time to think it through.

What did he want?

The problem was, you simply didn't just out of hand turn away insiders like W. Wade Wilson III, insiders who controlled big money, had almost unlimited influence, and served as the outlet for streams of power. While she often railed against such outside pressure from her seat on the HHS subcommittee, the fact was that there were times when Wilson and his ilk were needed.

Like when we need money for re-election

She stopped pacing and looked out the window. Being inquisitive had caused her a lot of grief in her life, especially when she was younger.

Well, maybe it was her hormones.

No, her hormones were just fine, thank you.

It was her rage that always did her in, a smoldering rage that never seemed to die. She'd raged against injustice, especially toward women. Raged against powerful men like Wilson, who always seemed to be at the core of every low down thing there was, no matter how large or how small.

She grabbed her purse from her desk drawer and headed for the door, wondering if just being seen in public with the asshole would be considered lying down with the enemy?

* * *

The Washington Five & Dime, contrary to its name, was a plush, extravagant restaurant within sight of the Capitol. It was pure luck that she was wearing her most expensive power suit, with a contrasting red silk blouse. Angelle felt in tip-top form.

From the moment she walked into the circular restaurant with Wilson—there were rumors people liked to go there because the design eliminated an obvious pecking order—they were treated like royalty.

The place had an overpowering masculine aura, all polished wood walls and tables, underlining what a battle it was being a woman in politics. It was obvious that many of her male peers thrived on the restaurant's atmosphere; they were everywhere, chomping on unlit cigars as if that was part of the required image that had to be maintained.

As they followed the maitre d' to their table, they both indulged in nods to various colleagues, many of whom didn't bother to hide their surprise. A heavy, oversize old-fashion glass of bourbon and water was set in front of W. W. She asked for iced tea.

The obsequious waiter was a little much. She'd been in the restaurant before but her recollections didn't include this much special attention.

"Angelle is kind of an—what shall we say—an unusual name?" Wilson said after a sip of his bourbon.

"You mean for a senator, don't you?"

"Actually," he said, chuckling, "it's sort of like naming a dog Lucky." He reached across the table to pat her hand. "No offense, Angelle." He took a long draw on his drink. "Lucky, my foot—

sooner or later that pup's gonna get run over by a car, or at the very least, tangle with a polecat."

Her name had been an annoyance during most of her life, although she did like the attention she received simply because of it. She'd developed an almost automatic response to those who questioned it.

"My mother loved romance novels; she thought Angelle Savage had a certain glamorous sound to it." She smiled and tilted her head to one side. "I really don't think she had anything celestial in mind."

There was more inane small talk that ended in response to the server arriving with their main course. Once the food was ceremoniously placed in front of them, the server's assistant refilled her iced tea glass and replaced Wilson's depleted bourbon with a fresh glass.

"You know they call you the 'angel of death' behind your back, don't you?"

"Sticks and stones, Wade." She dabbed at her mouth with a napkin. "I won't tell you what they call you, although I'm sure you know."

She glanced around the room to get a quick idea of how many people were watching them. She particularly enjoyed catching the ones who quickly looked away. "I know you didn't invite me here just because the food's good or because you wanted to play word games with my name."

"Touché, Senator." He sipped at his drink; his steely gray eyes hardened. "That was quite a little plum that just happened to drop in your lap a while back. Not too many junior senators get to sit on the HHS subcommittee."

"Wade, I'm having a rough day," she said. "I really didn't have the time for this sit-down with you, so consider yourself very effective in coercing me to come."

"All too true," he said, smiling as though he had four aces up his sleeve.

"No more small talk, Wade. Let's get on with it." The bastard was really starting to get to her. "Brass tacks, that's what I want or I get up and walk."

"Careful what you ask for, little lady."

"Okay, I've had enough—"

Wilson studied her for a moment, sipped at his second drink, and said, "Perhaps it's time you were made aware that I was the one who got you a seat on the HHS subcommittee." He waited for the response that never came. "Play it that way if you want," he said, "but be sure you understand that that kind of thing doesn't come easy, no, sir. I mean, not only are you a junior senator from freakin' Nevada, you're a damn woman besides."

"Whoa!" She looked at him speculatively. "How much flattery do you think a junior senator from Nevada can take at one expensive lunch?"

She stuffed a forkful of crab salad into her mouth, stalled for time, watched his eyes search hers. When she'd finished thoroughly chewing every morsel, she said, "Why on earth would *you* want me on that committee anyway?"

"Let's just say, I have my reasons, Angelle."

"If I had known—"

"You'd have turned it down?" He laughed aloud. "I don't think so."

"I'm not for sale, Wade. And if I were, I'd just as soon sell my soul to the devil. I'm at a loss as to what awe-inspiring feats you thought I could, or would, perform for you."

"We do have common goals."

"*We*? Why, you almost sound like a liberal, Mr. Wilson."

He reached for his knife and fork, cut off a huge piece of filet mignon, shoved it roughly into his mouth, then chewed it delicately. When he finally swallowed, he gave her an amused smile but the humor never reached his eyes.

"Why is it liberals always think *they* corner the market when it comes to social welfare?"

"We think that way because it's true," she said.

"An obvious misconception, Senator. I never want anything less than the very best for my fellow citizens, every one of them."

"*Rich* Americans, Wade. That's the difference between the lobby you represent and us so-called liberals."

"Be that as it may, Senator, it's pay-back time."

She slowly shook her head and hated herself for feeling so sanctimonious. "Wade, you and I could sit here and have lunch together every day, call each other by our first names, and it's still not going to make us working partners, let alone friends." She ate more of her salad and waited for his response.

Instead, he gave her a pleasant look and continued to consume his steak and side of crisp, cooked vegetables. Angelle decided not to push it, did her best to slowly pick out all the crab morsels from the stack of romaine, arugola, and red lettuce. When they both were about finished, she said, "You know, Wade, you probably could get me a seat on almost any committee. Hell, maybe even get me a cabinet appointment. But you know what?"

Chin down, eyes on his plate, he looked up at her without raising his head.

"It wouldn't change a thing. I mean, it should be crystal clear, even to you, that I'm never going to jump into bed with your insurance industry buddies." She reached across the table and patted his hand. "No offense intended."

He pushed his plate off to the side and set the drink in front of him. "When you get to be my age, Senator, you realize, never is just a long time. Understand, Angelle, I really don't want to be a ruffian with you. I really don't. But if you're going to play in the sandbox with the big boys, you're going to have to show a little more give-and-take."

"Is there a point to any of this?"

"Always a point, Angelle. Always a point." He pulled a notebook from his inside jacket pocket, thumbed carefully through the pages. "Does the name Joanne Paige mean anything to you?"

Her breath caught. She pulled her linen napkin from her lap and dabbed delicately at her mouth, her heart beating wildly. "I can't say that I recall meeting anyone by that name. No. I really don't think so."

He leaned forward, smiled, and said, "Allow me to refresh your memory."

* * *

Wilson slipped off his suit jacket, flicked a couple of gray hairs from one shoulder, and hung it in his office closet. He was very pleased with himself, pleased with the way he'd handled the Savage woman. Nice touch, taking her to the Washington Five & Dime where she wouldn't dare over-emote. He'd had more than his share of dealing with women in his sixty years and he'd found the one thing they were good at was crying, carrying on, and, in general, making men feel stupid, useless, and embarrassed.

He shook his head. Uppity women were particularly distasteful; it tickled him that he'd taken the supposedly tough senator down a notch or two.

In fact, if he was any judge of character—and if he was anything, he was that—he'd have to say he'd left behind one frightened female junior senator from Nevada.

He eased into his desk chair and reached for a new disposable cell. After punching in the numbers, he waited, tapping out the rhythm of "Dixie" on his desktop.

"Garrett. How're you doing? That California sunshine still holding up?"

"Caught me during a Bioethics Committee break," Rudge said, his voice tight with tension.

"Sorry, want me to call back later?" Wilson said, knowing Rudge would never put him off.

"No, no. It's okay. Actually, if all goes well, this should be our final session."

"Glad to hear that, Garr. I mean, this is the big one, right, the one where your people do the right thing?"

"That's the plan," Rudge said.

149

Wilson paused, evaluated the crisp, business-like response he'd come to recognize as Garrett Rudge's no-nonsense approach. The man was not only good at his job, but had been the foundation of the Desisto Project, even though he was a real pain in the ass if any little thing wasn't right on target. A little too soft for the game of hardball Wade played.

"Listen, Garr, I've got to go," he said in a mellower tone. "Just checking in, wanted to let you know everything's on schedule at our end. You're bringing Hygea along as we knew you would." He paused for a moment. "Good man."

When he hung up and placed the telephone back in the desk drawer, his thoughts were interrupted by the buzz of the intercom.

"Yes, Calli?"

"Sorry to bother you, sir, but Leonard is here."

"Send him in, would ya?"

He loosened his tie and slipped it over his head as the door opened. A man with a military brush cut entered and set a briefcase on the end table next to a large leather sofa.

"How are you, Lennie?" Wilson watched the barber's eyebrows rise in consternation. "Sorry, *Leonard.*" He'd used the diminutive intentionally.

"It's all right, sir." They both knew it wasn't; just a ritual to be played out every time the barber came to trim Wilson's hair.

Leonard walked over to the extensive wet bar and came back with one of the bar stools.

"How have you been, sir?" the barber asked as W. W. took his seat. They continued their usual banter as he was draped.

"Helluva day. Helluva good day!" He listened to the crisp sounds of the clicking scissors and marveled again how Leonard simply running a comb through his hair relaxed him immediately.

"You know, Leonard, sometimes I wish people would surprise me more often. Kind of boring that they're so predictable."

"Yes, sir."

"Now you see what I mean? I knew you'd say that. Kind of takes the fun out of things."

Wilson listened to the click-click of the scissors speed up even more. That too was predictable.

"You know, Leonard, you only have to push the right buttons and you can get people to do damn near anything. I mean, take this woman I know." He laughed wickedly. "You take her. I don't want her."

"Yes, sir."

"The woman works like a dog, keeps such long hours that her personal life is a disaster. She's spent most of her days dedicating herself to what she thinks of as public service. Then someone like me comes along and not only threatens to take it all away, but flush it down the toilet."

"Yes, sir. You sure you don't want me to touch up some of this gray? It'll make you look a good ten years younger."

"Maybe so. Maybe so." Wilson patted his flat abdomen. "But I think my disciplined lifestyle and working out does more to keep me younger looking than any bottle of dye." He continued to listen to the rhythmic scissors. "If only they had a pill we could swallow, eh, Leonard?"

"Yes, sir."

"Anyway, this hard-workin', dedicated woman made one little slip in her teens. Hell, you and I know that's what youth's all about—it's the right time to slip up here and there, if you're going to, don't you think?"

"Yes, sir."

"I mean, it was after that sixties-seventies crap— demonstrations all over the country in an uproar over Vietnam. Damn, I was too steeped in gettin' my education or I'd have jumped right into that war."

"I'm sure you would have, sir."

"Actually, kind of feel like I missed out ... not goin'." The clicking of the scissors caught him up again for a moment. "Still, the whole country was a little screwy then—even marijuana was acceptable in most crowds."

"Yes, sir."

"Ever try that stuff, Leonard?"

"No-o-o, sir. Can't say that I have."

"Give me a good shot of bourbon, anytime—sets you right back on your seat. Besides, don't know how anyone could stand the smell of that stuff."

"Yes, sir."

"Still, it's amazing how just a little slip-up all those years ago can come back to haunt you."

"Yes, sir."

"Ever slept with a man, Leonard."

"I'm sure you know the answer to that, sir."

"Right about that, Leonard. Anyway, this woman I'm telling you about was, shall we say, a tad indiscrete in her youth."

"Sir?"

"You know what I mean. But then, some youthful mistakes can be overlooked." He cleared his throat for emphasis. "Others merely become useful."

"I see, sir."

"I doubt it." He was quiet for a moment, then added, "Hardly had to dig very deep to find the dirt. Surprised no one beat me to it."

"Sir?" Leonard delicately ran a finger against the grain of Wilson's chin. "Doesn't look like you need a shave today, sir."

Wilson shook his head and held still as the barber put a puff of foam around his sideburns. "You know I'm a man of my word, Leonard. But if I wasn't, I'd sure enjoy helpin' the media mess up that little lady's reputation."

"Yes, sir."

"Her and her plebian ideas about care for the poorer members of our society. You and I know you only get what you pay for."

"That's certainly the truth, sir."

"Life's a bitch, isn't it, Leonard?"

"Yes, sir."

"And then you die."

Bette Golden Lamb & J. J. Lamb

Chapter 24

Gabe Harrington ignored the intercom buzzer even though he knew Dawn seldom used it except for urgent matters. Most of those emergencies always seemed to be related in some way to his wife, the esteemed Sen. Angelle Savage.

"Not now, for Christ's sake," he muttered.

Tomorrow's 10 a.m. deadline for his architectural review of the Escobar Condominium Complex was like a sledgehammer poised over his head. The half-billion-dollar project would not only provide much-needed housing for low income residents of Las Vegas, it would also have a substantial impact on the area's way-above-average unemployment stats.

His basic problem was that he'd found too many discrepancies—substandard materials, construction short-cuts, and inflated building costs—indicating the ECC developer hoped HUD wouldn't be looking too closely at the specifications.

But there was a lot of heavy pressure to see the project through to completion, starting with the entire Nevada congressional delegation. And, the HUD director had emphasized over and over that he expected to make the project a showcase partnership between the department and a coalition of faith-based organizations.

Caught in the goddam middle again. Should never have allowed Angelle to talk me into coming to Washington in the first place.

The intercom finally stopped buzzing. He exhaled a long sigh of relief, but before he could refocus his thoughts, Dawn barged into his office. He looked up into her blazing eyes.

"We had an agreement," she said.

"Yeah, yeah." He nodded toward the crystal quartz clock on his desk. "I'm running out of time. I've got to pull this stuff together."

"She's on the line—called three times already. I can't put her off again."

He slammed a hand down on the desktop, clawed a pile of paper into a wad and tossed it across the room.

"Does what *I* want, or who *I* am ever amount to more than a rat's ass around here?"

Dawn stood her ground, but her blue eyes were wide, on the edge of spilling tears.

He flushed, threw up his hands. "I'm sorry, all right?"

She stared at him, silent.

"Look, don't worry about it." He came around the desk, put his arms around her and kissed her on the neck.

She smiled, her lips barely moving, looking like a child—smooth, peach cheeks, pale blond hair

With an encouraging nod, he nudged her toward the door. "Tell her I'll call back in a few minutes." Dawn's satiny blouse fluttered with her rapid breathing as she took her soft curves, her dewy skin, and left.

He knelt and gathered up the mess of papers from the rug, flattening and setting them in order next to the telephone, which seemed to sit glaring at him.

Again he sat down, closed his eyes, and tried to ease the tension in his neck—it was getting harder and harder to do. He forced himself to look around the tiny office. He'd given up fancy decor when he went to work for the U.S, Department of Housing and Urban Development three years ago.

Toeing open the bottom desk drawer, Gabe peered into an array of odds and ends before reaching for a photo buried deep inside. He carefully lifted out the framed 8x10 and propped it up in the middle of the desk. There they were the happy couple, fifteen years ago; Angelle's face radiant, with dark, long, silky hair framing her heart-shaped face; he was all teeth and curly hair.

After a long moment, he gently tucked the photo back into the drawer and slid it shut. The phone continued to glare at him. He either called her now or nothing would get done.

He stabbed the auto-dial button.

The first ring was cut short with Angelle Savage's voice, heavy with menace. "Where have you been?"

"Right here—"

"I can't talk on this line. Anybody could be listening, especially that ditzy female assistant you sleep with."

"Cut it out, Angelle."

"I need to see you at home. Now!"

"Can't do it."

His wife's voice slid into a softer pitch. She wanted something. Wanted it badly. "Gabe, I don't interfere with your private life--"

"—and I don't interfere with yours."

A silent emptiness stretched between them. Finally she said, "I can't do this myself. I need your help, Gabe."

"You've never needed my help."

"That's not true. And whether or not you believe it, I still love you."

"Only when you want something, Senator."

"Look, I'm not the one carrying on an extramarital affair."

"This is a boring conversation, Angelle. Tiresome and repetitious. I'm on a
 deadline for the Las Vegas ECC Project. I can't rush off right now."

The weight of silence expanded, seemed to crush his chest. He would have to meet with her.

* * *

Gabe saw he'd arrived first—her car was nowhere to be seen, which told the tale since she never took the time to put it in the garage. Out of spite, he'd planned to ring the doorbell, wait for her to answer. But he couldn't do it. A neighbor might pick up on it, use it against her in some obscure way. Washington was cold and uncompromising. They were supposed to be a loving couple even though he'd heard the second-hand rumors that they were separated. It was a joke to think no one knew.

He pulled out his key, but before he could use it, Angelle opened the door and threw her arms around him.

"I'm so glad you came," she said, holding him close.

His heart took a runaway beat; he hated himself for the power he allowed her to hold over him. "Finally learned to park your car in the garage, I see," he said, gently disengaging himself.

"Oh, no. I simply decided the time had come to get a chauffeur. He puts the car in the garage." She took his hand and ushered him to the sofa in the large, two-story-high living room

He gave her a knowing smile. She'd only done what he'd suggested a long time ago.

"Hey, I'm not selling out. I need the extra time to work."

"Angelle, you don't have to explain anything to me except why you dragged me away from a project that's so vital—well, let's just say that for me, it's one of those do-or-die things."

"I know, the Escobar condos; the Las Vegas low-income project," she said.

"I'm flattered you remembered."

"Remembered? You just mentioned it on the phone. Besides, I have a vested interest in seeing that one through to completion, as you well know."

"Sorry. It's become a problem child."

"Getting you into urban planning was the best thing that could have happened. Escobar is one of the most practical developments we've seen in years. I can't imagine there could be problems with it that you couldn't overcome."

He didn't know how she did it, but she had the capacity to always catch him off guard, put him in an untenable place. He looked around the room, stalling. Each time he came into their Georgetown home, there was some additional piece of furniture, either antique or modern, but always in keeping with her uncanny sense of making opposites work together.

What had once held tasteful contemporary furnishings that reflected the Bauhaus school had evolved into a hodgepodge of what should have been clashing themes. In just a month since he'd last been in the place, a brocade drape with a sculptured valance had replaced simple, straight-line drapes.

"I hardly recognize the place," he said. "Is this what they call political chic or is it some designer's dream of heaven?"

She sat down on the sofa next to him, put a hand on his knee. "You've been gone for almost three months; back here no more than twice since then. What did you expect?"

"Angelle, I don't know what to expect. But being with you makes me sad and I've got too much to do for that. Just tell me what you want."

She stood, took off her suit jacket, revealing a shimmery red blouse. He noticed her hand was shaking as she took a cigarette from a sterling silver box on the mahogany side table. She gave him a guilty glance before lighting it with a matching silver lighter. She took a drag and held up one hand, palm out. "Don't say it. I know we gave up smoking. Together." Her eyebrow lifted, eyes turned dark. "But we're not together, are we?"

"Angelle, if you want to smoke, smoke. Just tell me why I'm here, and then we can get on with our make-believe marriage."

She took two more quick hits and stubbed out the cigarette; she sat down next to him again.

"I had lunch with W. Wade Wilson today."

He could feel the blood rise in his face. "What the hell could you possibly want from that bastard?"

"Exactly! I don't want anything from him. It's what he wants from me."

"That man is poison—"

"Don't play back the obvious to me." Her voice had a tautness to it. "I'm well aware of his reputation." Her face collapsed into grief—the same face he remembered when they lost their two-year-old son. He had no choice: he grasped her hand tightly.

"What is it? Tell me!"

"He knows about my relationship with Joanne Paige. Politically, the worst part is that she's a prostitute, has been for many years."

"Joanne Paige?" As the words escaped his mouth, he remembered: "That scamp you grew up with in Virginia City?"

"How can you be so judgmental? You didn't grow up in that hellhole; you went from birth to maturity in a single leap, no real bumps on the road. That scamp, as you put it, saved my life on more occasions than I care to remember. That scamp also killed Harlen Davis so he wouldn't kill me."

"Harlen Davis?"

"A big hulk of a guy who decided he was going to put a bullet through me if I didn't spread my legs for him." She shook her head and smiled weakly. "We both know how primitive that sounds so far removed from that corrupt little town in the West. But everything is basic there—eat or be eaten."

He wanted to say it wasn't much different than Washington, but he didn't. He had to get out, get back to his own life, his own world. "What does that have to do with Wilson?"

"I couldn't refuse her." She covered her face and began to sob. "Don't you understand? All she wanted was me."

* * *

Gabe Harrington's eyes drifted opened. He'd been dreaming about Billy again. Always the same dream: tossing his son playfully in the air; loud giggles as he caught him. The peal of laughter usually awakened, haunted him, as his mind's eye saw a small, silver casket being lowered into the cold, hard ground.

The details seemed to fill in with more intricacy over the years: white long-stem roses resting like a thorny spread on the coffin, large flakes of white snow falling on an already alabaster landscape; Angelle's pasty face streaked with rivulets of tears, her hair dusted a powdery white. Everything was pure. Everything was crystalline white.

Everything but his heart. It had turned black, vacant as the deepest hole in a far, empty stretch of space.

He turned to find Angelle studying him. She reached over to rake her fingers through his chest hair, then leaned over and kissed his neck.

"I've missed this," she said, her hazel eyes more green than brown.

He studied the deep lines in her forehead; she seemed exhausted. "I don't know how you manage to reel me in like some doomed fish whenever you want to." He slid a finger from her throat to her navel. "This isn't going to change anything, you know."

"I don't care what you say. It wouldn't have happened if you didn't want it to."

"I'm not so sure of that."

"You know you love me, Gabe."

"Loving you has never been an issue."

"Then what are you doing in bed with that Dawn something or other. Do you love her, too?"

"She has nothing to do with us."

"Do you think she feels that way?"

He thought of Dawn's baby blue eyes with their look of betrayal every time he spoke on the telephone to *Senator* Savage. "No. You're probably right."

"Looking for a younger woman? A younger body?"

His temper flared. "Why do women always think that men want a younger woman?"

"Isn't that the way it is?"

"Maybe. For some men. But I think it's needing to start with a clean slate."

"Clean slate?"

"Yeah. None of that emotional baggage that makes you feel old, beaten." He looked at the bedside clock. "I've got to get out of here. I'm going to be working half the night to get that project ready." He swung his feet over the edge of the mattress.

"Gabe, I need you." She took his hand. "Please help me find Joanne."

He stood and began picking up his scattered clothes, most of which were intertwined with hers. He snatched up her blouse, along with his shirt. Before he could stop himself he buried his nose in the silky material.

When he looked up again, he said, "You have a large, efficient staff, Angelle. Get one of them to act as your gofer. I've got my own busy life to live."

"A staff member? Have you forgotten what this is all about? Once the relationship is discovered it will create a media frenzy."

"So they'll think you're gay. So what?"

"They'll use it against me, make it harder for me to be effective. I'll be eaten alive by the media." Her nails dug into her arm. "Worst of all, it'll give them an excuse to toss another woman out of the power arena. Something they've been way too successful at already."

He turned and continued to stare at her as he finished dressing. "I'm sorry you're in a difficult place, Angelle, but our climbing into bed hasn't changed anything between us."

Her eyes shifted from velvet to stone.

When she turned away, he stood only for a moment before he moved towards her.

Chapter 25

A sinking feeling of emptiness awakened Melissa Yost.

Her eyes blinked open. Her hands reached up. Nothing.

Sudden pain rushed at her, curled around every muscle, every joint; a sharp chemical odor lingered in her nostrils and throat. She tried to turn, but it brought the burn of bile to the back of her throat.

Was she lying at the bottom of a black pit?

Confused.

Was this a bad dream?

She flung out an arm, felt around for Ted.

He wasn't here. Nothing was here.

She forced herself onto her hands and knees. Her head did a slow spin when she managed to stand on wobbly legs; she grazed her head on something loose. Reaching out, she felt heavy plastic coat hangers on a thick rod.

A closet? Was she in a closet? She shuffled around, realized she was in a large walk-in.

She stretched, explored the surface of a long, smooth shelf with tentative finger tips. She pushed a bed pillow and a blanket aside and wrapped her fingers around an iron. Jammed in a corner was woman's shoe.

What was she doing in an empty closet?

She turned too quickly and the darkness filled with a maze of bright colors. Her chest tightened, her heart raced—she could barely get air. She squatted, forced herself into a deep breathing trance that soon quieted her, allowed her to stave off panic. The swirling colors disappeared.

A thread of logic worked for her one second and was gone in the next. What was she doing in a closet?

Then she remembered: Someone had attacked her. Smothered her.

Chloroform? Was that what she smelled?

Oh, my God, this is what Ted was afraid of.

She'd been kidnapped.

He'd tried to tell her they were in danger, but she'd ignored him, and now she was locked away with an old, forgotten shoe.

* * *

Al moved around the hotel suite in nervous quick steps. He hadn't wanted to leave San Francisco for Washington, but Levi Black had put the squeeze on, said he owed him this one for screwing up the job at CORPS headquarters.

Shit! Wasn't my fault some old broad got caught in the crosshairs.

So here he was in this swank hotel, high above the streets of D.C. instead of out in the burbs, where it was quiet, safe, and out of the way. Black said keep her in the city, close at hand; they'd be moving her out soon.

It was a comfy spot, but he didn't like it. Not one bit.

He stopped pacing to look out the window at the snow fall. He could barely make out the people walking far below him.

It always amazed him how seldom affluent people looked at each other or anyone else under ordinary circumstances. More like they expected to be admired as they walked with their noses tilted up, unaware of anyone. It was all about them.

A piece of cake to bring the reporter's wife into the suite. He'd carried her through the lobby, his French beret covering most of his face, nuzzling her like a newlywed. Once in the suite, he'd dumped her into the walk-in closet. But he'd pulled a muscle and his shoulder was killing him, pain shooting down his arm like a spike of hot electricity.

And that made him think of Denny, blowing up that building in California, trashing the reporter's house. How did he ever hook up with such a freak? A lousy old reporter not only out-drove that young punk, but out-smarted him as well. Al was finished with that loser.

He stepped up to the closet and listened for a moment: Dead silence.

At first he'd worried they might have hurt the old broad. Black would have his ass if anything went south with this woman. But Billy, his hire in Washington, just shrugged it off.

"She's fine, man. That knock-out shit will keep her out for hours." With that, Billy'd flaked out on the giant king bed and gone to sleep.

There was no escaping it: Al's inner warning system continued to not only tickle, it shouted at him. Was he hooking up with another loser like Denny? They'd just nabbed a woman and he was already snoring.

Black supposedly knew his onions, and he'd recommended Billy. But he'd also recommended Denny. What did that tell you?

Still, if he couldn't trust Black ... well, forget about it ... they'd worked together on and off for years. When Black called him, he came. No ifs, buts, or maybes.

Then why was Al's intuition clanging away like a fire alarm? And he was stuck with this jerk Billy until the situation ran its course.

Look at him, curled up on the bed.

Well, he'd just have to cram on his George W. mask, with the creepy smile, and throw her on the bed by himself. Scare the hell out of the snoring idiot.

Al walked over to a huge flat-screen TV in the corner of the room and turned it on. It had been a long stretch since he had the time to catch up on his golf stuff.

Wonder how Tiger's doing?

* * *

Melissa tried to make sense of it. Where was she? A hotel, or maybe a vacant house? The iron, pillows and blanket on the one shelf suggested a hotel room. If so, probably upscale, considering the size of the closet. And it smelled clean and fresh.

She couldn't help but laugh at the irony—she had to get kidnapped to get out of that crummy, run-down mess of a hotel where she and Ted were supposed to be safe.

165

Where was the light switch? She felt along the wall on either side of the doors. Nothing; probably on the outside

She sat down on the floor, tried to think back.

Out of a dark memory she could hear two men talking to each other. So there was probably at least two of them. Her thoughts were interrupted by voices on the other side of the sliding doors.

Voices. Television. Someone had turned on the television. The comments were about golf. Golf? In the middle of winter? Sunny skies wherever the commentator was.

She needed to get out the damn closet and find a way to call Ted. And if she couldn't do that?

Can't think about that.

Instead, Melissa remembered when a creep broke into their house while Ted was gone, away on another assignment. The man pulled a knife, threatened to kill her. Focus and determination to survive made her strong; saved her

* * *

Al couldn't believe Billy was snoring so loud he could barely hear the TV announcer describing the golf shots.

Snort, hold your breath, snort, hold your breath. Creepy.

He put on the George W. mask, got up, and stepped over to the closet where they'd stashed the woman. His plan was to quietly open the door, pick her up, and carry her to the bed. Sure as hell better than her waking up in a dark closet—that could give the old broad a heart attack.

He tapped the rocker switch for the closet light, then slowly slid the door to one side, not wanting to startle the woman.

Before he'd moved the door more than a few inches, it shot out of his hand and crashed open.

And there she was, charging straight out at him, swinging up at his crotch with a steam iron and down on his head with something else.

Al cried out and crumpled to the floor, excruciating pain coming from both his crushed testicles and left temple. He tried to grab her ankle as she raced past him, but she was too fast. When he rolled back, his nose rested on a woman's spiked heel.

She was out of the hotel room door and gone before he could sit up.

Billy kept snoring.

* * *

Melissa ran full out, couldn't remember the last time she'd moved that fast.

She kept listening, looking behind her when she ran down the stairway.

Nothing. There was no one.

She didn't stop until she was through the lobby and out onto the sidewalk. A cab pulled up in front of the hotel with arriving guests—she jumped into the back seat, reached for the lock button and pressed down hard.

"Drive!" she shouted before he could even ask where she was going.

She looked back, then scooted down into the seat, smiled as she gave Bill Tana's address.

"There's an extra fifty in it if you put the pedal to the metal."

"In this snow storm? You gotta be kiddin'."

* * *

Bill Tana opened the door and stood there, his mouth hanging open.

"I need some money for the cab." Melissa said. "A hundred bucks ought to do it."

"What?"

"The cabby. He's waiting in your driveway."

"Oh!" Bill reached for his wallet, trotted out to the pay the taxi driver, and was quickly back. "How'd you get away?"

"Luck!" She looked around "Where's Ted?"

Bill grabbed her around the waist and rushed her into the house.

"Careful, people will talk," she said, forcing a lightness she really didn't feel.

"Did you call the police?"

"All I wanted to do was get away from there."

He took her into the living room, sat her down on the sofa, and just stared at her. Loud, wall-shaking rap music came from the upstairs.

"Ted?" she said again, looking up at Bill. "Isn't he here?"

Kelli Tana came into the room from the kitchen, dropped her dishtowel, ran to Melissa, and gave her a kiss and a tight squeeze. "How—"

"I'll call Ted," Bill interrupted.

"Where is he?" Mel asked. "I thought he'd be here with you."

Bill held up a hand, grabbed a phone, and punched in a series of numbers. "She's here," he said and hung up.

"What's going on?"

"Your asshole husband lost it when they nabbed you. Let's just say we're not on speaking terms at the moment."

"I swear, for two people who love each other, you get into more fights than a street gang."

Kelli laughed. "Ain't it the truth?"

* * *

Ted came crashing through the doorway, paused a moment, and looked at Melissa. Then they were in each other's arms, crying and talking at the same time.

"I should never have let you go off alone."

"And I should have listened to you."

"What happened? I thought I'd lost you."

"Did you think you could get rid of me that easily, Ted Yost?"

Ted looked at Bill and Kelli. "Has anyone called the police?"

"It won't do any good," Mel said. "I don't know the name of the hotel where they took me, let alone the floor and room number."

"And you can bet they were gone as soon as she was out the door," Bill said.

Ted kissed Mel again. "I can't believe you're safe and really here. How'd you get away?"

They all listened while she told them what happened.

"Those jerks didn't stand a chance," Ted said, squeezing her hand.

"The woman has stones," Bill said to Kelli.

"Listen asshole." A quick step and Ted was at Bill's side, staring long and hard at his friend. "I'll take that ten-thousand-dollar check now. Then I'm going to tear it up in front of you, and I don't ever want to hear about it again. Do you read me loud and clear?"

Then they were into a bear hug, pounding on each other's back.

"Asshole."

"Asshole."

Chapter 26

Ted and Melissa sat at the Tanas' dining room table. It was covered with so much food they barely had room for the place settings; the aromas made Mel's stomach growl like a lion on the prowl.

It was a huge spread of all the fun things a good deli can provide—piles of sliced pastrami, corned beef, a variety of cheeses; gobs of chopped chicken liver; huge bowls of potato and macaroni salad; puffy potato knishes; kosher pickles; corn rye; and on and on. Everyone was digging in, eating and talking all at once.

Even with their mouths stuffed, question after question was mercilessly thrown at Melissa, prodding her to tell the story of her kidnapping and incredible escape for the third time.

"The iron I can understand." Ted's voice was filled with the same awe as the first time he'd heard it, "but a shoe with a spike heel? Whatever made you even consider using it?"

Melissa laughed so hard she couldn't stop. "That's the trouble with men. You think to get something done, you need to run out, buy all kinds of materials, special gadgets and tools, and even then, you're still looking for more gizmos to accomplish the simplest task. Women use whatever falls into their hands and get the same job done without all the fuss."

"Unless there's another woman around," Bill had a big smile on his face, "then you'll talk it to death."

"Forget all that," Kelli said. "I want to know how scared you were." She placed a hand on Melissa's arm. "Now that you're safe, that is." She gave everyone an apologetic smile. "I'm such a dragon."

"My wife's a ghoul. Of course she was scared. I know I would have been."

"Yeah, but you're a wuss," Ted said.

Mel laughed, chomped down on a pickle. You two can't ever let up on each other, can you?"

The two men smiled.

"Not only was I scared out of my wits, I was confused and my imagination was in hyper-drive." Mel slathered two slices of bread with mayo and piled on a mountain of chopped chicken liver and a thick slice of red onion.

After a big bite of the sandwich, she said, "When I woke up in that damn closet and got myself together there was no time to be frightened. If I ever thought it through I would've gone into catatonic shock."

She reached for Ted's hand, looked into his eyes. "There was that one horrific moment when I thought I'd never see you again. I couldn't deal with that."

Ted jumped up and pulled her up into his arms. "I can't live without you, Mel." He gave her a big kiss that smeared mayo and chopped chicken liver all around both their mouths. "I'm never going to let that to happen again."

They kissed again until the Tanas started hooting.

"Think we could learn a thing or two from these guys?" Kelli said. She reached over to squeeze Bill's hand.

"I'll see what I can do about getting you kidnapped," Bill said.

Kelli slapped his hand, then smeared mustard on it.

"Yeah, well, this is the way we old folks get it on," Ted said, laughing.

"Watch who you're calling old," Mel said and nipped at his ear.

"Why don't you two get a room?"

"Seems to me, the last room you sent us to was nothing but a flea bag. And why the hell didn't you invite us to stay here in the first place? Some way to treat Patty's God father."

"Yost, you're such an ass. I did invite you. Told you these people would find you no matter where you touched down. But, no, you wanted to play the Tanas' noble protector. So I found the worst hotel I could come up with."

Mel and Ted both laughed.

"I tried to stop him," Kelli said, but we all know that's impossible."

The telephone interrupted. "Let the house princess who's way too busy to eat with us pick it up."

"Probably Tommy anyway," Bill and Kelli said in unison.

But a voice shouted down from the upstairs, "It's for you, Uncle Ted."

Just as Ted picked up the downstairs phone, Patty called out. "Please don't talk too long. I'm expecting a call from—"

"—Tommy," everyone said.

"Ted Yost here."

"It's me," Nathan Sorkin's voice was low and somber.

"I had a feeling it might be you, especially since you're the only one I gave this number to. What's happening back in San Francisco?"

"Myra died. Never woke up."

Ted sank back down into a chair, covered his face. It was a long moment before he could speak. "When?"

"Early this morning. Her sister called me about an hour ago. I was just getting ready to go over to the hospital. Insist on seeing her."

"Nathan, I'm so sorry. I feel terrible—"

"I know. I kept calling the hospital over and over, pleading with them to tell me how she was, what was happening. They wouldn't tell me anything."

"Nathan?"

"Stonewalled me. Again and again. When I called this morning, they finally said I'd have to get in touch with the family for information. Then I knew." There was a long pause. "My poor Myra."

"Nathan—"

"—we have to nail them, Teddy. They killed her when it was me they were after. She died instead of me."

Chapter 27

Dick Abrams loosened his tie, allowed his body to sink back into the familiar mold of his custom leather desk chair. He hummed a Beatles favorite as he rolled an electric razor across the sharp features of his face and enjoyed the soft buzzing sound. It was transcendental.

When he was ready to work again, he looked across the room at two large, framed pictures: President John Armistead Tyler positioned next to a painting of the President's ancestor, John Tyler Jr.

One of Abrams goals as Chief of Staff was to make certain *his* boss wasn't labeled with the earlier president's derogatory nickname, "His Ascendancy."

"Not on my watch," Abrams mumbled.

Still, placing those portraits across the room was an idiotic thing to do, but too late to correct it without getting a whole lot of grief from the media, the rest of the White House staff, members of the Cabinet, and probably the President himself.

He hadn't voted for this president in the primary, didn't even like him all that much. The man had the vision of a slug and it was downright childish in the way he played on his familial coat-of-arms. Who even cared that President William Henry Harrison caught pneumonia at his inauguration and died a month later, making John Tyler, Jr. president? It was all too long ago.

Yet, he and Tyler had been thrown together as a result of common party interests, ranging from rampant fiscal irresponsibility, to lack of party focus.

The populace was growing restless. Abrams carefully followed the reports of demonstrations filled with loud, nasty rhetoric. And guns! Guns were showing up everywhere.

At this rate it wouldn't take long before the U.S. he knew would be a thing of the past.

He'd walked away from a long Senate hitch that Indiana' electorate had given him almost automatically every six years. And he'd enjoyed being a Senator. But the White House, with its closed doors, kept him fired up in a different way. He was at the core of everything local and global, public and not so public. He could have impact. Really get things done.

Ambition's a killer.

And it didn't take long for W. Wade Wilson to present Abrams with the right opportunity.

Desisto was born.

While he hadn't grown to like Tyler any better, he had grown to dislike Wilson more and more. But Abrams knew W.W. was a survivor. That's what the country needed now. Survivors.

Wilson convinced him that redemption lay in making a significant change the Medicare system, a change that wouldn't be noticed until it was too late to stop it; provided they could slip it in under the wire, tag it onto an appropriations bill up for almost automatic congressional approval. The process didn't dare attract the negativism that previously had accompanied introduction of the Affordable Care Act.

Timing was crucial. Secrecy was paramount.

The simplicity of the plan made Abrams see success. They would have a real cost-effective solution with the kind of zeros that added up to a trillion. One that could not only halt the rise of Medicare costs, but could make the program's projected debt figures plunge until costs were stabilized.

Abrams knew he was being used by W. Wade Wilson and the people who owned him. But he'd managed to retain a certain amount of control by coercing the President into bringing on an opposition party member, Maurice Seldon, as his HHS Secretary.

The carrot: They could wipe out the deficit, fix a badly broken Medicare, and create a bipartisan flair that would keep the pointing fingers at bay.

And President John Armistead Tyler could nail the whole thing as his idea.

He found it interesting how certain important and memorable policies and programs, good or bad, were forever associated with the President at the time, whether he had anything significant to do with them or not.

A knock on his door, followed by the uninvited appearance of his assistant, brought Abrams back to the present. The assistant carried a tray with all the accoutrements for a bountiful coffee break. Abrams' eyes focused on, and immediately claimed, a large strawberry Danish, buttery and sugary.

"Good morning, sir," the young man said. "Thought it was about time for a pick-me-up."

Abrams looked at the twenty-something and once again kicked himself for not choosing a woman to be his personal assistant. But he'd been advised against it. Gossip in the White House corridors could be vicious. That and a couple of threatened, unearned, female sexual harassment incidents in the past dictated a male in his front office.

"Thanks," he said. This kid did a great job, but he was convinced women added a certain positive flair to the running of an office; they were not only more observant, but they were quick to let you know when a reality check was in order. They also had the kind of common sense that his testosterone-driven assistant wouldn't have for a few years, maybe never.

Abrams hadn't been sleeping nights and drinking the strong hot coffee was the only thing that kept him focused. The Desisto Project was giving him a sensitive stomach, and his wife was starting to complain about all the ultra-late hours and his absences from home for days at a time. With all the sex scandals popping out like teenage acne, she'd become suspicious. There were a lot of questions, the most specific one being: Was he sleeping around?

Hell, who had time?

* * *

The out-of-the-way, pseudo-Italian cafe in Alexandria had only three other sit-down patrons this morning, but, to Dick

Abrams' surprise, the place was doing a brisk pizza take-out business.

He pulled the food-spotted menu from between bottles of hot sauces with unfamiliar names, then glanced at his watch. Wilson was late.

It was after 10, the agreed upon time in this spot far from their element. A perfect place not to be noticed.

Abrams shifted on the saggy, torn vinyl seat, checked to see if he'd snagged the soft merino wool of his Hugo Boss slacks. Overhead, garish plastic flowers and imitation stuffed birds were suspended from the ceiling, drooping from layers of dust and greasy steam.

He was about to use his cell when the lobbyist appeared. Wilson started to sit down, scowled at the decrepit upholstery, then slid in across from Abrams anyway.

"How's it shaking," Wilson said, grabbing a menu.

Abrams spent a brief moment studying Wilson before he answered. The man was in terrific physical condition. It was no secret he was a fanatic about exercise even though he still ate all the junk food he could get his hands on. Word was he used to be a drinker's drinker, but found a way to retreat from conspicuous over indulgence to unassuming moderation. Some said he could still be the last man standing if the situation demanded it.

"I'll throw your question right back at you," Abrams said. "You're the man of the hour, or at least the one who keeps the clock wound."

A gaunt counter woman, who doubled as waitress, appeared at the booth with a carafe of coffee and filled their cups without asking. She set the pot down, wiped her hands on the sides of her wilted yellow uniform, and asked, "What can I get you boys this fine Virginia morning?"

"I'll have a slice of deep-dish pepperoni pizza," Wilson said. "But bring me a stack of rye toast to go with my coffee. Lots of butter, please, darlin'."

"And for you, honey?" she asked Abrams, her eyebrow lifting suggestively.

"I'll take Number 3 under the fruit section, with a side of plain yoghurt."

"Got it!"

"Uh, is the fruit fresh?" Abrams asked.

"As fresh as I am," she said and headed back toward the cash register to ring up a Goth teen couple who were waiting to pay.

"Since this is the last time I intend for us to meet," Abrams said, "tell me now exactly how everything stands; no lies, exaggerations, or omissions. I mean, I can still stop this thing anytime I don't like what I'm hearing. Or not hearing."

"You think I'd lie, Dick?"

"That must be a rhetorical question," Abrams said stone-faced.

W.W. turned bright red from forehead to chin.

"No, bullshit, Wade. Can I tell the President everything is set and ready to go?"

"Locked and loaded."

* * *

Wilson was royally pissed at Abrams. Although the lobbyist was used to being a shadowy player on the Congressional stage, this super-secret undercover stuff was beginning to weigh heavily on his shoulders.

He blasted the interior of his rented Audi with every profanity he could dredge up during the drive back to his office. Even the thought of having had to rent a car for the trip made him dig even deeper into his repertoire of vulgarisms to express his feelings for "that fucking Jew Abrams."

Plain and simple: He liked to be chauffeured. Didn't want the aggravation, the responsibility of maneuvering through heavy Beltway traffic.

"Asshole!" Wilson muttered for the umpteenth when he was back in his office. "Too bad that self-styled prince leads such a pristine life. He brushed the seat of his pants, getting rid of imaginary crumbs from the rundown pizza parlor. "God, how I'd love to slop something gooey and dirty all over that sanctimonious hide of his."

But his best efforts to dredge up any scandal involving Abrams, sexual or otherwise, had produced absolutely nothing, even after going all the way back to the man's high school years. Honor student, sports star, marriage to his college sweetheart, clean political campaigns for city councilman, state legislature, and the U.S. Senate. Not a chink anywhere.

"Gonna have to play it straight with that prick," he told the portrait of Edward Bernays that hung on the wall next to his desk. Wilson kept a stack of passes to the Smithsonian as prizes for anyone who recognized "The Father of Public Relations" without being told. He still had the original rubber-banded ten.

Regardless of what he thought about Abrams, the Desisto Project continued to be his primary concern. He knew it was the right time.

Desisto had taken on a life of its own and was moving with the speed of an avalanche. But without the White House connection—Abrams, Seldon, and the President—the whole kit-and-caboodle would keep on crashing down the mountainside into a bottomless crevasse.

Wilson had an unexpected chill, his scrotum tightened as he envisioned his drug company clients dropping him one by one. They'd made him more money than he ever imagined he could make as a political flack. And it could all disappear as rapidly as yesterday's news if he didn't stay on top of things, keep a tight hold on every part of Desisto, from CORPS to the final Senate vote on the Medicare funding.

His heart raced.

Shouldn't have let Rudge give me the jitters about the journalist. Should have just left that old has-been alone. All it did was bring him and his wife to D. C. Nothing but a mess of trouble, unnecessary trouble.

God, it was hard to imagine some sixty-something broad outsmarting two badass pros.

All that drama and expense just to keep one old blogger at bay. Shit!

Sen. Angelle Savage and that Nevada whore were the last pieces. Once they were set into the humongous Desisto jigsaw puzzle, the picture would be complete.

If not, he might well spend the rest of his days sunning himself in The Caymans.

Wilson looked out his office window, saw that it was snowing again. He thought about the cold waters of the Potomac and how sitting by a pool on a Caribbean island, sucking up a piña colada, sliding his hand up into the crotch of a lovely island woman might not be such a bad life.

No, no, no! A little trouble had never put him on the run, and he wasn't about to start running now. He barked a harsh laugh and sang out to Edward Bernays and the empty office,

"I'm a D.C. man, I am, I am."

He smacked the flat of his abdomen with the palm of his hand, sat taller in his chair, and reached for the phone.

Chapter 28

Garrett Rudge tapped in his password and scrolled to the ICU AM Report that he was looking for. The Della Paoli update was written by Sarah Silver, RN and signed off by Terence Emory, MD.

Sarah Silver, RN? That could be a real stroke of luck.

He loosened his tie, pulled out a handkerchief and blew his nose.

Or maybe not.

The morning update covered the projected Desisto target; Della Paoli's physiological and neurological systems. Rudge scrolled through most of the report before skipping to the conclusion:

Diagnosis: Locked-In Syndrome. Condition: Moribund. Prognosis: Grave.

"Good news," he said to the empty office. The sound of his own voice jarred him back to reality. The words were hollow.

For years and years, he and his cohorts had railed against euthanasia in all its guises.

Even Congress had put on a big show with the Terry Schavo case. Their cry: Don't Americans deserve the best care possible to the end?

All talk.

The real goal: Drive costs down.

It would be political suicide to push for more birth control or abortion. Forget the ethics. It was the perception not the reality that brought the votes.

The population was exploding and the cost of healthcare with it. Putting end-of-life economies into place was the easy answer.

His mind kept tricking him into visualizing Della Paoli—a person in trouble with no one there for her. No advocate in her corner

And the numbers weren't going to be there for her either.

Right now, six other Hygea offices were poised and ready—they had no ethical problems with the directives, the protocols Rudge had sent. They'd all fallen into line, each with its own candidate—six Della Paolis. Their fingers were on the THAT WAS EASY button.

Rudge broke out in a full sweat.

It was at times like these that dark memories of his twin sister Evie reached out to him. He could swear he felt her hand squeezing his.

* * *

"Mrs. Paoli!" Dr. Terence Emory said, standing by the woman's bedside. "Can you hear me?" He ran his fingers through his matted hair, didn't like the way it felt. He quickly checked his watch—8:00 pm.

Man, after 48 hours, I need a shower and some sleep

"Mrs. Paoli!" he repeated, lowering his head until his lips were close to her ear. "My name is Doctor Terence Emory. We're trying to help you. Do you understand?"

The lack of response made him uneasy. Emory straightened and looked down at the patient, glanced again at her chart, and said, "Mrs. Paoli! Can you hear me?"

He knew his display of irritation was causing a negative reaction among the nursing staff.

"Let's try something different," he said in a more conversational tone. He needed to get this over with before he could go off duty. He took one of Della's hands.

"Are you awake, Mrs. Paoli? Just a nod is okay." He waited, knowing from her test results that probably wasn't going to happen.

"Okay," He gently squeezed her hand. "Don't even worry about trying to open your eyes. Just move them back and forth or up and down; either way will do."

* * *

Della disliked the man speaking to her. His voice was cold and it came from far away. She could barely make it out. But what if he was her only contact with the outside? She made a supreme effort to do as he asked.

* * *

"Ah," Emory sighed, watching her eyes flick back and forth under her lids. The doctor pulled a chair close to her bed and sat down. He was encouraged, but wanted to make certain that what he'd witnessed was not some kind of erratic reflex.

"Very good, Mrs. Paoli. Can you do that again, move your eyes?" He watched and waited, surprised at the tension he felt. She responded with distinct movement. It was the most positive response he'd experienced from a patient during the 48 hours he'd been on duty.

"Excellent!" he said as much for his own benefit as for hers.

Emory sat back in his chair, exhausted. With the cutbacks in staff, he was living more and more on the ragged edge.

He stared at Della Paoli's chart and once again went through the computer readouts clamped firmly between blue carbon filament covers—history (what there was of it), ER notes, nurses' notes, doctors' notes, orders, diagnostic test results.

Everything they knew about the woman was in this computer read out. He slumped and forced himself to acknowledge that within the hospital system, this patient had no identity, no substance, no reality without the chart he held in his hand. But it really told him nothing about the human being in the bed.

Frustrated, he scanned the information again, checking and rechecking, hoping to find some clue that would allow him to do something positive for her before he was forced to dismiss her from the ICU ... the satellite ... his mind.

Emory closed the chart and dropped it onto his lap. He pinched the bridge of his nose, sighed, and talked to the patient again.

"Mrs. Paoli, you've been in a very serious automobile accident. At first we thought you'd injured your spine. But after running many tests and taking numerous scans and x-rays, we know that's not the problem." He hesitated, searching for the right words.

He looked down at the old woman and took a tissue from the bedside stand, gently blotted the perspiration from her face. He could feel heat radiating from her parchment-like skin and knew she was running a fever without checking any of the various electronic or telemetry readouts to confirm it.

"You probably suffered a stroke and lost consciousness while driving your car. Our tests indicate a clot is blocking the signals from your brain stem that control movement and speech. That's why you haven't been able to talk or move."

Emory sighed and stretched his neck muscles. He was feeling the numbness that usually overcame him during these 48-hour stretches.

It didn't help knowing that this woman was doomed—time, her age were all against her—only a very small percentage of stroke victims suffered this type of total incapacity. The "Locked-In Syndrome" was simply rotten luck.

It was the rareness of her case that kept him riveted to the chair, had him devote more time than he normally would have given to a patient. He mentally reviewed the statistics for people in her condition. For one thing, it was unusual for someone like her to survive even this long. Nevertheless, he felt a sense of loss, a sense of sadness and pain over the fact he could not save her from going through this ordeal.

He was surprised by his emotional response—he thought he'd finally learned how to bury all those kinds of feelings.

Emory knew what her life would be like confined to a bed, unable to care for herself or even communicate meaningfully. She had a right to know the facts, but he couldn't bring himself to just spill it out. He stared at Della while swallowing down a lump in his throat.

God, I hate this. This isn't what I signed on for.

He'd wiggled his way into Galen because it was in a mostly affluent community. He'd faced all of the old and destitute patients he ever wanted to see while in medical school. He simply didn't have whatever special commitment it took to deal with indigent, isolated patients.

Like a number of doctors in their early training, he'd identified with many terminal patients under his care. He became certain he had whatever it was that was killing them—brain tumor, lung cancer, emphysema, heart attack—he developed the same symptoms. Everyone of them. But each time he'd survived.

Now, as he sat staring at Della Paoli, he envisioned the blood clot lodged in her brain. Death would definitely be preferable. But there she was, alive, locked-in, no different than any other prisoner in solitary confinement—shut out from a world that gave her no hope of release or escape. He doubted anyone would ever hear her voice again.

Emory pictured himself in Della Paoli's situation. He clutched at the almost unendurable pain growing in his stomach.

"Mrs. Paoli," he said, "in medicine we try to never use the word never. I know you're unable to move right now, but that doesn't mean you never will."

He cringed at the lie.

"You should be able to regain full use of the muscles that control your eyelids. So, you will be able to see. You may even regain limited use of the rest of your body. How much, I don't know. There's no way to know for sure."

And now you know the truth.

Again, he grasped one of her hands, took some deep breaths. He was beginning to feel better.

"You see," he said, "every person is different in their response to illness." He glanced at his watch; he'd spent much too much time with this woman and he no longer felt threatened by her condition. Actually, she had been much simpler to deal with than if she'd been conscious pushing him into a tight corner where she would demand more information than he thought she should have.

Emory stood, stretched, and signaled for the nurse to bring the patient's sedative. As she approached he said, "She'll need some rest." He waited while the nurse injected the medication into an intravenous port.

* * *

No, no. Don't go I don't want to rest.
I need to know more. I need you to tell me.
More. Please!
She frantically moved her eyes under the lids.
Stay.
Please stay.
I'm here.
Stay.

* * *

Emory looked down at the woman and shook his head. He'd made his decision. It wasn't difficult since it was totally in line with Garret Rudge's most recent protocols. He was definitely off the hook.

"Mrs. Paoli, I think it would be best if we moved you to another part of the hospital. I'm sure you'll be very comfortable there and we'll do all we can to help you."

"So soon?" the ICU nurse asked.

He put both hands on the back of a chair and stretched. "I think so."

Whatever empathy Emory felt earlier was now sublimated, tucked away. All he saw was an old woman who had not moved her body a fraction of an inch since he'd started talking to her.

Following the nurse back to the station, Emory said, "Let's have her moved out to the hospice unit."

"Not Med/Surg?"

He shook his head as he looked over at the patient's bed with all the machines that surrounded her. Even though policies were changing, not always to his liking, he still wanted to be an integral part of the medical system. He hadn't gone through all those years of training to step aside because healthcare operated in a different world than when he started.

"She's an administrative problem now."

Dr. Terence Emory was satisfied he'd done what he could for Della Paoli. Before going off duty he took one final look around the unit.

"Where's Myra Jackson?" he asked. "The patient brought in from the explosion downtown. I don't remember transferring her."

"You didn't. She died early this morning—septicemia, toxic shock, you name it, she went out with all of it."

The nurse indicated the final chart on the desk should he want to look at it. "Not too many people survive a ten-inch stake blasted into the middle of their chest."

"Yeah, her chances were pretty slim right from the start," Emory said. "Helluva surgery. Everyone was talking about it. Can you imagine all those foreign bodies, all those splinters?"

"Yeah," the nurse said. "It was a mess."

"It's probably better this way."

"Probably," the nurse said, turning away.

Chapter 29

Jumbo elbowed Death out of the way as they entered the Capital City Whore House. They walked through the lobby, smirked at each other, ordered a couple of whiskeys and sprawled out on a ratty sofa. When they plopped down, they dug their boot heels into the rug that looked like it was held together by an uninterrupted smear of mud and grease.

The air smelled of sweaty socks, dirty underwear ... and sex.

The gun-toting madam, probably in her mid fifties, maybe younger, maybe older, barked a coarse laugh at nothing in particular as she slopped their drinks down in front of them. Jumbo flicked out a credit card, which earned him a heavy grunt.

"Cash only, buster," she said in a voice well-worn from hitting the booze and sucking on unfiltered Camels hour after hour, day after day, year after year.

Jumbo pulled some crumpled bills from his jeans pocket. She gave him a pasted on smile, but it didn't take much for him to see that she could turn into a pit bull if he dared say or do anything to ruffle her fur.

Like shoot my balls to kingdom come.

Death ogled the line of women dressed in stained satin and tattered lace teddies. He rubbed a finger back and forth across a tattoo of a skull and crossbones and the faded word "Death" on his forearm. He snickered.

Jumbo barely glanced at the whores, who were all phony smiles and sexy poses, licking and sucking at their lips. He studied the layout of the cat house—several patched-together doublewides with minimal furnishings.

The place had a good reputation—the madam knew how to deal with county law enforcement and health officials. Bribes bought advance warnings of sheriff's raids whenever righteous citizens or a new hot shot district attorney tried to close down the place. The owner simply hitched a truck onto the mobile units and wheeled the whole enterprise into another of the three counties that intersected at a common point on the high desert mesa, each no more than a few scorpions away from the other.

The cat house wanted no trouble, so the madam worked hard to keep the law away and her whores out of jail. She was very much aware that some of her customers had a tendency to get nasty, lusting, and likkered up. Sometimes they would start shooting at anything that moved. So, on the wall near the front door was a large, bold-lettered poster with the Capital City Whore House Rules:

Guns collected at the door
Cock wash a must
No exceptions

Jumbo continued to study the layout, took a small sip of his whisky and tried to calculate the number of bedrooms and exits.

He didn't like the pair of Dobermans chained to a huge doghouse near the front gate, and the chain link fence surrounding the trailer complex was solid. But the beady-eyed, stubby-fingered bouncer at the front door hadn't exercised in a long time and probably got paid in nooky. He'd be no problem.

The gig wasn't impossible, but it wasn't going to be a pushover either.

"You boys see anything you like yet?" The madam was getting impatient. Wanted them to fuck and move on. "Sure one of our ladies can do anything you have in mind."

Death stood, mumbled to his friend as he pulled at his crotch. "You do your thing, I'll do mine."

"Keep your mind on the job, not on your pecker," Jumbo whispered. He watched his companion grab a busty brunette and lead her off to one of the rooms.

When Death disappeared down the hallway, Jumbo said to the madam, "Don't these girls have names?"

"You're not marrying them, for crissakes. What do you care? A fuck's a fuck." She tapped him on the shoulder. "So what's it gonna be, big guy?"

He wasn't ready, didn't have enough information. But the madam was getting antsy. He'd better do something—keep his ass from getting tossed out of the dump. It was getting busy and the johns were rolling in, most of them acting like regulars—grungy-looking ranchers, a lot of them grinning, toothless. She glared at him, wanting him off her mind.

He rose stiffly and tossed down the rest of the rotgut. "I like to know the name of the whore I'm fucking."

The madam glared at him for a moment, a glint of distrust in her eyes. Then her expression changed, and she started reciting names of the girls in one long sentence.

"Did you say you had a Joanne?" He stood, wiggled his hips, and said, "Tell her to stand back. Jumbo's coming."

* * *

Joanne Paige sat in her room drinking decaffeinated green tea and reading a pamphlet on "How to Become a Real Estate Agent."

Dream on.

From a distance, because she was petite and waif-like, she looked thirty-five instead of the forty-four she really was. She lied about her age constantly. After putting on fresh makeup, the mirror kept telling her that not even the drunkest of the johns would soon believe she was thirty five.

At least she didn't have AIDS.

It had been a long day. She felt old, wasted. Every week she expected Lorene to tell her she wasn't earning enough and The Capital would turn her out, the same way the top-of-the-line escort services and several upper class houses had.

Then she'd have no crib space. She'd be out in the cold. This was the end of the line. Trying to make a miserable buck as she aged out of the game was only going to get harder and harder and she'd promised herself that there was no way she was going to become one of those pick-up gals at truck stops along I-80.

She shrugged her long, blonde hair over her shoulder, noting how limp and dingy it had become. She ran a hand over her face, moved down her neck, and gingerly touched her left breast where some miserable asshole had bitten through the skin, leaving a dark bruise behind.

"Jesus, I hate this," she said to the mirror as she adjusted the straps on her lacy black bra.

She tossed on her robe and padded down the hallway to the "Staff Only" bathroom; it was its usual mess. She turned the shower water up as hot as she could stand it, grateful that there was any heated water left at all.

As the streams beat down her back, she studied a line of old track marks on both arms. Ten years of using had scarred her forever, yet she never stopped hoping the tell-tale marks would somehow disappear. It had been five years since she stopped cold turkey, but that pitiful creature, the user, still lived inside of her, starving, screaming for "just one more."

She was back in her room and into her skimpy lingerie outfit again when she heard her name being called.

"Yeah, I'm in here."

"Someone asking for you by name, sweetheart." Lorene stuck her head in. "Didn't know you still had fans."

"Ever-popular me," Joanne said.

"Yeah, well, get your goodies ready before he changes his mind."

Joanne straightened her bed and waited.

* * *

"I don't remember you as ever being one of my regulars," Joanne said. She stood in the middle of her room, looked the john up and down.

"You remember all the guys you've boffed?"

"No, but being asked for by name is special."

"Well, don't worry your pretty little head about it. I'm just going to make sure you don't forget me this time."

He grabbed her by one wrist, spun her around and shoved her down onto the mattress.

* * *

By the time the last customer left The Capital City, Joanne was exhausted, couldn't remember the last time she was so beat. Probably didn't eat enough today. Each day she found her appetite shrinking another notch.

Was she trying to kill herself? Did she wish she was dead? Maybe.

She dropped onto the bed, was drifting off, her mind finally emptied when a hand clamped tight over her mouth.

She struggled to breathe, to move more air into her lungs. She grabbed hard at the rough hands and tried to see her attacker, but the predawn light and the closed blinds only gave off silhouettes.

She thumped her legs into the mattress, twisted and turned her head, but she still couldn't breathe.

She heard the door open—someone else came in, jumped on top of her, sat on her arms. She tried to kick again, but a cord was wrapped around her ankles and cinched up tight.

"Okay, get off her, you dumb dick. Can't you hear she's not getting any air?"

"Yeah, so?"

"I told you before: a dead broad is worthless to us. We gotta get her out of here ... alive. And keep her that way."

Blindfolded, on her back, she lay perfectly still. She sensed that the man clamping her mouth liked to cause pain, would hurt her even more if she struggled.

"Will you stop hammerin' me," hand-over-her-mouth said in a whiney voice.

"Or what?"

The room was suddenly silent, she could smell their sweat, taste their anger.

Then, "Did you cut the fence?"

"Piece of cake. Those Dobermans gobbled up that doped hamburger almost before it was out of my hand. They'll be snoozin' for hours."

* * *

"I've got to get back to Nevada, Gabe. I've got to find Joanne. I can't believe she would do *anything* to hurt me. No matter what that slime Wade Wilson says."

"People change, Angelle."

She tried to quell her desperation as she tossed a hard look at her husband. "Haven't we, though." Her voice was coated with bitterness.

"My dear Senator," he said, pointing a finger at her, "our crawling into bed again doesn't make this my problem, *or* allow you to talk to me like that. How you stay in office, what you do to stay in office, has nothing to do with me. So stop throwing those daggers or I'm out the door."

"I'm sorry," she said quickly. "You're right. It has nothing to do with you and me."

"Well, what the hell *is* it about?"

She lit a cigarette and inhaled deeply. The smoke curled around her face as she walked back and forth in the bedroom. Finally, she sat down next to him.

"Wade Wilson wants me to attach a Medicare-related rider onto an upcoming must-pass appropriations bill."

"What's his *real* interest in all of this?" He snatched the cigarette away from her and roughly stubbed it out an ashtray on the bedside table. "Dammit, will you tell me what the hell is going on?"

"You might be sorry you asked,"

He reached for her hand. "Tell me, Angelle."

The words came out in a rush. "Mainly, it's all about Wilson's agenda to cut Medicare costs. It could even be a stepping stone to getting rid of the program entirely."

"Come on, Angelle. No one is going to stand for that nonsense. What's going to happen to the old people in this country?"

"If they're in good health, they'll probably have no problems."

"And if they're not?"

"Well, then there sits the rider—tagged to legislation to authorize palliative care or selective euthanasia, under certain medical conditions."

"Do you really think something like that will fly?"

"If they can stay under the radar, keep it nebulous and loose, it will ride on through before there's too much in the way of opposition, especially if I'm the one to tag it on. Everyone knows I'm a liberal who sleeps with no special interests." She looked closely at him. "Even my husband ... most of the time."

"Typical political subterfuge shit," he said, ignoring the jab. "Why you want to continue to be a part of this Washington nightmare is beyond me."

"I've worked hard to get where I am. Can't you, of all people, see that? I wanted to make a difference. A real difference. I can't walk out on that commitment."

"They'll destroy you, Angelle. You'll end up being a sacrificial goat if anything goes sour, or at the very least you'll come off looking like a hypocrite."

"Not if I can find Joanne and talk to her."

"So your future is on the shoulders of a Nevada hooker?"

"What difference," Angelle said, "does it make who or what she is?"

"Listen, *I* don't care how she earns her money, or that you had a fling with her way back when. But how do you think your electorate is going to react?"

Angelle laughed without humor. "I'd like to think that in Nevada we're a simpler, more down-to-earth bunch of humanoids. But truth be told, we're probably not."

"And I'll bet they expect their elected officials to be straight as an arrow, and I mean that in the biblical not the fiduciary sense."

Angelle dropped down onto the bed. "It was so long ago, Gabe. Another lifetime."

"That won't matter and you know it."

"You're right. Once the media puts together my lesbian affair with Joanne, and the fact she's a prostitute, it'll bring me down."

Angelle's eyes closed and she was quiet for a moment. "I loved Joanne ... still do. And even though I haven't seen her for a long time, she saved my life, and I'm not being theatrical about that. She killed a man who would have destroyed me."

"Did the law ever catch up with her?"

Angelle threw her head back and laughed until tears ran down her face. She held out a hand, palm up. "Really, I'm not laughing at you. It's just that I don't think you could ever truly understand Virginia City and its unwritten code of ethics. I mean, how could a nice Midwestern boy like you ever understand?"

"Everyone's accountable to the law, Angelle. Everyone."

"That may be true on television, or maybe even in some parts of the real world. But that's not the way it always works in my remote little home town. Besides, the man she killed had a lot of enemies. Any number of people could and would have murdered him for any number of reasons, most of them quite legitimate."

"So he wasn't popular," Gabe said. "The law is still the law."

"Sounds good. Sounds right." Angelle walked to the bedroom window and stared at the hot tub in the small back yard. "They found his body in one of the deserted mines. And what a fluke that was—couple of tourists wandering off the beaten path. They weren't looking for trouble, just adventure."

"I guess they got more than they bargained for," Gabe said.

"They called it an accidental death. Interesting, especially since he had a hole the size of quarter in the middle of his chest. They cremated the bastard almost immediately."

"Did he have a family?"

"Oh, he had a wife and two pre-schoolers. They still live in Virginia City, and from what I hear, they never hurt for money. Word at the time was that there was a contract out on good ole Harlen for playing fast and loose with someone else's money. Joanne just beat them to it. Did them an unexpected favor."

"When was the last time you spoke to her?"

"You mean, when was the last time I was in bed with her? Isn't that really what you want to know, Gabe?"

"No, it isn't, which still leaves my question unanswered."

"For one thing, it was over when I left for college." Angelle reached for a fresh cigarette and held it between her fingers, unlit. "But I ran into her about five years ago."

"What happened?"

The door bell chimed. Angelle threw on a robe, patted her hair, and moved out of the bedroom toward the stairway. She turned back to Gabe for an instant.

"Nothing happened. We were both dumbstruck. We hugged each other ... and walked away." Angelle ran her fingers through her hair again, tightened her robe. "It was weird. We never said a word."

She was back in a moment carrying a large, flat envelope of Priority Mail. She held it carefully with her fingertips as though it was a delicate flower. She sat on the edge of the bed, pulled the tab, and removed a piece of lined notepaper.

"Oh, my God! Someone's taken Joanne. She's been kidnapped."

Bette Golden Lamb & J. J. Lamb

Chapter 30

W. Wade Wilson's mind was filled with the Desisto Project. All its machinations rolled through his brain, buzzing him with scenarios of failure, scenarios of success, one piled upon another. His brain simply wouldn't shut down.

He stood at "his" spot along the edge of the Potomac, hoping to clear away all the confusion.

The best time was always in the spring when everything smelled fresh and new, giving him instant revelation. Things would automatically fall into place. Even summer and fall were almost as effective But now the water was choppy, frigid, and the ground was covered with snow; his mind remained cluttered.

He stared at the surface of the water, muddy with the reflection of the dark clouds that had covered the D.C. area for several days. He pulled his coat collar tighter against his neck— protection from the harsh breeze that swept across the landscape. It took his breath away.

There was hardly a soul in the park. Why would anyone come out in this kind of weather? This was certainly the right place to be alone.

His meeting with Dick Abrams had left him uneasy. For the first time since the whole Desisto thing started, an unusual weight of anxiety crushed his chest.

Wooing the right people from the insurance and the healthcare industries, HMOs, hospitals, politicians, along with anyone else who could help, had been intense. But his strategy remained persuasive; the same he'd used time and time again.

The one where no one was left holding the bag.

Even the Affordable Care Act hadn't gotten in his way. or slowed down the industry.

It was uncanny. Like the people in the industry had been waiting for him, expecting him to call. When he approached them, they jumped right in and poured out the massive amounts of money needed to grease the wheels of the legislative process.

Yes. This was his thing—being in the right place at the right time with the right people. It was the heart of not only his successful lobbying operation, but his entire public relations career.

Public relations, lobbying—fancy names for the hardcore business of peddling influence.

The past six months had been amazing.

Now he was in the endgame, at the finish, holding the final piece to a massive jig saw puzzle. And the image embossed on that last crucial piece was Angelle Savage.

He pulled a silver flask from the inside of his overcoat and tossed down a stiff jolt of bourbon. He capped the flask, studied it for a moment, reflected on how it was a poor substitute for one of his exquisite Waterford cut-crystal old fashion glasses. The heft of the glass was right and he barely moved it to make the liquor swirl in a tiny eddy, releasing the intense aroma.

The Desisto Project had started him drinking heavily again. And he knew he'd have to stop soon, before he did something stupid. Something his old friend Levi Black would not be able to mop up.

He exhaled a deep breath and a cloud of frosted moisture puffed out in front of his eyes.

Damn but I could use a break. Been thinking of that way too often lately. But a stint in the Caribbean would be just the thing—hook up with some lovely brown sugar for a week or two.

Get my juices flowing again.

Stream of consciousness carried him to the last woman he'd been with.

Couldn't have been more than twenty-five. Tight, moist skin. Voluptuous! Only word to describe her. Cost me a pretty penny. Worth every cent.

After three wives, he'd learned to stay away from permanent relationships. Brief liaisons worked out much better.

Dangerous sometimes.

But the women knew who was in charge, and they collected big bucks. Clean. Simple.

Too bad everything in life doesn't work that way.

Maybe, just maybe, after this whole Desisto thing gets going, I'll turn my back on all of it. Walk away.

The lie dissipated before it had time to nestle in his brain.

Being in charge made him think about Dick Abrams again. He took another large swallow from the flask, flinched at the freezing cold of the metal opening.

He didn't like the way Abrams had spoken to him today—like he was some minion that could be dismissed at will.

But he couldn't work up a resentment—the booze had made him feel better and lightheaded at the same time. He turned from the river and started walking back to his BMW.

* * *

Wilson's phone vibrated in his pocket. He tapped the button on the steering wheel to make the Bluetooth connection, then realized the call was coming in on the disposable cell he was carrying. He pulled out the phone and clamped it between shoulder and ear, hoping to avoid being spotted by some vigilant cop who hadn't written enough tickets for the day.

"Yes?"

"My boys picked up the package. Right now it's stowed in the trunk of a plain-Jane sedan, headed for an appropriate storage place."

Wilson pulled over and parked. "Please, Levi, tell me they didn't damage the merchandise."

"Have I ever let you down, man? That kind of business is always handled with the greatest of care."

"Yeah. That's what I expected with the California package, and look what happened."

"Hey, I'm sorry about—"

"—all I want to hear is that everything is being taken care of. Because if anything goes wrong this time, if the package is damaged in any way, no one's getting another dollar. They understand that?"

Wilson could hear Levi Black struggling to hold back some wiseass remark. Although he'd been extra careful with this Joanne equation, he wasn't crazy enough to think this whole mess wouldn't find its way back to his doorstep if there was a slipup … of any kind.

"Got it."

"Don't use this line again—it will be gone immediately after this conversation."

"Just don't forget I'm out-of-pocket for the front money for these guys, and they didn't come cheap."

"I'll get in touch with you the usual way, and then we'll settle."

"Yeah, okay, but they won't be too happy about any delay in getting paid."

He took a deep breath and watched the snow falling on Washington, hoped the roads weren't getting too slick to drive. "I'll let you know when it's safe for them to release the package. Not one minute sooner. Until then, the merchandise stays safe and sound. Otherwise, we all go down."

* * *

Wilson pulled into his townhouse garage and slid out of the car. He walked over to a nearby trash can and stomped down on the disposable cell until it was nothing but a pile of shattered plastic and ruined circuits. He scooped up the pieces with the broom and dustpan he kept nearby and dumped the disintegrated cell into the trash. It would be gone with tomorrow's garbage pickup, never to be traced back to him.

As he dusted off his hands, he saw that they were trembling.

The door from the garage opened into the kitchen; he quickly crossed the room and went straight into the living room and peeled off his overcoat and scarf. He tossed them onto a very proper burgundy Queen Victoria sofa that was rarely used to sit on, then he quickly started the gas fireplace, before pulling back the drapes. The cold, gray day that had already chilled him to the bone was now seeping into the townhouse; he couldn't stop shivering.

Wilson stepped back over to the sofa, pulled a colorful, woven throw from off the back, and wrapped it around his shoulders. He returned to stand in front of the fireplace and allowed the flames to warm him.

Thinking back over the past couple of days, he again realized it had been a mistake to kidnap the old newsman's wife. But had it done any real harm? He didn't think so. The woman got away, and neither she nor anyone else was injured, and apparently the police hadn't been notified. With luck, the newsman would back off long enough for Desisto to be finalized.

Wilson's trip to the river side had calmed his agitation. His focus had returned.

Congress had let the country down, had not been doing its job to protect the fiscal health of the United States. It was up to him and all the others to push Desisto. Save the country.

And it didn't matter that the President and his Chief of Staff, and the Secretary of HHS, and Hygea, and the whole healthcare industry were backing the scheme.

None of that mattered.

Because without Joanne Paige, the likelihood of Savage delivering the legislative rider would evaporate.

The success of the whole Desisto operation rested on the shoulders of Sen. Angelle Savage of Nevada, and one goddam, washed out whore.

Chapter 31

Nathan stood in the shadows at his apartment window, stared at the moon. It amazed him that something so far away could appear so clear, so spectacular. Tonight he thought he could even make out the craters that clustered to make it look like the legendary man in the moon. And right here in his tiny place on planet Earth everything around him was flooded with the eerie white glow of a heavenly satellite millions of miles away.

At one time, instead of becoming a history teacher, he'd thought he wanted to be a physicist or an astronomer, but he had realized he was too grounded, needed people too much for those heady occupations. So instead of dealing with space, time, and infinity, he remained earthbound where every ordinary 24-hour cycle now seemed to diminish his very existence.

Before he retired, there was at least laughter in his life every day. Teaching in middle school had kept him young and engaged. He would watch children with all their pent-up energy, their exuberance, and they would make him smile. Not a peaceful or quiet bunch, but there was a kind of joy in being around them. Now everything was grounded, but it was also too serious.

And too quiet.

He tossed stray thoughts aside. Right from the beginning Ted Yost had said he needed to come clean, tell everything he knew. But he couldn't . He'd promised.

Promised.

Suddenly he was crying.

"Poor Myra," he muttered. "You didn't deserve to die that way."

Life wasn't fair. The relatives he'd lost in the Holocaust— people he'd never even gotten to know. They didn't deserve to die that way either.

Cruelty, heartlessness seemed to be the human condition. That or indifference. Well, he'd never been indifferent about anything before in his life, and he wouldn't start now.

He looked at his watch. 10:00 p.m. in D.C. Too late to call? He left the window and walked through the apartment, let the moonlight guide him.

He'd given his word and he never went back on his word. He didn't want to reveal his Washington connection; but if he didn't tell Ted there was a good chance everything he'd worked for was going down.

He opened the drawer in a small bedside table and lifted out an address book, opened it to "S", and looked at the name for a long time: **Sen. Angelle Savage**

Nathan met her eight years ago. From the start she'd come out in favor of senior rights, a strong voice against raiding social security. He made it his business to meet her and they'd become instant friends. About a year ago, she began leaking info to help CORPS stay ahead of legislation meant to undercut Medicare.

It was that complicated and that simple.

He picked up the phone and dialed, was surprised that someone answered at the other end almost immediately. "It's me, Senator. Nathan Sorkin."

"Hello, Nathan. And you can cut the Senator stuff. We know each other too well for that."

"I know it's late, Angelle, but we need to talk. I'm in a situation here."

"I'm listening."

"I've kept my promise. I've never given your name as my Washington connection. But everything is happening so quickly. It's all falling apart."

Heavy breathing at her end of the line, but she didn't speak.

"Angelle?"

"I'm here." Another long stretch of silence.

"Angelle?"

"Nathan, I 'm in the middle of a big, big mess and I can't discuss it with you or anyone else—"

"—I need to identify you as my source. The one who has been leaking information to me."

Angelle Savage was crying. Her sobs were loud and painful.

"I'm sorry, Senator."

"It's not you, Nathan."

"What is it? You know you can trust me."

"Nathan, on Wednesday I'm being forced to carry a rider to the Medicare funding bill. It concerns selective euthanasia."

"Selective euthanasia? You're going to do this? "

* * *

Angelle Savage walked outside the townhouse with her phone, shivered at the cold, but couldn't stand to be closed in anymore. Gabe followed, stood next to her, draped a jacket around her shoulders, and wrapped an arm around her shoulder.

"I'm being blackmailed, Nathan."

"Blackmailed? About what?"

She took a deep breath, leaned closer to Gabe, and saw the snow had stopped.

"I had a sexual relationship with a girl when I was a teenager. She's now earns her living as a prostitute."

"Oh, my God! Who's behind this?"

"At this point, it doesn't matter. What does matter is if I don't tag on that rider, they'll not only release the information to the press—"

"—tell the *momzarim* to go to hell—"

"But, Nathan, they've kidnapped Joanne … the woman—"

"—kidnapped her?"

"They've sent me a warning. They have her and if I don't cooperate, they're going to hurt her, maybe kill her." Her throat was tight; she was so close to hysteria she bit down on her lip to keep from screaming.

"Go to the police. Now!"

"I can't. I just can't! That woman saved my life a long time ago. I can't risk hers now. No. I won't do that, no matter what the cost."

"Are you sure they've taken her? Have you tried to reach her?"

"I haven't seen Joanne in years. I don't even know where she is. But I won't take the chance. I can't let her down."

Chapter 32

The Tanas' dining room table and the surrounding floor were a jumble of newspapers, reference books, and laptops. Ted, Bill, Melissa, and Kelli drank cup after cup of hot, black coffee, trying to stay focused, but it was getting harder and harder to concentrate.

Ted suddenly slapped a palm down on the tabletop. "Bill! Did you ever remove that bug from your telephone line?" He picked up his cup and took a finishing gulp.

Bill rolled his eyes and looked over at Kelli. "The dude can really ask dumb questions sometimes, and he's supposed to be a Pulitzer ace." He turned to Ted. "I not only removed it, I stomped that sucker into submission and buried its remains in the garden. I hope it doesn't kill my plants."

"The question popped into my head, I had to ask it."

"Okay," Bill said, spreading his hands over the hodgepodge of papers on the table. "Where do we stand with all of this?"

Ted held up a fistful of notes. "I've tried every contact I could think of at the wire services, newspapers, local radio and TV stations, and all the networks. No one knows squat about proposed changes for Medicare."

"Did you get to Maria Weiskott at PBS?" Bill asked.

"Yeah. She mumbled something about a rider, but I couldn't get anything specific out of her. I tried to dig deeper, but she cut me off as though I'd hit her with a Taser."

"Hold it! A rider?" Bill looked up at the ceiling. "Wait! Wait!" He jumped up and began pacing around the table. "Damn it! I may have heard mention of a rider, too. Can't quite put my finger on it." He clamped his head with both hands. "Give me a moment or two; it'll come to me."

"Are you kidding me? Time is what we don't have a whole lot of."

Bill held up a hand. "Let's think about this logically. What do we actually know at this point?"

"Hygea may be pushing selective euthanasia as a means of cutting costs for terminally ill patients. At least, mentioning the subject hit a raw nerve with Garrett Rudge. And he has an ethics committee that's been meeting on end-of-life procedures for the past six months. The committee's scheduled to vote next Monday on whether or not to approve that policy for Galen."

"Where'd you get the committee information?" Mel asked.

"Mostly from my old friend, John Bradberry," Ted said. "But some of it came from Nathan Sorkin's hidden Washington connection."

"Sorkin wouldn't give you the name of his connection?" Kelli asked.

"Believe me, I tried, but he said his lips were sealed. Not even a hint as to who his source is."

"Yeah, well, we're all smart enough to know that even a positive vote by every medical ethics committee in the nation isn't going to make something like this fly without legislation to back it up, make it legal," Bill said.

"It has to be a Congressional insider," Ted said.

"We have a friend who's high up in the Social Security Administration," Mel said. "Did you try him?"

"Nope, but it's a good idea. Give him a call. He might know something."

"Use the phone in the den," Kelli said, "and I'll go make us some sandwiches."

"How about Ted and me giving you a hand," Bill said. "We could all use a break."

Before the food was half ready, Melissa came into the kitchen.

"That was strange ... really strange," she said. "After I got through the usual pleasantries, I told our friend at Social Security we were in town on a mission for CORPS. That put a big stop to the conversation." She plopped down on a kitchen counter bar stool. "Suddenly it was, 'nice to hear from you, gotta go, goodbye.' No 'let's get together while you're in Washington' or anything else." She grabbed a slice of cheese from a sandwich-in-the-making. "God, and to think of all those times we've had him over to dinner when he was in the Bay Area."

"There must be someone who can help us," Kelli said.

"Hey, gang, let's not give up yet," Bill said. "Even if Congress takes Friday off, as usual, we still have a couple of days left in this week to dig into things."

"Doesn't Congress recess for the holidays sometime soon?" Ted said.

"Next Thursday, the fifteenth. They'll be gone until the new session starts on January third."

"So there's going to be a mad dash to wrap up any pending legislation, particularly if it involves funding."

"Exactly." Bill leveled a finger at Ted. "Hey, you, you're the fly in the ointment here. You've come to town representing CORPS and shut down most, if not all, of your insider contacts. Looks like no one wants to have anything to do with CORPS."

"Yeah," Ted said. "So what do you suggest?"

"Get on the horn to Sorkin. If the man has information, we need it. Now!"

"But—"

"No 'buts,' damn it. The man asked for your help and then holds out on you? You can't let him get away with that, not after what happened to Mel."

Their eyes locked.

"Well?"

After a long moment, Ted said, "I haven't wanted to push, what with Myra's death, and the bombing of the CORPS offices."

"Ted, I don't think you have a choice," Mel said. "You have to put more pressure on Nathan."

"Okay! But he's a stubborn old fart."

"And he's going to stay that way unless you start showing us some of that old Yost don't-let-'em-off-the-hook interviewing

213

technique." Mel gave him a big, phony smile. "It's either that or give up investigative journalism for all time and get serious about your golf game."

Bill roared with laughter. "Better stick to the news, big guy. I've played golf with you and trust me, there's no future for you there."

Ted gave him the finger and picked up the phone.

* * *

"Nathan, it's me, Ted."

There was no response but he could hear strained breathing at the other end.

"Are you there, Nathan—"

"—I'm here."

"I think you know why I'm calling. Either you give me the name of your Washington source or Mel and I are on the next available flight back to San Francisco. We're running out of information sources here ... and time."

"I planned on calling later."

Ted hated the heaviness in Nathan's voice, the sound of a beaten man, but he couldn't let Nathan off the hook. "Hey, old man, maybe it's time you joined those rocking chair folks in some retirement home. You know, the ones who sit on their asses, never take a chance, hope someone else will do what has to be done."

"*Yop tvayu mat!*"

"Don't think I want to know what that means."

"Okay, Mr. Big Shot newsman, you've let *us* down? *You* were supposed to dig out the information so I could protect my Washington source. That's why we hired you in the first place. You were supposed to find it on your own."

"Stop it, Nathan! We don't have time for you-did-this, I-did-that nonsense. I need every goddam name you have, and I need them now."

More heavy breathing.

"It all started out as just a rumor," Sorkin said, almost in a whisper. "Came from someone inside the Feds. Just a stupid rumor about the healthcare people pushing for changes in end-of-life treatment."

"Yeah?"

"I didn't even believe it. The only reason I followed up was that I got the same information from my D.C. person. But I had to promise not to reveal where it came from. I was in a spot. Like I said, *you* were supposed to find it, Ted."

"So give me the info now."

"Someone, or some group—and it's very high up—is pushing for legalized selective euthanasia. And I just found out a rider that will make that happen is being tagged onto a piece of shoo-in legislation that's up for a vote sometime soon."

"Like sometime before Congress adjourns on the fifteenth. That means we've got five working days, at best, Nathan!"

"I know. I know."

"And you were planning to drop this little bomb on me when?"

"Believe or not, Ted, I was going to call you later tonight."

"Pacific or Eastern time?"

The silence grew between the two men. Finally, Ted said, "This day is not finished, Mr. Sorkin. Stay right where you are! I'll get back to you within the hour."

Chapter 33

"Maria, I need the back story on this rider you mentioned. Does it have anything to do with Medicare?"

Silence.

"Look, I know you don't want to talk about this, but remember: you owe me ... you owe me big time."

"Yost, I have no time for this. I've got to get over to Bethesda for a big National Endowment for the Arts to-do. In fact, I'm standing here getting ready to get into my car. Besides, I thought we'd finished this conversation earlier in the day."

"Not to my satisfaction. I'm up to my neck in alligators. I need you to toss me a lifeline."

"This better be serious. And it'd better be quick, Yost."

"My wife was kidnapped earlier this week. Is that serious enough?"

"I'm listening."

He laid the whole package for her, explained what he was needed, and why.

After a long moment with no response, he said, "Don't hold out on me, lady. I really need this information ... a lot of people need it."

"I can't help you, Ted."

"Don't tell me that. Just give me this one and I'll keep my mouth zipped forever about how you got that Guantanamo exclusive that landed you a spot on *60 Minutes*. After that, we'll be even."

"You're making this very tough."

"I know, Maria, and I'm sorry. But I've run out of time. I've no place else to go."

"What are you going to do with the information?"

"Whadda ya think, run it up the flagpole and see if anyone salutes? Damn it! Stop the rider, that's what I'm going to do."

Several seconds passed, then she said, "I'll give you what little I know. But you have to swear that attribution never lands on my doorstep. This PBS gig is the best assignment I've ever latched onto. If I lose it, well, you know what the news world is like out there. There ain't no jobs no more."

"Not a peep." Ted heard her sigh.

"There's something floating around called the Desisto Project, which fits in with what you've dug up. We tripped over it while working on an in-depth medical feature about the elderly."

"Go on."

"It leaked during an interview I did with Maurice Seldon, Secretary of HHS."

The hairs on Ted's neck prickled. "Yeah, I know who he is. What happened?"

"I was grilling him about the financial picture for long-term care."

"And Desisto?"

"It was literally a slip of the tongue; he screwed up. He'd referred to a rider and something called Desisto. When I pushed for more details, he told me to forget it. Said that if I ever mentioned any of this again, it would be worth my job, if not my head."

"The asshole threatened you?"

"He wasn't kidding."

"And it worked, didn't it?" Ted said.

"Back off, Ted. I gave it my best shot."

"No, Maria, *now* you're giving it your best shot."

* * *

Bill Tana stood at the window of his den. Snow covered everything in the back yard, including his favorite plant, a huge hydrangea. Under the clinging snow, there was nothing but a skeleton of dead sticks that needed to be lopped off at the ground. He was always impressed when in spring and summer it turned into this massive ball of beautiful, puffed-up pink clusters. This past spring he'd finally gotten around to putting a penny in the ground and it actually worked—the blossoms turned blue. Robin's egg blue.

Pretty damn amazing.

He forced himself to turn from the window when he heard Ted winding up his phone conversation with Maria Weiskott at PBS.

Ted's involvement with the advocacy group had seemed lame. Then he'd done a little research and discovered that the older generation was beginning to understand that its sheer numbers represented a lot of political clout. Politicians may have treated them like pushovers in the past, but that was changing.

And if someone like Ted was hooking up with CORPS, the name of the game was certainly going to change much more rapidly. Maybe something would finally be done to stop Social Security funds from being shoved into the general fund, *borrowed* to pay for other programs. .

Looking into the living room, he saw Kelli and Melissa going through a list of politicians and administration officials, then making an occasional call. As he watched, he was impressed with how lucky two reprobates like Ted and he were to have found such amazing women.

He walked over to his bookcase and absently read the titles on an eye-level shelf that held many of his favorite books, both fiction and non-fiction. He suddenly stuck out a finger and touched the spine of one particular novel, *She,* by H. Rider Haggard.

Something kept curling around in his head, a piece of conversation he'd overheard at his PR firm, about the same time he'd passed on the Medicare blurb to Ted. Had to do with a fast-moving piece of healthcare legislation. When he'd tried to find out the specifics, he was given the run-around. The only real thing he heard was that the junior Senator from Nevada was involved.

Oh yeah!

When Ted hung up the telephone, Bill said, "Don't know what you found out, but I think you're about to tell me I'm pretty damn smart. Not only that, but resourceful and even good looking."

"And that you're beautiful—a beautiful pain in the ass."

Bill laughed and held up a restraining hand. "Don't be so hasty with the criticism, Ted Yost. I just recalled a bit of office chit-chat that pointed to Senator Angelle Savage as being ready to pop with some action this coming week, possibly having to do with healthcare legislation.

"You're kidding."

"Cross my heart."

"I take back all the bad things I ever said about you, although it would have been nice if you'd remembered this crucial information earlier."

"Hey, no one's perfect."

"That's for sure," Mel and Kelli said in unison.

"Man, I need to get some shut-eye," Bill said. "I feel hung over."

"Sucking on beer bottles for hours will do that," Ted said. "It's getting late and I could use some food. Why don't we lock it up for the day and get back to it in the morning."

"Works for me, man."

But Ted remained seated, doodling on a scrap of paper. "Damn! That Galen Hospital committee is meeting next Monday ," he said.

"What about it?"

"The timing has to be more than coincidental."

"Timing with what?" Bill said.

"Look at what we know, or think we know—efforts to introduce selective euthanasia, a possible healthcare rider tagged to must-pass legislation, Congress adjourning for the year."

"Plus an undercover scheme involving Medicare, with the code name *Desisto.* "

"I just don't understand how Weiskott could sit on this information." Ted shoved a bunch of papers away from in front of him. "I mean, I get it that the PBS gig is a great career move, but there was a time when you couldn't hold that woman back. If she had even the hint of a good story, she ran with it. She was one helluva reporter."

Bill ran fingers through his hair with shaking hands. "Journalists gotta eat, too."

"Yeah, but what happened to honesty? Truth?"

"If you're talking about the truth, the whole truth, and nothing but the truth, I may not be your guy. Probably not since day one of my getting into public relations. I'm making a very, very good living, my friend, by frequently avoiding the truth, making useless and obnoxious things sound useful and innocent."

"You knew what you were getting into right from the start," Ted said. "What's changed?"

"Hell, it sounded exciting at the time. You know, hanging out with D.C. insiders, courting the power brokers, getting to know things the average citizen knows absolutely nothing about. It was good in the beginning."

"The druggie kid scores big."

"Something like that," Bill said. "But maybe it's time I got out of the PR game."

"Be careful what you ask for, guy."

Bill walked into the kitchen, opened the fridge, and pulled out another beer. "Get you anything?"

"How about a Coke?"

Bill filled a large glass with ice and poured the cola over it, gave it to Ted, and dropped back into his chair. He banged his beer bottle down, dry-washed his face with both hands, and shouted, "W. Wade Wilson!"

"The lobbyist?"

"Insurance industry, White House, Congress. I'd bet my last dollar that he's the one behind this whole shebang—this Desisto thing. No one else could orchestrate this kind of project and keep it under wraps." He picked up his beer and drank nearly half of it. "Dammit! I should have been on it when his name first came to mind."

"I'm not following you."

"This guy Wilson is a nightmare."

He's a lobbyist. What else do you expect? Don't really know much about the guy—"

"You gotta be kidding! Blogging has not only hog-tied you to a desk, the brain circuits ain't firing."

"Awright, already. Spit it out."

"W.W. is not only the most powerful healthcare industry lobbyist in Washington, he's a slime bag. Doesn't care what he's pushing as long as there's lots of money in the game. And he's smart, stays out of the limelight so there's no finger-pointing. But his connections lead everywhere, including the Oval Office."

"So you think the President is behind this thing?"

"Damn straight!" Bill walked up to Ted, pinched and jiggled his cheek. "You're turning into such a sweet old guy."

"Do that again and this sweet old feller will have you sitting on your ass."

"Well, get with it, think about it," Bill said. "Who has the most to gain politically—say a year from now? Da-dum! Election time! Start eliminating some of those zeros for Medicare spending—cut back on hospital services, expenditures that deal with the elderly, and man, you're in. And the good news just goes on and on."

"But if this came out, it would sink Tyler," Ted said. "The President would be out, along with anyone riding his coattails."

"Maybe, maybe not. But either way, this just the kind of behind-closed-doors thing Wilson loves to handle. He'd have all of them right in his pocket."

"This is even nastier than I thought," Ted said.

"What really rips me is it's a sneaky, heartless way to deal with old people who have no resources—people who are poor or dependent only on Medicare." Bill finished off his beer. "It's a simple equation—poor, sick; old, dead."

"Deadly simple."

"Hell, Ted, this is supposed to be the greatest country in the world. That's no way to treat *anyone*."

"At least they die drugged up, pain free." Ted held up his soda, and watched the ice swirl into a tiny eddy. "We all die. No way out of it. And there are worse ways to go."

Bill stood and headed out of the room. He tossed over his shoulder, "Yeah, but who wants to die on somebody's daily short list?"

* * *

After they finished dinner, Bill said, "Time to call Sorkin again."

He and Ted were still sitting around the dining room table and Kelli and Mel were in the living room. No one wanted to be the first to give in and call it a day, like everything would fall apart without all of them present.

Before Ted could respond, the phone rang. Kelli picked it up, listened, and handed it to Ted. "It's Nathan Sorkin."

"I know you were going to call me back," Nathan said, "but I couldn't wait any longer."

"Lay it on me. What do you have?"

Nathan's words spilled out, running together. "I hope this still helps. I'm sorry I haven't been totally straight with you. I've been stalling, but—"

"Hey, slow down, man. Take a breath or two. I can barely understand what you're saying."

Mel walked a cup of coffee to Ted, carried away his empty dinner plate.. He started drinking it right away.

"I know I should have told you from the start ... but I gave my word. I wanted to tell you, almost told you—"

"Nathan, just tell me now."

"Senator Angelle Savage."

"Yeah. The one from Nevada. We were just talking about her."

"Then you know?"

"Know what?"

"She's my Washington leak. And next week, she'll be the one carrying the rider—"

"—that will be tagged on to an appropriations bill that's expected to coast on through without a hitch," Ted said. "And undoubtedly the President plans to sign it the next day before anyone's had a chance to challenge it."

"When did *you* find out she's the one?"

"Does it matter? We're involved in a fucking flood, too fast and too big to stop."

"I'm sorry, Ted, I should have told you about Senator Savage. Maybe if you'd known sooner we could have stopped it."

Ted snatched the last chocolate chip cookie from a dish that had been stacked high a couple of hours ago. He was agitated, angry. "Yes, it might have helped if you had trusted me sooner."

Nathan's voice hardened. "Well, here's something you don't know, Mr. Ted Yost. Savage got bushwhacked into carrying the rider."

Ted had a sudden migraine. He hadn't had one in years, but his head was pounding and his face was being squeezed in a band of steel.

"Nathan, tell me what needs to be done. Is there anything we can do to stop Savage?"

"I'm not sure."

"Then tell me everything you know, and I mean *everything.*

Chapter 34

Garrett Rudge was into a slow boil. What he wanted was an update from all of Hygea's six administrators around the country with a single conference call. That's the way he preferred to do business. All this secrecy meant he was stuck with having to call each and every one of the six facility head honchos individually on a disposable cell phone. It took extra time; it took extra energy; and he was running out of both.

Looking over his shoulder, second guessing everything had gone on way too long. For God's sake, he'd barely even used his land line in the past six months—and for some reason that irked him even more.

There'd been no complaints when he'd informed the different Hygea people that he'd be calling at an unspecified time outside of work hours. They all knew Hygea was a 24/7 commitment. That's just the way it was. And if they were doing their jobs, got the yes votes from their committees, they would all be ready for the 'go' word. Ready to start the wheels of the future turning.

It had been a long day and a grueling task going over each facility's plan of attack, then making certain they were all in synch with his master scheme. He'd already spoken to five of the facility administrators, and was now making his sixth and final call. Everyone would be primed and ready when he got the legislative green light on Wednesday.

"Good evening, Larry," Rudge said. "Running a bit later than I intended; hope I'm not cutting into your dinner hour. Have I kept you from anything?"

"No, no. Just been sitting here reading a book"

And that really yanked Rudge's chain. He'd been working non-stop all day with damn little time to even go to the john, much less read anything that didn't have to do with Desisto. It only confirmed his impressions along with everything else he'd read about the man—capable; unflappable.

"I see," Rudge said. "So it's all lined up. No last-minute hitches."

"Look Garrett, I've done my job. I've got one candidate and two backups if something unforeseen pops up. Remember, this is Chicago. Our fair city has its share of poorbies. The field doesn't get any more fertile."

"Poorbies?"

"You know, *Medicare A* people. No close families to run interference. Isn't that what we're shooting for?"

Rudge sat back in his desk chair and realized that this man was the ideal Hygea executive. *Does what he's told with no second thoughts.*

"Funny, Larry, all the others administrators are ... well, maybe anxious isn't the word ... but they sure as hell are antsy."

"Antsy? You've got to be kidding. I've been working on this project for six months, just like you and everyone else. If I don't have it together by now, I deserve to get my ass booted off the train."

Supercilious bastard.

"Good," Rudge said, "because I need to know you're completely committed to the project; there can't be any reservations by anyone."

"No need to worry about me, Garrett. I'm ready to go; Chicago's ready to go."

And right then, Rudge knew that if he ever did find his way to a Washington appointment, Larry would be the one to fill his seat with no trouble at all. Rudge would just have to make certain it didn't happen before he was ready.

* * *

Silence.
Darkness.
Emptiness.
Della Paoli forced her eyes open.

She looked from side to side.

I can see.

She wanted to shout with joy. But her lips remained dead and useless.

Then her mind went blank

What happened?

Everything was a blur, a swirl of everything. Then nothing.

Lost. Confused.

Where am I? Not at home. My room doesn't look like this.

To the right, moonlight splashed through the vertical blinds of a narrow window. To the left, another bed—neatly made, but empty.

And then she remembered:

I'm in a hospital.

How long?

Quiet. Too quiet.

Where's the hum? Click of machines, people?

A doctor was here. Said I was in some kind of accident. But something else is wrong.

She looked down to where her arms were tucked beneath the sheets. She tried to lift her hands, concentrated on making the sheets move. Then closed her eyes and imagined her hands picking up flowers.

Everything remained smooth, undisturbed. Her arms hadn't moved.

She took a deep breath, tested her legs, went through an imaginary exercise of walking through the park.

Nothing.

Can't concentrate, can't understand, can't put it together. Everything's a jumble of bits and pieces.

What will they do with me? Send me away? To a nursing home?

No, no, no!

She didn't want to go. Rows and rows of wheelchairs; people like empty shells staring out into space—no dreams, no future.

She closed her eyes, forced herself to look at her body again. Everything remained undisturbed. Not a ruffle. Nothing.

There was an IV next to the bed. She watched the fluid drip, feeding slowly into her arm like an icicle melting into a quiet pond.

Drip, drip, drip.

Then she heard it. A sharp intake of breath and the quiet breathing of another person.

Someone was in the room with her.

Who's there?

Her eyes probed the shadows. She concentrated until her vision adjusted to the darkness in the corner of the room.

Two eyes stared back.

* * *

Garrett Rudge edged out of Della Paoli's room. He would never be able to explain the need to see her. All day he'd fought the urge until there was nothing else to do but go.

As he watched her open her eyes, he knew she must be trying to move beneath the sheets tucked neatly around her. That's what he would do. But he also knew there was nothing she could do for herself. Not one single thing. She might as well have been a turnip.

But if it had been his sister Evelyn, would he have allowed anyone to take away a single moment of her life?

No. Not one second, no matter what her condition. He would have stopped anyone who tried to end her life.

But this woman had no champion. No advocate to fight for her life.

She lay in that bed understanding everything, doing nothing.

Would he have wanted his twin to live like that? A stone with a brain? Would he really?

No.

The questioning was over. This woman would cost Medicare hundreds of thousands of dollars for who knew how long—weeks, months, years? And to what end?

Della Paoli had been the right choice for Desisto.

Chapter 35

Garrett Rudge's fix for insomnia was a long, hot shower—pounding water that cascaded over his body, breathing in the thick steam. It usually relaxed, even sedated him. But it hadn't worked this time. After crawling back into bed, he tossed and turned, fought with his king-sized sheets until he'd created a mountain of linen bunched up all around him.

Fear, failure, disaster created a paralyzing trio of thoughts that spun through his head.

Six months of weekly meetings with the constant indoctrination of corporate culture, business philosophy, and vital healthcare statistics should have done the trick for each and every one of the committee members. Their heads should be filled with not only all the information Rudge had given them, but what they needed to do.

One fact remained: he either got the yes votes he needed on Monday or he was through.

Thinking about it was exhausting.

In the beginning the challenge had been to keep the committee members from bolting from their conference room chairs so he could feed them the same boring material over and over.

Then he had to carefully weave in the financial relief that selective euthanasia could bring.

Was there something he'd overlooked?

He flung the balled-up sheets onto the floor.

Ted Yost? CORPS? They kept popping into his head. What happened to them? They seem to fade away much too easily.

He sat up, scooted back into the pile of sweaty pillows. Restless, he pushed out of bed, edged up to the railing of his bedroom loft and stared down into the black hole that hid his living room.

He thought about Della Paoli as he went down the stairs, the wall-to-wall carpeting soft under his bare feet. She had been at the edge of his thoughts all day. He wanted to know more about this chosen, ideal candidate for the Desisto Project.

He walked through the living room, but the atmosphere was thick, difficult to breathe. Here in the stillness was the place where he most often thought about his twin sister, Evelyn, and that final moment when his twin sister left this world, left him.

At the end, her face had shown a moment of sadness, a smile that revealed an eerie beauty, as though she'd discovered something wonderful. Would it be the same for Della Paoli as her last second was snatched away?

Rudge went to the wet bar, found the decanter of aged Spanish brandy. He lifted a small snifter and poured until the liquid reached the brim. Unable to swirl and inhale the aroma as he usually did, he drank it down in a single gulp.

Evelyn and Della Paoli were not all that different. Both were victims of diseases that the universe randomly tossed at them, like seeds scattered in the wind.

He'd known his sister. Known who she was. But Della Paoli? Who was she? What kind of person was she?

He slapped a hand on the wet bar. "What difference does any of that make? Della Paoli, John Doe, Jane Doe, who cares? It's what has to be done."

He shuffled back through the living room, clamping his still-stinging hand in his armpit.

"Fuck it! She's going to die one way or the other!"

He stopped in front of the entertainment center, tapped the controls of the iPod-audio system link. Immediately the whole condo was filled with the rich sounds of Bach's Concerto in D-Minor for Two Violins.

The structured rhythms of the music began to soothe him. Even before the concerto ended, his fears and priorities were in place again: The Desisto Project was necessary—for him, Galen Hospital, Hygea, the nation.

Satisfied, he forced himself back up to his bedroom.

"I need this, Evie," he shouted back into the darkness.

* * *

"Damn it, Willa, it's three o'clock in the morning and I can't go on anymore about today's committee vote." Cliff Michaels paced around their living room, looked at his wife. "Enough!"

"Well, maybe we'd be cozy and warm in our bed if you'd had the balls to talk about all of this sooner," she snapped. "This isn't chopped liver. We're talking about someone's life."

"You think I don't know that?"

"Do you, really? I mean, I don't understand how you could keep something this significant from me for almost six months."

Cliff sat down next to her, tried to take her hand. She yanked it away, refused to allow him to touch her. He slumped, bowing his head almost to his knees. He knew she wanted to put the matter to rest as much as he did. But they continued to fight.

"It didn't seem real to me, not until today. Hell, what do I know about medical economics?"

"That's why you were there. To learn."

"You've got to be kidding. I'm on that committee for only one reason." He held out a forearm. "See that, woman? That's black skin. And that's exactly why I'm there."

"What they want and what they get are two different things."

"What's that supposed to mean?"

"Christ, I think you spend too much time with idealists, Cliff. Save the land! Save the whales! What about getting down and dirty and mixing with the rest of us?"

"That's a cheap shot. You've never taken any more than a passing interest in anything I've found important."

"That's not true!"

"The hell it's not! Those idealists are trying to do something for the planet. Dammit, why are you picking at that? Do I have to explain all of it to you.?"

"Of course not. You're just overreacting."

233

"Really? How many rallies have you attended with me? How much time have you put into saving the air we breathe?"

"You know damn well where my extra time and energy go, Cliff. It's not that I think what you're doing is unimportant, it's just that you've never needed my help; the black children I tutor do."

"You're dead wrong. I do need your help. The planet needs your help. It's past time for you and everyone else to wake up to that fact."

She stood and circled aimlessly about the room. After about the fourth circuit, she walked up to her husband, stopped in front of him, and stared hard into his eyes.

"You're so goddam selfish," she said.

"What do you mean?"

"I mean, there are all kinds of people out there who are ready to help you. And the issues you feel so strongly about cross all color lines. Most intelligent people today, regardless of their background, race, or education, are concerned about the environment." She shook a finger at him. "But how many of them want to dig in and help poor blacks? Even our well-to-do brothers and sisters seem to have lost interest."

"That's a shot between the legs."

"Is it?"

"Is there some point to all this shit?" he said.

"You bet your black ass there is."

"Well, what the hell is it?"

She glared at him for several seconds, then plopped down on the couch, put a hand on his knee. "That committee you're sitting on at Galen needs some contrast to all those white faces. With you there, it makes it look like they have a group that represents the entire community."

"Isn't that exactly what I said?"

"Not exactly. What I heard was you feeling resentful and sorry for yourself. Why not think of yourself as someone who represents millions of blacks, not just the committee's token black. Can't you do that, Clifford?"

"I only know how *I* feel. I have no way of knowing how millions of blacks feel."

"You fight against the useless slaughter of animals, the rape of the land, the contamination of the air we breathe, but you don't get that millions of people could be eliminated simply because they are black and poor?"

"Yeah, I get it. But there's not much I can do about it."

"So not knowing what to do, you do nothing? Those kids are not going to make it, Clifford. Not unless we help them. And regardless of the rhetoric, most whites simply don't give a damn."

Cliff closed his eyes. "I should never have agreed to sit on that damn committee."

"Are you kidding? What if they'd chosen someone who was there just for the prestige? What then? You have a chance to make a difference. Take it, run with it."

"Run where?"

"They're going to let that woman die because she's alone and poor. That's murder. And she's a white woman. If they can get away with this one, they won't even think twice when it's a poor black or Hispanic, or any other minority."

"It's not murder, Willa."

"Like hell it's not."

"Ease up, will you. Most enlightened people today believe in euthanasia."

"I think people also want the right to decide for themselves. I sure as hell don't want the government or some goddam corporation making that kind of decision because it's the economically expedient thing to do."

"I wish it was that clear-cut for me." He stood, turned off the table lamp, and walked through the darkened room to the patio door. He stared at the shimmering dots of street lights that seemed to float down the hill and out to the bay. The deck door slid open smoothly and he stepped out onto the moonlit deck, lifted his eyes to the clear, star-filled sky.

Willa followed him, slid an arm around his waist.

* * *

Reverend John Bradberry lay awake in the semi-darkness.

A high, full moon seemed to highlight the empty space beside him where his wife should have been.

Audrey was in the spare room. He was alone for the first time in many years. He wanted to march down the hall, beg her to talk to him. But three days of silence had killed his courage to face her.

He forced himself off the bed and started to slip into his robe, then tossed it aside. The Bible on the bedside stand stared back at him. It brought no comfort.

The hallway was dark, but when he pushed open the door to the guestroom, moonlight was shining through a window and highlighted the bed.

For a long time he stood and stared at the outlines of her body lost in the covering blankets. He silently rehearsed what he wanted to say.

"Audrey?"

"I'm awake, John."

"I'd like to talk to you. There are things I need to tell you, things about me, things that—"

"Not now, John. Just come to bed." She moved over.

"Not until you know the truth."

Audrey sat up, propped a pillow behind her head, and turned on the bedside light. He avoided her eyes and began to tell her about his life in Southeast Asia during the Vietnam War.

"When I went there," he said softly, "I was fresh out of seminary. Idealistic, ignorant about life. No matter how I tried, I couldn't absorb the death and destruction all around me."

"It must have been was awful."

He felt her eyes searching his. "I lived with a Vietnamese woman and her children. They became very dear too me. Being with that woman saved my sanity. She was the only one I could hold onto in a world filled with blood and violence. Without her I would have gone mad."

He sat down heavily on the bed and described the death of the woman's youngest child; how he felt responsible for the disappearance of the older child.

"I was so crazy. I might have kept her, done something." He swatted at the tears, the beads of sweat on his face. His voice dropped to a whisper as he spoke of his hospitalization.

"In the end, it was my faith in God that healed me. But I swore that I would never again be vulnerable or powerless."

"John, did you marry me for my money?" She blurted it out as though she hadn't heard a word he'd said.

"Audrey, I didn't even know who you were before I went to that dance. I was visiting; I didn't know anyone. And then you appeared out of nowhere. It's true that I was impressed when I learned about your family's wealth; but I didn't know before we met."

"You really didn't marry me for my money?"

"No, I didn't."

She was silent for a long time. When she did speak, her voice was soft and low. "I had no illusions about my physical beauty. I was ... I am ... a plain woman. That any man could want me for myself was not an option. I simply knew that no one would."

"Don't you understand, Audrey? I married you because you were a warm, caring, and loving woman; I needed you desperately. It was pure luck that your father scared away anyone else who might have taken you from me."

"I want to believe you, John."

"You know that no one could stand to be around your father, regardless of his wealth. He was a failed human being and I know how miserable he made your life."

"*I* didn't have a choice," she said. "But you? How did you tolerate him?"

He stared out the window at the moon. Several seconds passed before he could find the right words.

"He was a God-send for me," he said, gazing at her. "Incredible? Oh, no, not incredible. I came to love your father. He became my personal redeemer. His very being provided me with the daily punishment I needed."

"I don't understand."

"Can't you see he was the lashing I earned for my life in Vietnam, for what I allowed my life to become afterwards—using your father's money—your money—to buy up tenement after tenement, profiting from the despair of the poor, the displaced? He was the torture I deserved for forcing all of those people onto the streets as the properties were condemned. That I profited from all of this only gave me the need for even greater punishment."

Audrey reached over, clasped his hand.

"Every day I ask myself, what happened to all of those people, where did they go?"

"Stop it, John!"

"I cursed the day your father died," he said. "Who was going to punish me for all my sins now?"

"You've suffered enough."

He turned away, his head bowed. "Audrey, can't you understand? How will I ever find God again? I've lost my way."

She wrapped her arms around him, rested her head on his shoulder.

"We can help those people, John. Use our money to find homes for the poor, the homeless. They still need you."

"How do I make it up to you? How do I make up for all the years I've taken your love for granted?"

She squeezed him closer, kissed his cheek

"Love me, John. Just love me."

* * *

Robert Holt sat in his living room staring at an unopened bottle of Chivas Regal. It was eight p.m. and he was still sober.

He had been sitting in the same chair since dinner, staring at a half-eaten bowl of canned tomato soup. He'd turned on the television then put the volume on mute; the flickering images of the programs' characters and action moved without his understanding any of it, or even wanting to.

He thought only about past committee meetings, recreating them in his mind.

Garrett Rudge's immediate objective was obvious: He wanted Della Paoli "put down." Using the euphemism for killing injured and sick animals struck him as dark humor. He wondered if they would use the same terminology for people, or would some marketing genius come up with a more acceptable, more romantic expression, perhaps something grandiose like "the final trip of a lifetime."

He resented that Rudge expected absolute obedience from him, made it plain without using the actual words that his job and his retirement pension depended entirely upon whether or not he performed to Hygea's expectations.

And Rudge's real agenda?

He'd listened to the words, heard the rationale, but it didn't wash; something was being left out.

Holt stood up and paced through the house, going from room to room, opening and closing closets and cabinets for no reason. He couldn't stop thinking about the ethics committee meetings. The implications numbed his mind.

Before the last meeting, he'd tried to escape the reality of the proceedings, hiding in a fantasy world, where no one was ever desperately ill, or where no one ever died. It was all a waiting game. Waiting until he could come home, sit in this chair, drink his Scotch.

At this last meeting, the fantasy died. He heard every interchange, every word.

Selective euthanasia.

Holt returned to his chair, sat, and buried his face into his hands. The pain of losing his beloved wife overcame him. He reached out, opened the bottle of Scotch at his side, and poured until his glass was full.

He gulped it down, poured again.

* * *

"Love these weekends, when we're both off," Zach Wolfe said, a wide smile spreading across his face. "I mean here we are at La Ginestra, waiting for a fantastic meal, and not worrying about another thing in the whole world."

Sarah Silver laughed, thoroughly enjoying seeing Zach so happy. He reached across the table and squeezed her hand.

"That's the first time I've heard you laugh this evening; actually, in several days," he said.

"I know. It's been ages since I felt this relaxed."

Zach took in a deep breath. "And can you smell that garlic? Right now I feel like a real, live person instead of some HMO's puppet."

She took a sip of her Chianti and looked out the window at the leisurely flow of casually dressed people. It was good to just sit and observe. On Sunday, people were more likely to be into a don't-need-to-hurry attitude, while on Saturdays, they were always more frantic, intent on getting everything done or having a good time.

Zach squeezed her hand again. "Is it so difficult to talk to me?"

She ignored the question, turned back to the window and tried to embrace the easygoing manner of those strolling by.

When was I ever carefree?

The waiter brought their antipasto, and with a flourish set the plate filled with salami, prosciutto, melon, copa, provolone, olives, and pepperoncini on the red-and-white- checkered tablecloth. Then he put down a large basket of toasted garlic bread.

"Too much, as usual, Gino." Zach immediately snatched a piece of sourdough, topped it with layers of meat and cheese, and began munching.

Gino pointed at them and said, in a phony Sicilian accent, "Need fattening; too skinny." The three of them laughed. Sarah knew Gino was a UC Berkeley grad student who often helped his parents in the Mill Valley restaurant, doing everything from washing dishes to serving food to cooking, all the while pretending to be fresh off the boat from Italy.

Zach nodded in the direction of the departing Gino and said, "What about those perfect, white teeth of his? I swear there was a Disney-like glint on a front tooth; it blinded me for an instant. Man, I'm so dentally challenged compared to that guy."

"Too late to work on your genes," Sarah said.

"Guess so."

Sarah studied his relaxed, smiling face. "How come I feel so awful and you're dancing on air this evening?" She played with her fork, sliding it back and forth between a slice of salami and a dark Sicilian olive. "All I can think about is that conference room with Rudge doing his Three-D talk."

"Three-D?"

"You know: death, dying, disaster," she said. "And not necessarily in that order."

"It *was* pretty grim."

"All my fears about the future of nursing, medicine, and healthcare make me wonder why I even bother to get up in the morning."

"I guess we're both worry warts. I haven't been sleeping too well. The whole scenario keeps me awake." Zach cut a piece of copa into small pieces before scooping all of it up with a fork and shoving it in his mouth. "The whole system is in such a state of flux, almost anything is possible."

"Rudge keeps going on and on about how many hospitals have shut down over the past ten years," she said.

"It's true, we're losing our turf. And when that asshole talks about thinning our overcrowded population to meet reduced available care and facilities, I get the chills."

"Remember the woman with locked-in syndrome I told you about?

"Of course, who could forget that?"

"They moved her out of ICU," Sarah said. "She was barely stabilized and they sent her off to hospice. Terence Emory signed off on her. Period. End of discussion." Sarah felt the hair prickle on the back of her neck "They're sending her off to die. It's a scenario out of a sci/fi novel."

"Terrance Emory is a company man. He'll do as he's told. The one I'm disappointed in is Holt. He sits at those meetings like a lump of clay, lets Rudge run the whole show."

"If Rudge hits me with one more statistic, I'm going to scream … scream right there in the conference room."

"What else do you expect? He's only interested in making big bucks for Hygea; screw the patients, nurses, physicians, and everyone else."

"Still. not much of a Hygea fan, are you?" Sarah said.

"I spent years trying to organize the community docs against the Hygea takeover. Only a few listened; the rest were too independent. Now most of them work for Hygea, or some other HMO-controlled facility." He grabbed another piece of bread and stuffed it into his mouth. "Ironic, huh?"

"Zach, I've got to admit, I'm on the fence about this whole euthanasia business. The idea of patients suffering—well, that's not why I became a nurse."

"Nor why I became a doctor." He picked at the antipasto, shoved some of the meat around on the plate. "You and I weren't together when my Mom was dying."

"You've always been reluctant to talk about that."

He was silent for a moment, then it all came out in a rush.

"When I think of all the years I tried to get her to stop smoking. Years before she was diagnosed with COPD. Then the complications, pneumonia." He took a sip of his wine. "In the final stages, when she couldn't breathe on her own, there wasn't anything anyone could do for her. After a week of watching her drown in her hospital bed, I gave her what she needed to die. But to this day, I wonder whether it was me who really needed to be comfortable—or her."

Sarah took his hand. "A difficult time."

"Yeah, but dying quicker, according to Rudge, saves not only a lot of suffering, it saves a lot of money."

"Maybe it's time for you to move on, Zach. Do something else."

"Like what? I'm a doctor. It's what I've always wanted to be. And hospitals like Galen have me by the balls; I need them to survive, and don't think they don't know it."

Bette Golden Lamb & J. J. Lamb

Chapter 36

Joanne Paige was choking on the rag stuffed in her mouth and she couldn't loosen the bonds that tied her to a straight-back chair. Her throat was so dry she could barely swallow her own spit, if she had any spit to swallow. She began to retch—so hard her chest was instantly sore and tight.

Please don't throw up, please don't throw up.

If she did, it was all over. When the spasms finally stopped, she looked around.

The room was dark except for a slash of light that came from under a door. She could make out the outline of a bed, a window with drawn drapes, and a TV sitting on a chest of drawers. She took in the familiar odor of stale liquor and cigar smoke. A motel room, an apartment?

Was this some sicko's far-out sex fantasy?

Her temple throbbed with pain, and with it came the memory. Two men had snatched her from the Capital City Whore House.

She'd just gotten comfortable in her favorite flannel PJs, was drifting off to sleep when two bozos pounced on her, gagged, blindfolded her, and dragged her out. She'd fought hard when they'd tried to shove her inside some kind of car—braced her arms and legs against a door frame and earned a bop on the head for her efforts.

Now she was really scared. Her heart raced, breathing was difficult.

Why would a couple of goons snatch her? It made no sense. Her head spun with questions. It's not like she hadn't heard of other girls being taken, but they were usually the young ones and worth a few bucks. Hell, she was forty-four and on the way down. They must have mixed her up with someone else. No one was going to deliberately steal her from a crib or park her ass in a ship container and tote her off to some sheik or Asian sex factory where blonde women were a big plus.

Shit, they must have known after they got me out of there, must have seen that they had the wrong whore. Why didn't they turn me loose?

Her chest hurt like she had a bad cold or the flu. She remembered the big hand covering her face, choking her. She started to shiver, strained hard to hear any kind of sound from the other side of the door.

* * *

"Hey, Death, what the hell's your real name?" Jumbo tapped the ash from a fat Cuban cigar into an empty fast-food container tray they were using for an ashtray. He looked from the cards in his hand to the discard stack between them, and then to the three unrelated cards that had kept him from going out for two turns. He only needed another 60 points to hit 500 Rummy.

Death glared at Jumbo. "Fuck you!" He tossed out a discard.

"Now don't go mean on me, man." Jumbo looked at the card that had fallen, smiled, and reached out to pull in all the cards but one. He gave Death a crooked grin as he arranged the three-and four-card runs, slipped in the three cards in his hand, and said, "Out!"

"Fuck you."

Jumbo grinned again. "Count your cards."

"You won, asshole." He swept the cards off the table, poured the last inch from a bottle of tequila into a plastic cup, and downed the liquor.

"Hey, I wanted some of that."

"So go buy another bottle." Death pushed back from the table, got up, and went over to plop down on one of the twin beds.

"Before you get too comfortable, why don't you go check on the broad?"

"Want her checked, you go check. She ain't making no noise."

"Got a gag in her mouth, dummy. How's she gonna make any noise."

"How the fuck should I know?" Death picked up the remote and turned on the TV. "I still think we shoulda taken her over to Reno instead of keeping her here."

"Black said keep her in Carson City, so we're gonna keep her in Carson City."

"Ain't nothing to do in this goddam town."

"What we're doing is watchin' the broad."

"Fan-fucking-tastic! He turned off the TV, got up and stomped into the kitchenette, opened the mini-fridge, and stared at the small cache of food they'd brought in with them along with the takeout. He yanked out a package of salami, another package of sliced American cheese, and a bag of bagels. He ripped open a bagel, stuffed several slices of meat and cheese between the two halves, and started chewing.

"Hey, that's supposed to last us for a couple of days, unless Black calls us from Washington before that."

"Fuck you!"

* * *

Washington?

Why were they talking about Washington? So far away. Joanne didn't know a soul there except Angelle. And Angelle didn't know where she was.

My lost Angelle. Went away to college. She was never mine again after she came back and got all involved in politics. People said she asked about me, but she couldn't have wanted me hangin' around with all that big stuff she got involved in. Got herself elected to all those different jobs, then she was gone. Gone away to Washington.

Joanne strained against the rope that lashed her to the chair. There seemed to be a little give, but not enough to do her any good.

Got to get loose, get out of here.

Frantic, she strained, pulled really hard against the rope. All it did was make her head buzz—like it always did when she focused too hard on something. Messed up from the meth. Yeah, she'd put the drugging behind her, but it didn't change anything except everything hurt so much more now that she was straight.

Never going to walk away from the life. Whoring is all I know. No future, only a past. A past of drugging and whoring. Waited too long.

She was still having trouble breathing. Maybe it was those big hands that had clamped down over her face, choked her. It hurt where they smashed her head, and a terrible sadness was welling up inside—then she was crying, remembering.

* * *

Joanne was a good shooter—could take the eye out of a rabbit. Kept her foster father from nailing her, especially after she threatened to blow his balls off if he ever touched her again. Actually, he was a much better man to be around after that, and he treated her foster mom a lot better, too.

Joanne usually loved the deserted mines but tonight she knew in coming to this old mine she was surrendering to her worst nightmare. The blackness quickly smothered her, blocking her retreat.

She'd decided to meet Harlen here, the creepiest mine shaft off Six-Mile Canyon—she was here to save Angelle. She patted the revolver stuck in the waistband of her jeans, felt better for an instant. The gun was as clean and well-oiled as the day it came from the factory. Hadn't been that way when she bought it off some kid who'd heisted it and needed a quick forty bucks for some meth.

Poor little Angelle. Joanne had wanted her to come to the mine, too, so they could face Harlen together. But Angelle was too scared to stand up to him, to fight back. Joanne would have to take care of it by herself.

The four-cell Maglite cut through the darkness; she could make out the large overhead timbers that kept tons of ore from crashing down and collapsing the tunnel. Even now she could hear chunks of rocks dropping.

She loved the old gold and silver mines, had been through many of them exploring, sometimes alone, sometimes with other kids. They were a great place to go to cut class and get high. And whenever she wanted, or needed, to get away from her foster father, she'd hunt for a new mine to explore. She'd almost been buried for good once. Scared shitless, but never gave up; finally dug her way out. Never told *anyone* about it.

She could hear Harlen Davis getting closer, could see the bright beam of his flashlight. He moved with heavy steps, scuffing his boots in the loose gravel.

He was big, ugly, and mean. And he was coming to get what he wanted and expected from every girl in the area. And she'd promised to let him have it.

"There you are you little tramp," Harlen called out. Before she could say anything, he grabbed her and started running his hands up and down her body, across her breasts, between her legs.

"What's this?" he shouted. He pulled the gun from her waistband. He looked at the small Smith & Wesson .38 Special and laughed. Threw it on the ground.

"Did you think you were going to stop old Harlen with that little pop gun? You're sure a stupid little thing even if you do got beautiful tits."

He continued to laugh as he stripped off her t-shirt, jeans, and panties. Forced her down.

"Stop it!" she screamed at the top of her lungs. "Leave me alone!"

"Pussy's gotta keep a promise. You promised Harlen. Gotta keep your promise."

She tried to roll away, but he unbuckled his belt and opened his fly. She was trapped as he rammed inside of her. She reached, reached until her hand closed around the butt of the gun.

Not even drugs could erase that moment—the horrendous blast tearing at her ears … the look of surprise on Harlen's face … the blood pouring over his shirt. Bright red blood that started in the center and spread everywhere.

He died on top of her—a dead weight with chest rattles that echoed through the mine. In death, his body pressed down harder, harder until she couldn't breathe.

* * *

Can't breathe.

"Stop struggling, bitch." A mouth slobbered into her ear and spit ran down her neck as she tried to move away from him.

He cut away her gag and bindings, picked her up, threw her on the bed, and ripped off her pajama bottoms.

"You damn whore." He laughed and laughed. "Gonna ride you like an ole gray mare.

"Leave me alone. Get away!"

"Give it to me. Now! " He shouted in her face; the air between them filled with the smell of booze and garlic. And spit flew everywhere.

She punched his head, his shoulders, but he wouldn't budge.

"Jumbo's gone. You and me are gonna have some fun." He squeezed her breast until she screamed, then moved his lips over her mouth; she bit down until she tasted blood.

"Fucker!" He punched her in the face. Then again.

She turned wild, scratched his eyes, and finally struggled out from under him. He yanked her by the hair and the sound of a switchblade snapping open silenced her.

"Move one more inch, you bitch, and I'll carve your face so bad even yer friggin' mother won't know ya."

Chapter 37

"Yes?" The man on the other end of the phone had a no-nonsense voice and it was filled with suspicion.

"My name is Ted Yost and I need to speak to Senator Savage. It's urgent."

"Is that Y-O-S-T?

"That's correct." Ted could hear the shuffling of papers.

"Your name is not on her approved list of callers, Mr. Yost. I suggest you call the Senator's office and either speak to someone there, or leave a message."

"Did that. Got me nowhere."

"Yes, well, this is her residence and she doesn't conduct business from home, especially at this hour."

Ted was on hyper-drive, caffeine had gone down as easy as drinking water and his emotions were all over the map. It was now or never. He had to stop the rider.

He placed a hand on his chest; it was being squeezed in a vice and he could barely breathe.

He would not accept no. No was not an option He *had* to speak to Senator Savage. And it had to be now.

"Look, tell the Senator that Nathan Sorkin told me to call—he was the one who gave me her number. I'm working with him and CORPS."

Ted heard a verbal exchange behind a muffled mouthpiece.

"Mr. Yost, this is Angelle Savage. Thank you for calling. Nathan spoke to me about you." A sudden pause told the story. The Senator was definitely under the gun. "This is a terrible time for you to call—"

"I know," Ted said.

"You know?"

"I know everything about the rider on Wednesday ... that they've taken your friend to blackmail you."

Several seconds passed. "Nathan shouldn't have told you."

251

"Senator, he's your friend, and he knows you're in trouble.

* * *

"Mel, I wanted you to stay with the Tanas. Bill can handle himself and you'd be safe."

"Are you kidding? I'm not letting you out of my sight again. The last time we were separated, I ended up drugged, snatched, and stashed. Believe me, I'm much safer here with you. If we go down, we go down together. And this time, Teddy bear, I go down fighting." She pulled a set of brass knuckles out of her purse, slipped her fingers through the holes, and held her hand up for him to see. "Kelli gave them to me, said they would even the odds. Not even that heavy."

"Put those things back in your purse before the cabbie turns us in to Homeland Security." He smiled but was serious at the same time. He looked up at the rear view mirror but the driver was minding his own business. "You're becoming a regular thug, you know that? I'll bet those kidnappers are sorry they ever met up with you."

She gave him a big smile and slipped the brass knuckles back into her purse as the car came to a stop.

"This is it," the cabbie said. Ted leaned forward and paid the fare. He and Mel walked up to the entrance of an elegant, two-story brick townhouse. Ted thought the white Greek columns were over-the-top, more like a movie set. But every house on the block had the same facade.

Before they could ring the bell, the door swung open and a tall, lean man in his late forties stood at the threshold.

"Yes?"

"I'm Ted Yost; this is my wife, Melissa."

The man studied them, looked as though he was going to ask for identification, but instead said, "Gabe Harrington," and held out a hand. "I'm the Senator's husband. Sorry I gave you such a bad time on the phone." He stepped aside. "Come on in."

They moved into the foyer, where a grand sweep of staircase curved down from the second story. The living room was highlighted by heavy burgundy drapes, obviously made to imitate ancient tapestries. The room was a quirky mix of the old and the new, very comfortable, but could have been featured in *Architectural Digest*.

The Senator, elegant in an emerald green suit, rose from the sofa. A tall and stately woman, she held out a hand, first to Ted, then to Mel.

"No need to tell me what a mess I've gotten myself into. I already know." With a sweep of her hand, she offered them a seat on the opposite sofa; her husband sat down next to her. "I'm sorry, I'm forgetting my manners. Would you care for something to drink?"

Ted and Mel both shook their heads.

"Look, Senator, I know how hard this is for you," Ted said. "But we need to get the Joanne Paige problem out into the open and discuss it. And there isn't a lot of time."

"Tell them, Angelle," her husband said. "Nothing else has been working."

"Look, I don't need a lot of details," Ted said. "Nathan's told me most of it. They're threatening to kill your friend, expose your past sexual involvement, if you don't do give them what they want."

"That's right."

"Senator, do you have any idea who's behind all of this?"

The Senator stood and walked to the window as though she were looking out, even though all she could see were the closed drapes with their intricate needlepoint patterns. She briefly fingered the coarse material as though there was comfort in the touch. "I think I can fend off the gay thing and Joanne being a prostitute, but I can't live with her being tortured or murdered."

Ted shook his head.

The Senator turned to face them again. "You probably think she can't be much of a person." Tears filled her eyes. Gabe moved to her side, put an arm around her waist. The rumors of their separation were either false or the Harringtons were very good actors.

"Take your time, Angelle." Gabe said. "You don't need to tell them if you don't want to."

"But I need to." She reached for her husband's hand and they walked back to the sofa together. "Joanne and I grew up in a small Nevada town, a place where everyone knew each other's secrets. Joanne was my only real friend—she saved my life. How could you *not* love someone like that, someone who would give up her life for you? We were lovers until I left for college. Then, I left town, left her behind."

"Never saw her again?" Mel asked.

"Years later I ran into her. But it was a brief contact." Tears ran down Angelle's cheeks; she swiped at them with the back of her hand. "I never asked what she was doing with her life. I treated her like a stranger." Her hands covered her face. "I could have helped her."

"It's not your fault she's a prostitute," Gabe said.

"Maybe not, but I feel responsible. I was so ambitious, embarrassed to even talk to her—she was dressed in trashy clothes and wearing gobs of makeup. I couldn't wait to get away. That's the kind of friend I turned out to be."

"Do you think they'll really hurt the woman?" Mel asked.

"Yes!" Angelle reached into an end table drawer. "This is the note they sent me yesterday." She held it out to Ted and he read it aloud.

Senator Savage:

We have your "friend," Joanne Paige. If you want her to live, you know what to do on Wednesday. Her life is in your hands.

Do the right thing and she'll be released. If not, you've been warned.

The words hung in the air.

"What do you plan to do, Senator?" Ted asked.

"I don't know."

"Will you carry the rider?"

Angelle straightened like a rod of steel had been jammed up into her spine. "Mr. Yost, I don't speak to anyone in advance about pending decisions, political or otherwise .You have no right to ask that question."

"We know what a desperate situation this is," Melissa said. "But you can't run away from this."

"And you can't give in to them," Ted said. "You can't give them the rider."

"And my friend? They'll kill her."

Angelle Savage's face sagged and she seemed to age several years. "I won't let them kill Joanne. Even if it means doing something despicable, even if it makes me despicable. I'll do what has to be done."

"You can't!" Ted said. "You know you can't. Think of all the people this involves."

"Joanne is only one person" Mel said. "This rider could mean millions of people will die."

Angelle stood suddenly. "Do you think I don't know that? Do you think I'm stupid, unfeeling?"

"Are you sure it's not your political career you're worried about?" Ted said, pointing a finger.

"Mr. Yost! Stop that right now," Gabe, said. "You're underestimating my wife."

"Senator, do you have any idea who sent that note?" Ted said.

"I don't know who sent it, but I know who's behind it. It has to be the work of Wade Wilson. It's got his MO all over it."

"The lobbyist?"

"The filthiest man in Washington politics. He's the kind of egomaniac who sets things in motion and disappears when it's time to pay the consequences." Angelle looked away from the Yosts.

"But it might not be him," Ted said.

"Wilson all but threatened me with exposure the other day. He gave himself away by emphasizing the word 'friend' in that note."

Ted was doubtful.

"Don't you see? It has to be him. This is a massive power struggle. We can't even imagine the amounts of money involved." Her eyes pierced Ted's. "He warned that everything was on the line. I didn't take him seriously enough. How could I imagine he would do something *this* dirty?"

"Do you think he was also behind my kidnapping?" Mel said.

"You were kidnapped?" Angelle said. "And they let you go?"

Melissa shook her head. "Let's just say, I managed to get away."

The Senator's face was a pasty white. "Oh, my God. If they took your wife, they *will* kill Joanne." She turned to Melissa. "But, why you, Mrs. Yost?"

Gabe's voice filled the room. "Damage control."

Angelle Savage stood abruptly. "I'm sorry. Sorry for all the people who are going to suffer because of me. Sorry for being so … so selfish. But I have to stand by Joanne. I can't allow them to kill her."

Chapter 38

Ted was agitated, couldn't calm down as he paced back and forth in the *Washington News-Sentinel* reception area. He'd tried to sit, but kept sliding out of the room's sculpted plastic chair.

Hell, face it, waiting for anything was not his strong point. And he was especially uneasy coming to his old friend, Hy Muller, to dump this whole mess in his lap. It could either be a great coup or a flat-ass dud.

Stop speculating. Think.

He pulled out his notebook and scribbled down the mantra he'd used since his college days.

Time the crusher,
the killer,
the enemy,
Time.

The repetition organized his thoughts.

At least all the parts of the puzzle were in place. Desisto *was* a conspiracy. No other word for it. And it had begun with Hygea's Garrett Rudge and his agenda to gain approval for selective euthanasia. A new national end-of-life protocol.

John Bradberry had refused to believe the ethics committee would go along with the Hygea proposal, and that that would be the end of it. But Ted wasn't as optimistic.

Angelle Savage seemed determined to save her friend, make everything legal by slipping in the necessary rider onto a Medicare appropriations bill. A bill that had to be passed before Congress adjourned for the holidays.

Time. There was no time.

He shifted back and forth in his seat again. Was it only yesterday when possessions, money, and power weren't foremost goals? Sure, people wanted all of that, but personal values counted for something.

Time had put him out of step with a world where ethics and altruism were all but gone. Corporate greed had finally set the pattern for everyone, right down to the man in the street..

He hunched over in the chair, studied the floor in the newspaper's reception area. Muller had tried to put him off until Tuesday, but Ted had insisted on a face-to-face meeting today, telling him only that he had a time-sensitive, exclusive story, with serious national implications.

Ted dug into his wallet and pulled out a hidden, crumbling one-dollar bill. He pressed it out with care. Written across George Washington's face were the fading words:

I owe you one, buddy—Hy
And I'm here to collect, my friend.

The door flung open and a bald man about Ted's age, dressed in wrinkled slacks, rushed toward him. The two men collided into an embrace, pounding one another on the back.

They stepped back and got an eyeful of each other. "Son of a bitch! How the hell are you?" Muller said. "Come on, we'll play catch-up in my office."

They entered the work area, where reporters sat at their desks, tap-tapping on computer keyboards, finger-fucking smartphones, and yammering into the mouthpieces of head-mounted telephones. Ted felt a twinge of nostalgia, wanted to linger, but Muller pulled him through a door, its clear glass imprinted with: Hyman Muller, National News Editor.

"Grab a seat, man." When he saw Ted pondering two wooden chairs stacked high with newspapers, magazines, and books, he added, "Just toss that stuff on the floor. I'll probably never get around to looking at half of it."

"How do you do it? I mean, how is it they haven't tossed an old guy like you out the door?"

"Yeah, I wonder that every day." He laughed as he sat down behind a desk cluttered with almost as much paper debris as the chairs. "Except I'm smarter than most of those dudes out there,

258

and twenty times faster digging out all kinds of stuff by phone *and* online." After Ted managed to clear one of the chairs, Hy pointed toward the news room and added, "'Cause they're young doesn't mean they're smart."

"Keep trying to convince myself of that almost every day."

Muller leaned forward, arms sprawled across his desk, and said in a conspiratorial tone, "Ask me, they don't teach those little shits how to be closers once they do get a foot in the door. And they hang around here longer than asparagus pee, but they stay just as green."

Ted shook his head. "No, man. That's not it. It takes talent and passion. Two things you've always had."

Muller leaned way back in his chair with a confidence that said he'd done it many times and knew just how far he could go without tipping over backwards. "Been following your blog. Some good stuff. Even stole a line here and there."

"Thought I recognized my style in some of your better pieces."

That earned him knit-eyebrows and a piercing look. "All right, man. It's time to stop this small-talk shit. Why in hell did you think you needed to drag me in here when I was home thinking about possibly getting it on with the wife? And by the way, that's not so easy to accomplish these days. So this better be good; it better be damn good."

Ted pulled the dollar bill from his wallet and placed it gently on the desk in front of Muller. "I've always known that someday I'd have a reason to collect on this. Today's the day."

Muller lightly touched the bill; his eyes went soft. He looked at Ted, the wise guy attitude gone from his demeanor. "You saved my ass in 'Nam, man. Without you, my career would have been shit-canned."

"We were both lucky to get out of there in one piece."

Muller stood, then quickly sat back down and pretended to be interested in sharpening pencils he'd gathered from the top of his messy desk. After a long moment, he said, "I couldn't write shit anymore. If you hadn't filed my copy, I would have been history."

"Yeah, talk is cheap, real cheap. I noticed you didn't sign a fiver as an IOU. And by the way, push that bill back over here. I might need it to tip a cabby."

Muller laughed. "And you call me cheap?"

The room became silent, each of them lost in his own thoughts. Muller was the first to speak again. "Okay, what is it you think you know that might make the front page?"

"I'm sure you're following the Medicare funding bill that's scheduled for a floor vote on Wednesday."

"Oh, yeah. Routine procedure. No one expects a fight on that one."

"You may be dead wrong." He watched Muller's eyes squint with suspicion. "There's a cost-cutting rider in the wings that's going to drastically affect Medicare policy and procedures. The wheels are in motion to hang it onto the funding bill. Senator Angelle Savage is carrying it—it's top secret stuff."

"Does this rider have a number or is it a figment of someone's imagination?"

"Oh, it's real all right. But I don't think it's been assigned a number yet."

"That's easy enough to find out, provided you can tell me what it's meant to do."

"Legalize selective euthanasia."

The seasoned editor's mouth dropped. "You shitting me, Ted?"

"Wish I was."

Muller cupped his chin in one hand, turned his chair to look out the window, then spun himself back around. "I can't believe something that big hasn't been picked up by one of my people. And if what you're saying *is* true, some heads are going to roll."

"Not only is it true, Hygea is in the process of lining up its string of hospitals to initiate the policy as soon as the legislation is signed off by Congress and the President."

Hy moved his pencils again, sharpening several of them down to stubs. "You say Savage is doing this? Man, that doesn't make any sense at all. I can't think of a single thing in her voting record to indicate she might go along with something like that, let alone come up with it on her own."

"Pressure. Something personal; someone has a hook in her."

"And how the hell did you get wind of all of these shenanigans?"

"CORPS brought me into it."

"That old folks group? Sorkin's people?" He shook his head, tapped a finger on the desktop. "Something's not kosher here, Ted. I mean, I have a pretty good handle on the balance of power in this city and while Savage is an up and coming star, she simply doesn't have that kind of weight. And even if she did, I can't see her torpedoing herself like that." He paused again. "Someone outside the hallowed halls of Congress has to be pulling the strings. The trick is to find out who's the big *kahuna* on this one."

"Try W. Wade Wilson, the—"

"Fuck," Muller shouted. "I know who the hell W. Wade Wilson is, that asshole. Who in Washington doesn't? Anytime you suspect there's a camel's head in the tent, put your money on old W.W.W."

"And if he could be exposed?"

"A lobbyist with his kind of White House connections isn't very likely to be thrown to the media wolves, although you can bet your ass we've tried. And it looks like we might get another chance if your story pans out." He pointed a finger at Ted. "If there's anything else you can tell me about all of this, now's the time to put it on the table."

Ted looked at the National News Editor and swallowed hard.

"There is something, Hy, but you have to promise not to use it."

"That depends on what it is. But I'll tell you this, it's a rare day when we hold back on anything."

261

"This needs to be one of those days, because there's a good chance someone might die if you don't."

Muller cocked his head to one side. "Isn't that a bit melodramatic?"

"What if I told you a close personal friend of Savage's has been kidnapped, and if Savage doesn't follow through on that rider, that person will be killed?"

"Shit!"

"It's a tough one, I know. And there's no attribution I can provide to make this a page one story. But there must be some way you can run with this. People have to start asking questions, put a stop to what's happening."

"The Senator won't help us?"

"It's not that she won't, she can't."

"Well, if what you're telling me checks out, even one little bit, I'd say we have the proverbial tiger by the tail."

"And you'll hold back on the kidnapping?"

Muller chewed at his upper lip. "I'll try," he said. "That's the best I can promise."

"I wouldn't expect anything more." He stood, held his hand out to Muller, and looked down at the "I owe you one" dollar bill. "We're even now," he said. "Keep the buck."

Muller laughed. "Naw! You take it. I wouldn't want to be responsible for some cabby not getting a tip."

Chapter 39

Calli Salvio sat at her desk feeling sorry for herself. It was Monday morning and she'd had a miserable weekend.

First, she had to work late Friday, then Saturday night turned out to be really bizarre when she had to fight off some guy she'd picked up at a local bar. He'd turned weird on her, wanted to get into kinky stuff she hadn't signed on for. Without her kickboxing, she'd have been stewed, screwed, and tattooed. Well, at least the first two.

And Sunday? God, she'd spent nearly the whole day moping around, hating herself for being so stupid. What was she thinking anyway? Getting loaded and going off with a total stranger? He could have killed her.

For the hundredth time, she wished she was back in Henderson, Nevada.

Senator Savage had done her best to land her a good job, and Calli had all but nailed the slot as a research assistant with an important subcommittee. But— the big but—at the last minute a senior Senator's daughter aced her out, leaving her high and dry, with all the other good spots filled..

Now she was running at top speed, sometimes seven days a week, as W. Wade Wilson's lackey. Senator Savage had tried to talk her out of taking the job, but the pay was top rate. She was disgusted. If she wasn't so broke, she'd quit. Or at least that's what she kept telling herself.

She opened her purse and pulled out a small compact and peered into the miniature mirror, lightly pressed her fingers on the puffiness around her eyes as though that would make it disappear. Drinking and crying were a bad combination.

Calli closed the compact, looked around her tiny office space, which was really just an open reception area outside of the big man's cavernous office. She felt like a drone. Yesterday she was wallowing in self-hatred. Today it was self-pity.

Political science and history were her passions and she'd been excited just to be here—far from Henderson. She'd visited every monument, every memorial, and toured the White House, Smithsonian, and Library of Congress. But it had all become just a backdrop for a bust-your-butt, dead-end job. This wasn't what she'd hoped for when she hit the books like a fired-up nerd for four years at UNLV.

And what about her long-time fantasy about being a part of exciting D.C.? The dream that she would be steeped in government, part of the whole, complex political scene? Poof—that was out the window. Instead, she was slaving away for this creepy lobbyist who kept everything a big secret. The man had more to hide than Pandora's Box.

It was all too, too boring. She wasn't even a valuable assistant; she was a get-the-coffee, answer-the-phone *girl*. Not what she'd come to the Capital to do. She could have stayed in Nevada and done that.

Calli massaged her neck, rotated and stretched her arms.

Enough wallowing.

She tried to push her negative thoughts aside. Instead, she focused on her left forefinger. The nail had been bugging her all morning—it was rough and would probably ruin her stockings if she didn't smooth it. She sighed, opened a drawer, pulled out an emery board, and began filing down the offending nail.

It was rare she heard anything through Wade Wilson's solid door. But right now he was screaming into the phone, his Southern accent unexpectedly missing.

She slipped the nail file back into her drawer and stared at her phone. There were three extensions—two were his private lines, the other one the main line. She'd eavesdropped on some of his calls before, but they were mostly routine conversations with healthcare executives. They hadn't been worth taking a chance on getting caught.

Calli looked around her empty space, patted her hair in place, and pressed down on the button of the lighted extension; she held her breath and picked up the phone.

* * *

"Damn it, Levi, you said you'd stay on top of this like fleas on a dog. I mean, I want you to tell those two cowboys they need to stay put until you tell them otherwise."

"They just want to know how much longer this gig is going to last. The Carson Capital Motel is nothing but a dive. They're bored."

"Bored? You have to have some kind of brains to be bored."

"They're just hired help, Wade. Hired help."

"I know. I know."

Levi Black made a noise that was someplace between a grunt and a nasty laugh. "You didn't offer enough green to get smart muscle."

"Yeah, yeah," Wilson said. "It's just that things are a bit twitchy at this end, if you know what I mean. Coming down to the final hours for this bitch."

"The whore?"

"No, not her. I'm talking about this latest fuck-the-kitty thing I got going. Got too much skin exposed."

"Okay. I'll do what I can to calm down that pair. Just keep in mind that they're not the straightest cues in the rack, and Carson City is not Reno. It *is* boring," Black said.

"I'm not paying them to have a good time. Offer them more money, if you have to. But they've got to stick to the plan, Levi. No side trips. Not a single one."

"I'll give them the word again. But I think they're spooked— the broad's seen both their faces and I get the feeling they'd like to take her out into the desert and leave her there … permanently."

"Damn it, Levi. No harm is to be done. You know that better than anyone. For crissake, man, she's a nobody. A fucking nobody." Wilson took a deep breath. "Just make sure she gets enough money to keep her yap closed when this is over."

Black started laughing. "That might have worked yesterday, Wade. But one of the dorks lost it and cut up her face." He snorted into the phone. "She'll have to wear a bag over her head, 'cause her johns won't think she looks too good anymore."

"Morons! How did you let that happen?"

There was a long pause. "You know, Wade, it's a good thing I don't do this for money 'cause you couldn't pay me enough to put up with all your shit."

"Sorry, Levi. Shouldn't be taking this out on you. I mean, it's like they say, you get what you pay for. I shouldn't have been so cheap."

"No argument out of me."

"Okay. Let me think about it; I'll get back to you. And try to keep those assholes from pulling off anymore dumb stunts."

"I hear ya."

* * *

Calli's head was pounding with a headache. She waited for her boss to hang up then immediately hit the line for the call back number. But "Unknown caller" was all that came up on the screen. She wrote down the name of the motel and its location and stuffed the paper into her purse.

What was she going to do? She closed her eyes, held on tight to her desk to keep the room from spinning.

The outer door to the office opened and Senator Angelle Savage, and a man she didn't recognize, walked in.

"Hi, Calli. Good to see you again. By the way, I may have that research job for you that we talk about. Probably at the beginning of the year." The Senator reached across the desk for Calli's hand. "Is something wrong? You look a little pale."

Calli was lightheaded and weak. "No problem, Senator. And the first of the year would be great. I just hope I haven't been bugging you too much."

"No, no! I just wanted you to know that I haven't forgotten you. She turned to the man with her. "Ted Yost, Calli Salvio. "This young woman is from Nevada, too. One of my constituents. I even think she voted for me."

Calli smiled. "You know I did!"

"We have an appointment with W. W. Could you let him know we're here, please?"

Calli smiled and picked up the phone. When she hung up, she said. "Go right in, Senator. Nice to meet you Mr. Yost."

Angelle gave Ted a let's-get-it-over-with look and they entered the office. As the door closed, Calli saw Wade Wilson stand up and offer to shake hands.

* * *

"Let's cut to the chase, W.W.," Angelle said. "Where have you got Joanne Paige stashed?"

"You folks from Nevada have such a colorful way of expressin' yourselves," Wilson said. "And who are you, sir?"

"I'm Ted Yost. A citizen and friend of the Senator."

"Enough!" Angelle said. "Get Joanne on the phone for me. Now!"

"What makes you think I even know what you're talking about? That name? Never heard it."

"Have you forgotten about our lunch at the Five and Dime so soon?"

Wilson turned to Ted. "Now you see why women can be so difficult. I haven't got a hint of an idea of what this little lady's talking about."

"Listen, you supercilious son-of-a-bitch," Angelle said. "We know damn well you have Joanne, know you're holding her to keep me on the straight and narrow. But as long as you have the woman—no rider."

"Angelle, my dear, you're just ramblin' on and on. I don't have a whisper of what you're talkin' about. If I even had an inklin', I'd say we're at an impasse." Wilson's voice turned to steel. "And if I were playin' that game, then you would know: No rider, no Joanne. That is her name, isn't it, Senator?"

He abruptly stood, looked first at Ted, then at Angelle. "And I think you'll find that I don't blink first."

* * *

Calli stood with her ear pressed against the door but couldn't really hear everything. They needed to talk louder. Still it all fit together with Wilson's earlier telephone call.

What was she going to do? She couldn't go home to Nevada with her tail between her legs—she needed this job for now.

She was behind her desk when the Senator and Ted Yost walked out of the W. W.'s office, slamming the door behind them.

"Calli, you'll definitely be out of here the first of the year, even if I have to create a job for you myself. Trust me!"

"Senator," Calli whispered, "here's something I think you should see." She nodded toward Wilson's door.

Calli handed the Senator a folded piece of paper. She'd written down everything she'd heard on the phone earlier.

"Help her!"

Chapter 40

Della Paoli was levitating—lifting higher and higher.

Warm, strange energies infused her body.

Splotches of deep purple and cadmium yellow floated all around, bursting into towering irises, sunny daffodils.

Her eyelids fluttered open and the colors disappeared, replaced with a room that circled in an underwater smear of dizziness. She shut her eyes against the swirl. When she dared look again, everything was still.

A smothering silence closed in around her—there was no sound other than the oxygen rattling through her chest, along with her labored breathing. Her heart began a wild thumping that echoed in her ears.

She still could not move her body.

She looked at the corner of the room, remembered someone had been in the shadows watching her. She'd seen a person.

Or had she?

How could she know what was real or what wasn't?

Tears ran down her cheeks.

Will I ever see my apartment, my flowers again?

She studied the IV next to the bed. It was the one constant in her life; it was there when she closed her eyes, it was there when she opened them. She watched the fluid drip slowly, feed into her arm, enter her veins, swim its way to her heart.

* * *

Bob Holt lay in bed, drenched in sweat. He glanced at his clock—a little before five. Going back to sleep was not an option.

His mind jumped ahead to the question Rudge would force him to present to the committee today: Should Medicare patients receive only "care-for-comfort" if their prognosis lacked total recovery?

And this time Rudge would really need him, need his vote.

He headed for the kitchen, fighting the gnawing need to add a stiff shot of Chivas to his coffee. His hands shook violently when he poured his first cup—he added nothing to it. Nothing to his second or third cups.

The initial warm comfort of the coffee soon flipped into caffeine jitters. He forced himself to eat a light breakfast of sourdough toast and V-8 juice, but before he could rinse the dishes, he was racing to the bathroom, where he lost it all.

Exhausted, he staggered back to the bedroom, flopped across the bed, and stared at the double closet he'd shared with his wife. All these months and he still couldn't bring himself to touch or give anything of hers away. And buried among her sweaters on the top shelf was a .38 police special.

He arrived at the hospital at 7:00 a.m., an hour earlier than his usual time. After touring every satellite at least twice, upsetting the nursing staff with his repeated drop-ins, he knew the time had come to get out of their way. Leave. No one wanted administration watching their every move, and asking inconsequential questions. Even the doctors were beginning to toss hostile glances. No one said a word, but body language told him it was time to disappear.

He returned to his office to wait for Garrett Rudge's arrival.

While he sat staring at his office door, his thoughts returned to the woman who was destined to become a prototype for Desisto.

His stomach wrenched and his hands started to shake violently.

No! No! I can't vote against her! I can't!

He was on the bitter edge of breaking down, of breaking a long-standing rule: Do not drink at work.

One experience of almost getting caught nipping Scotch had ended that habit. He swore he would never take that risk again. But the bottle still remained in the locked bottom drawer of his desk.

He moved to his office window, still thinking about

whisky, how it would burn its way down his throat. Then Rudge's Mercedes pulled into the parking lot.

Holt glanced back at the desk drawer where the liquor was hidden, shook his head. He slipped into his suit coat, gathered the papers he would need, and squared his shoulders as he left his office. Holt and Rudge walked into the conference room at the same time. They nodded their usual unenthusiastic greetings to one another, and took their seats. The other members of the committee were already seated.

The Administrator could feel the CEO's eyes probing him, but Holt refused to make further eye contact. While the nervous tension started to invade the room, an iciness that started at his ankles and rose to his neck made him shiver; yet his palms were wet with perspiration.

Holt did a quick visual roll call—Silver, Wolfe, Bradberry, Michaels, Rudge, and himself, plus a woman from the Medical Secretaries department, who would be responsible for the minutes of the meeting. When he turned back to his notebook, he could sense Rudge continuing to study him as he opened the proceedings.

After Holt turned the meeting over to Rudge, the CEO stood to speak but was instantly interrupted by Rev. John Bradberry

"Yes, John?" Rudge said. "You have something urgent to put before the committee?"

"Yes!" Bradberry said sharply. "We must postpone this meeting."

"Your request is out of order."

"And that's an inappropriate response."

Rudge's face reddened. But before he could respond, Bradberry continued.

"Advocates for the elderly have been noticeable absent from these proceedings. Neither CORPS nor anyone else, has been informed about these deliberations, let alone invited to—"

"Come, now, Reverend, Galen's had a standing ethics committee since the mid-eighties."

"This is not the same kind of committee. In fact, *that* long standing hospital group continues to function on a regular basis." He looked around the table. "Our panel is *not* part of the Galen Ethics Committee. Our existence has never been made public, nor have we invited other community members to attend."

"And your point is?" Rudge asked.

"I think Bob should adjourn today's meeting until we can notify relevant community leaders about our agenda and request their input."

"That's totally unacceptable," Rudge said.

"Reverend," Zach said, "I understand your concern, but we've been struggling with this for six difficult months. Personally, I think we should get on with it."

"Exactly my point," Bradberry said. "Getting on with it? Is that the kind of atmosphere we want for something like this—"

"I don't think additional time and input," Clifford Michaels said, "is going to make our decision any easier."

"This is not supposed to be easy." Bradberry shuffled papers in front of him. "We're dealing with complexities here that far outweigh anything—"

"We're all aware of that, Reverend," Rudge said.

"Who represents Della Paoli?"

"We all represent her!" Rudge snapped.

"Do any of you even know what the woman looks like?"

"She would be the person who cannot move any part of her body." Rudge said. "Is that the answer you want?"

Bradberry pointed at Rudge. "That's a cheap shot."

"You're being obtuse, Reverend. This is a community problem; the people on this committee represent the community."

Bradberry looked around the table again. "Far as I can see, Clifford and I are the only so-called community members. And you've spent six months bombarding us with a bunch of corporate PR." He glared at Rudge. "All the other members of this committee have a biased connection to Galen and Hygea."

"Reverend, you're not the only one concerned about patient needs. I'm just as concerned as you are, so is the hospital staff," Sarah Silver said.

"Then why have these meetings been kept under wraps?"

"Because we can't allow the public to dictate hospital policy," Rudge said.

"I think you're giving the public short shrift."

"Really? How many people do you think would appear if we ran a newspaper ad announcing an open meeting of the Galen Ethical Review Committee?"

"I have no idea," Bradberry said. "But if you mentioned selective euthanasia, you'd probably have to hire an auditorium to handle the turnout."

Rudge looked around the room for support. Everyone avoided his eyes. "I think people are as well informed as they want to be!" He turned to Holt. "However, if Reverend Bradberry wants to put the question of postponement to a vote, then we should call for a second."

"I see nothing wrong with that," Holt said, still refusing to look in Rudge's direction.

"I second the motion" Michaels said.

"May I have a show of hands opposed to Reverend Bradberry's motion?"

At first, only Wolfe held up his hand. Then Michaels did the same.

"All right," Holt said, holding his breath, "those in favor?"

Bradberry's hand shot up immediately. Holt followed with a tentative half-raised hand, eliciting a stony stare from Rudge. "Sarah?" Rudge said. "Apparently it's up to you to break the tie."

She rearranged herself in her chair, glanced quickly at the other committee members, and said quietly, "I abstain."

Rudge, unable to contain a smile, said, "It appears we have a tie."

Reverend Bradberry snapped his pencil in two, tossed it down on the table, and leaned back in his chair, eyes closed.

* * *

"Moving on," Rudge said, fully in charge again, "we're going to hear from Patricia Evans, one of Galen's social workers. She's been investigating the designated case of Della Paoli." He nodded stiffly toward Bob, who used the intercom to call in the case worker.

Patricia Evans entered with a determined step, took a chair, and opened a slim file in a poised manner.

Rudge wished Holt had selected someone who projected more warmth. He cursed himself for not having taken care of it himself.

The case worker glanced at the committee members, then began to read unemotionally from her report:

"I'm Patricia Evans, senior staff social worker with Galen Hospital. I was assigned to the Paoli case two days ago.

"The nature of my investigation was to look into the woman's background; find and communicate with any relatives and friends; report on any findings that would be relevant to her treatment and ultimate disposition.

"Unfortunately, I was unable to obtain any useful information from the patient herself. And the only other data available was on her driver's license.

"Using that as a source, I went to her apartment and spoke to her landlord and neighbors. No one seemed to know much about the patient.

"She lives alone; her husband died approximately six months ago from a heart attack. She apparently has no children, nor other close relatives; and she's lived at her present address about five months."

As she stopped to turn a page, Bradberry interrupted. "Are you saying that after five months in one place, no one knew anything about this woman beyond what you've told us?"

Evans looked up from her reading. "One neighbor did seem to have a little more background than the rest, but—"

"Is this information in your report?" Bradberry said.

"No! I wasn't able to confirm her statement."

"I'd like to hear it anyway," Michaels said.

Rudge waved a hand for Evans to continue.

"Essentially, Mrs. Paoli told her neighbor that she'd spent most of her life moving from place to place. Apparently, her husband was a traveling musician."

"Did Mrs. Paoli work?" Silver asked.

"She supposedly worked as a waitress at various times, and also took occasional house cleaning jobs." Evans paused, then added with an edge of impatience, "I think we could save some time here if I read the statistical data."

Rudge winced at her tone of voice but Evans looked down at her file and continued:

Della Paoli. White. Sixty-six. Born August 2, 1947.

Widowed approximately six months.

No known children. No known blood relatives.

Occupation: Flower vendor

Resides in a one-room furnished apartment, rent $500 per month, plus utilities.

Owns an eight-year-old station wagon.

Checking account: $23.14; savings pass book showing $502.34. No evidence of any insurance —supplemental medical, life, or automobile beyond PL & PD.

Evans flipped her folder shut with a heavy sense of finality.

"She has no one at all?" Silver said, her voice dropping almost to a whisper. "Not even a close friend?

"That's what my investigation indicates."

"I thought you said something about her working as a waitress and house cleaner," Wolfe said. "Yet, you list her occupation as 'flower vendor.' I don't understand."

Evans cleared her throat. "According to her neighbor, Mr. Paoli had a five-thousand-dollar life insurance policy. The proceeds apparently were used to cover funeral expenses, and open a flower stall."

"Sounds like she was doing fairly well on her own," Wolfe said.

"Not necessarily. She didn't own the flower stall, she merely rented the space at an exceedingly low rate. This, I discovered, is not unusual—surrounding businesses like the color and atmosphere of a flower vendor, so they make it financially attractive for a person to operate one. All that was required was the first month's rent and enough money to purchase her first inventory. After that, it should have paid for itself."

"Did you question the surrounding merchants?" Bradberry asked. "Perhaps they might be willing to help her."

"Of course I spoke to them. They didn't know her very well, and they didn't seem to be interested in her situation."

"But you said she did have automobile insurance?" Holt said, his fingers drumming rapidly on the table.

"Property damage and personal liability only. The only insurance of any benefit to Mrs. Paoli is her Medicare."

"I wonder what prompted her to sell flowers?" Silver said.

"I have no way of knowing that. I've told you everything I was able to learn."

Wolfe asked Rudge, "Do you have copies of Miss Evans' report for us?"

Rudge nodded. He picked up the copies and passed them around the table. "Now, if there are no other questions—"

"Just a moment," Wolfe interrupted. "I'm really uncomfortable with the sparseness of the information on this woman."

"Miss Evans can't be held responsible for obtaining what isn't there," Rudge said.

"True," Wolfe said. "But it might help if she could provide us with her professional insight."

Evans looked at Rudge who nodded his permission.

"As I reported, the woman's life is a virtual blank." Evans stopped and thought for a moment. "Considering her physical condition, she has very little to sustain her—no family, no friends, no support group."

Most of the committee members were visibly uneasy. After a long interval, Rudge said, "Thank you, Miss Evans."

The social worker nodded, picked up her folder, and left the room.

* * *

Clifford Michaels interrupted his detailed note-taking, looked up at Rudge. "Garrett, after listening to Ms. Evans' report, I realized that there must be thousands, or millions of Della Paolis out there."

"No doubt. And your point?"

"I'm thinking about those who work hard for every penny they get," Michaels said, "yet never have much of anything—the kind of people who are never going to own a home, be able to buy a new car, or ever have more than two or three outfits of clothing. How many of them will face the same fate as Della Paoli when they're terminally ill or physically and mentally helpless?"

"We've covered that, and quite thoroughly, Clifford," Rudge said. "Some people will simply have more choices than others."

Michaels stared at the ceiling. "There is a huge difference between have some choices and having none."

"Don't you think you're overreacting?" Rudge said

"Overreacting?" Bradberry interjected before Michaels could respond. "Not if you add in old people, poor people, handicapped people, street people, black people, brown people, yellow people, red people, you have staggering numbers of those who will find themselves in the same hopeless situation as Della Paoli. Do we simply say, 'Sorry, there's no more space, no more money for you'?"

Rudge's face turned a bright red. "You've gone far off track, Reverend. Our only concern here is with one person, Della Paoli.

She's alone, she's very ill, she's helpless—probably terminal—and without financial resources."

"Society may not be doing much for people like Della Paoli," Bradberry said, "but as Ms. Evans pointed out, she does have Medicare. She doesn't have to be tossed out into the street."

"No one's talking about tossing her into the street," Rudge said, his voice getting louder. "But let me be blunt about this, Reverend: her only real prospect is to rot in some extended care facility, at great expense to the taxpayers. This committee has the unique opportunity to set a precedent which will allow patients like her to die with dignity."

"I've had it up to here with that 'death with dignity' crap," Michaels said, raising his hand to eye-level. "We've each seen all kinds of people die, under all kinds of circumstances. There's never anything dignified about it. It's a dirty, messy business."

"But everyone has to cross that threshold," Bradberry said. "At least it deserves as much dignity as we can provide."

"John, that's a nice bit of philosophy," Holt said, "but the truth is that we don't want to see others dying, slowly or in any other way. It reminds us of our own mortality."

"Don't you think we should have the right to determine the time and place of our own death, if at all possible?" Silver said.

"Yes, I do," Holt said. "But in Della Paoli's case, we don't know what she wants, or if it's possible to know what she wants."

"Bob," Wolfe said, "I know what she wants. So do you. It's what any of us would want."

"I certainly don't want someone standing over me, deciding whether I should live or die, not have any say in the decision?" Holt said.

Rudge's eyes bored into him.

"Wait a minute," Silver said. "Considering Mrs. Paoli's condition, you really don't know what she wants?"

"No, I don't"

"She's paralyzed, man," Silver said. "She's completely helpless. For me, being trapped like that, with a functioning mind, would be the most terrifying existence."

"That's *your* opinion, Sarah," Bradberry said, "but that still doesn't tell us how Della Paoli feels, does it?"

"And she'll never have that ability," Rudge said.

"Who the hell made you God?" Michaels said. "I understand, she can communicate in a rudimentary manner."

Rudge could see that Holt wanted to support Michaels. Twice he cleared his throat, ready to speak again, but one glance from Rudge stopped him.

"No one is trying to play God, Clifford." Our goal is to find a way to help Della Paoli."

"True, she may be the woman of the hour," Bradberry said, "but that's by no means the extent of it. Not by a long shot."

"I'm not sure I understand your meaning," Rudge said.

"I mean, would you and Hygea have needed this committee and six months of meetings if Della Paoli was your sole concern?"

"Right now," Rudge said, "all any of us need to be concerned about *is* Mrs. Paoli."

"You're a liar, Garrett Rudge," Bradberry said, pushing back from the table. "How can you sit there and deliberately lie. This is supposed to be a medical ethics committee. What we decide will have an effect on all of society, not just the patients of Galen Hospital."

"Reverend, you've made a lot of noise here this morning," Rudge said. "You've pounded us with your 'the sky is falling' negativity. But you've yet to come up with any constructive counter proposals."

"Garrett, I don't have to prove you're wrong. What you're doing here is unethical, short-sighted, and flat out deceptive.

* * *

Bob Holt sat with notebook open, pen in hand, playing the role of dedicated administrator to the hilt. But his entire body was damp and clammy, clothes soaked with sweat.

He believed the Reverend, knew he spoke the truth. But his inner voice was more of a whisper than a shout. And he was frightened.

He visualized the gun in his closet waiting for him. Then he shunned even that fantasy. He knew he would never use it.

If he was ever going to change his life, the turning point was in this room. It was now or not at all.

But he needed to think.

Wanted his Chivas. Now!

He watched Rudge become more and more aggressive. The man was ambitious and his future was probably riding on delivering the right vote. It was now or never for him, too.

Rudge continued to stare hard at him as though he was accusing him for Reverend John Bradberry's gaining the upper hand, bit-by-bit.

"I think this committee needs to express itself in regard to our prototype," Rudge said, standing again.

"Express ourselves in what way?" Michaels said.

"What action the hospital should take with respect to Mrs. Paoli's future treatment."

Bradberry jumped in almost before Rudge had the words out. "Oh, for God's sake! Stop making it sound like a hypothetical exercise. This is a human being we're talking about, Garrett. She will die very shortly without effective medical support."

"I'm suggesting that Bob," Rudge said shifting from foot to foot, "call for a vote. Should we continue or discontinue aggressive medical treatment for Della Paoli?"

"I propose we have an open ballot," Sarah Silver said.

"Why on earth would we do that?" Michaels asked in surprise.

"As the Reverend said, this is not a hypothetical exercise. I think all of us need to openly share the responsibility for this woman's fate."

* * *

No!

The exchange brought Holt fully to the moment. He looked directly at Rudge.

"Will you consider an open ballot?" Rudge said.

It took all of Holt's strength to respond with a weak nod.

"Then I suggest you put the question to the committee."

When Holt didn't respond immediately, Rudge added, "I would like to make one final comment. I ask only that each of you carefully consider the quality of life and the future Della Paoli faces." He paused, looked at each committee member. "What would you want for yourself?"

Holt looked into Rudge's eyes, then glanced down at the sheet of paper Rudge had given him some time ago.

"The question before you is," he said in a quavering voice, "should aggressive medical treatment be continued or discontinued for Della Paoli? Should the committee vote for the latter, medical care will bypass present medical protocols."

The sounds of shifting chairs cut through the heavy silence. Holt said, "Starting on my left, Sarah Silver, RN?"

"Discontinue treatment."

"Dr. Zach Wolfe?"

"Discontinue treatment."

"Reverend John Bradberry?"

"Continue treatment."

"Mr. Clifford Michaels?"

"Continue treatment."

At one level, Holt knew what was expected of him. At another, he stood apart, viewed the room, its participants in a large animated diorama.

The exhibits looked at him, eyes wide, bodies frozen in place. Frozen in time.

But he was slipping away. Only a single finger kept him from falling into a bottomless black hole.

And if he could just hold on, he could go back to the comfort of his soft nothingness.

"Discontinue treatment."

Chapter 41

Garrett Rudge carefully set one foot in front of the other, forcing himself to move at his normal pace. It was the hardest thing he'd ever done.

Someone spoke to him in the corridor almost breaking his concentration. He nodded and kept going, hoping that he had given an appropriate response.

He made it to his office, and once inside he collapsed against the door, let it hold his weight for a moment. Deep breathing helped, but his head remained fuzzy, and his heart was erratic, like a wild, trapped creature. He held a hand tight against his chest and made his way to his desk and fell into his chair. Eyes closed, he waited to feel normal again.

It's done.

Then he stared at the phone.

No, it wasn't done unless *all* of Hygea hospital ethical committees came through with their positive votes—*everyone* had to have a positive vote.

Without realizing it, he was restacking piles of papers that were already perfectly aligned. He caught himself and stopped, forcing his attention to the set of clicking silver balls on the edge of his desk. He pulled an outer ball, released it, and submitted to the orderly, relaxing click, click, click that followed. He could feel himself returning to his daily world of purposeful, directed action.

At least now all communication to the other Hygea offices could be on the conference line. No more disposable cells, no more hiding, no more secrets.

Don't kid yourself, there are enough secrets here to bury you and everyone else. Don't lose sight of that. Ever.

He sighed, reached over and pulled out a new cell from the bottom drawer.

Twenty minutes later, Rudge put through the last of the calls to the administrators, this one to Chicago.

"Hi, Larry. It's me, Garrett."

"So, are we set?"

No wasted social niceties. The man was all business. "You're the last one, Larry. Did your committee meeting go well?"

"I could have taken that vote two months ago; it was that solid."

"I'm sure you could have. But I'd like an answer."

"Garrett, it was a piece of cake."

* * *

W. Wade Wilson checked his watch again: 3:30. Where was Rudge?

His office seemed small today, almost claustrophobic. But his moping dissipated when he heard the muffled ring of the cell in the desk's bottom drawer. He yanked it out. It could only be Rudge. "'Bout time," he muttered to the empty room, taking a quick sip of his now-cold coffee.

"Wade?"

"Who else were you expecting to answer?"

"Right."

"So, Garr, how's the day goin'? Did you hit the magic number?"

"In the end, they bought the package."

Wade Wilson took a deep breath, let it out slowly. "Good! That's real good. But remember, Garr, they didn't just buy it, you sold it to them. I'm damn proud of you."

"Thanks, W. W."

"I'll call you Wednesday as soon as everything is in place and the vote is in on the appropriations bill. Then we can crack a bottle of champagne and celebrate. You're a real American...a patriot, Garrett Rudge. The country's gonna owe you a lot."

"Wade—"

"Gotta go now, Garr. We'll talk more later."

W. W. immediately hung up before the Hygea CEO could say anything else.

He stared hard at the mug of coffee and the spill-ring it had left on the surface of his desk. He reached out and pulled a tissue out of the small box he kept on the opposite edge, mostly for those who needed it when they sat across from him. No denying the facts—he had a way of making people cry. All for a good cause, of course. Methodically, he rubbed back and forth over the mess until it was gone.

He reached for his phone and punched in Angelle Savage's private number. Without her, it all goes south.

"This is Senator Savage."

"Angelle, just a reminder—that vote is coming up in two days and I'm counting on you.

"I want my friend back, Wade. Make no mistake about that. If you don't follow through with your end, I'll not only have you thrown in jail, I'll make it my business to hurt you in any way I can."

"You do your part and I promise you'll see Ms. Paige right quick."

"You son-of-a-bitch, I don't trust you."

"Well now, little lady, ya can see why the world has become so cynical." He paused and chuckled, then let the silence grow between them. "Trust is the foundation of our political careers, my dear. As soon as you do what you're supposed to do, you can have your little lesbo girlfriend back."

"Bastard!"

"Senator, I may be a bastard, but I'm a man of my word."

"Listen, Wilson, I don't know how, but you're going down, if it's the last thing I do."

* * *

Dick Abrams sat back in his chair and wondered how he had ever allowed himself to get involved with W.W. Wilson. If anyone asked him, he could honestly say that lobbyists held way too much power. They irked him and he worried about them constantly. You never knew for sure whether they were truly on your side, or just playing you, no matter what the issue.

Nothing but a bunch of leeches.

And Wilson was the biggest and sleaziest. But the money from the drug and healthcare industries was stashed in that bastard's pocket. And that support was needed to ensure Tyler's success at the convention and in the primary and general election.

And W. W. does get things done.

The President had buzzed him three times already wanting to know about Hygea, each time reminding him of Senator Savage's need to attach the much-needed rider.

Like Abrams needed reminding.

He'd never trusted anyone left of center, yet here they were being forced to place all bets on some liberal from Nevada, of all places. And if Savage didn't climb on board as, W. W. had promised, things were going to get ugly.

Either come up with some other *real* money to drive the deficit down, or President John Armistead Tyler would be walking out of the Oval Office with his tail between his legs.

But save a trillion dollars in Medicare and *that* will capture everybody's attention.

Selective euthanasia was not going to be an easy sell, but it was doable. When the public was given the right spin—only the people who were penniless and terminally ill would be affected—chances are the voters would swallow it.

Abrams learned a long time ago, no one wants to accept being a poor schlub, barely making it from paycheck to paycheck. They may shiver in their cold-water flats, but they're still certain that one fine day they, too, would become rich.

Dreams die hard.

The cell in his pocket vibrated against his leg. He swallowed hard, answered the call.

"Yes, W. W."

"Hygea did it. The entire organization."

"Any problems?" Abrams said.

"Not a one."

Abrams thought W. W.'s usual chuckle sounded ... off.

"The only major thing left, of course, is for Savage to drop the rider into the right slot."

"And you're sure she'll do it?"

"I think our President will be signing the funding bill before Congress flees town on Thursday for the Christmas holidays. He'll do it quietly, of course. Too early for any hullabaloo."

Dick Abrams sat up, then leaned all the way back into the chair, looked around his comfortable office, and let his gaze settle on the portrait of John Armistead Tyler.

"You damn well better be right, Wilson."

Chapter 42

"You're going where, to do what?"

Ted Yost looked at his wife, held his hands out to his sides, and said, "I'll just be gone overnight."

"Provided you don't get killed."

"Bill and I have worked out a plan."

"Oh, great—dumb and dumber. Who the hell do the two of you think you are, Castle and Beckett?"

He risked a small smile. "Beckett's a woman."

"Whatever!" Mel stepped to the other side of the Tanas' living room and plopped down in one of the reading chairs. "I'm not going to try to stop you," she said, "I mean, how could I? But I'll tell you this, don't be surprised when … and if … you get back, I'm not here."

He walked over and bent down to give her a kiss goodbye, but she turned her head away.

* * *

"That was one God-awful flight," Bill said as he and Ted walked to where their rental car was parked and waiting for them. "Who would have thought there could be that many winter storms between D.C. and Carson City? I would have been a lot happier in something much larger and with more engines; thought I was going to puke a couple of times."

"Sorry, but going commercial wasn't an option," Ted said. "No direct flights available to Carson City or Reno, and nothing at all until tomorrow. It was a charter a plane or forget it."

"Yeah, but you know I really do hate to fly … in *anything.*"

"Well, we're here, on the ground, and in one piece. Now let's go see what we can do to get Angelle Savage off the hook."

Ted took the car keys to the Jeep Liberty from the female rental agent and asked. "How far to the Carson Capital Motel?"

She gave him a quizzical look. "Are you sure you want the Capital? There are a lot nicer places to stay around here."

"Carson Capital Motel is the one, for better or worse," Ted said.

"Suit yourself." She opened the car door for him. "Take Airport Road to Highway Fifty, west to Three-Ninety-Five, then north. It's just past the city limits."

"Thanks." He started the car and as soon as Bill was seat-belted in, accelerated out of the airport. He barely slowed at the first intersection, hung a right, and punched the accelerator again.

"Take it easy, cowboy," Bill said. "I may have left my stomach back at that last turn." He straightened in his seat. "And getting stopped by a cop isn't going to—"

"I know." But Ted continued to speed ahead. "I'm worried we may already be too late to save the Senator's friend."

"My guess," Bill said, "is that those pricks who nabbed her are probably just a bunch of yahoos. All talk, no bite."

"We can't afford to take that chance. They may be idiots, but that doesn't mean they're not dangerous. Anyway, thanks for coming along. Don't know what I would have done without you."

"Probably never would have gotten out of the house," Bill said, then cringed as Ted ignored a red traffic light. "Mel was pretty pissed at you."

"Got that right."

"Man, don't you think it's way past time you gave that woman her due?"

Ted was silent for a moment, looked up to check the rearview mirror, then added another 5 mph to their speed. "There's a good chance I'm going to lose her, Bill." He used his sleeve to wipe away the tears that were clouding his view.

"Hey, man, I'm in no position to be giving marital advice, but it's obvious you're going to have to work pretty damn hard to win back that woman … and I don't mean with candy and flowers."

"But why now? Why not twenty, thirty years ago? Why'd she hang around all this time if she was so unhappy?"

"You really are a dummy sometimes." Bill tapped Ted's head with an index finger. "Duh! She loves you, you dip-shit."

* * *

"What's your take?" Bill asked after they'd slowly circled the single-level building twice. The only exterior light came from a dim, blinking sign: Carson Capital Motel; and, over the office door, "Apartments Available," showed in dull fluorescent script.

"I think if we go around one more time, someone's going to get suspicious and call the cops." Ted pulled to the curb, turned off the lights, and let the engine idle.

"My guess is they're in that room in back where the Dodge four-door pickup is parked," Bill said. "Seems only logical they wouldn't want to be in the front part of the motel"

"I agree. And it doesn't appear there all that many people staying here. And probably for good reason."

"Sure wouldn't be among my top ten choices."

Ted let out a humorless laugh. "Did you see the number on the door where the truck was parked?"

"One-eleven."

"Good," Ted said. "We'll try to get a room on one side or the other. If it's the wrong one, we'll try something else until we find them."

They drove around to the entrance and went in.

"Like a room in the back," Ted said to the clerk through a round, metal speaker plate in the thick, bullet-proof Plexiglas. "Two queen beds."

"Only got doubles."

"Then doubles; it's not critical."

The night man turned to the key cabinet on the wall behind him, put on a little show of pretending it was going to be difficult to find an appropriate room, then looked around as he pulled a key, gave them a pleased-with-myself expression, and said, "Got it. Room one-fifteen. Cash or credit?"

"Been here before," Ted lied. "I'd prefer one of the even-numbered rooms, like one-ten or one-twelve."

"Those ones are housekeepin' units—sittin' room, bedroom, bath, kitchenette. Cost you more." Bill stepped up to the window to stand next to Ted; they both stared at the clerk, said nothing.

"Okay. Okay. Have it your way." He went back to key cabinet, quickly exchanged #115 for another key and said, "One-ten, will that do it?"

Ted nodded. "Whatever." He tossed a credit card into the tray beneath the see-through partition. He signed for the room, took back his credit card, and pulled out the #110 key.

"How long you plan on stayin'?" the desk man said.

"Don't know," Bill said and pushed through the door. When they were both outside, he added, "Shit. What does he care how long we're going to stay? This place is nothing but an overpriced pimple on a coyote's ass."

"Got that right. But if this is where we're supposed to find Joanne Page, making a scene with that jerk would be counterproductive."

Bill gave him the finger.

They piled back into the rented Jeep and drove around to the back of the run-down adobe building. They parked on a pile of fresh snow in the #110 slot, next to the huge Dodge Ram crewcab. There were still no other vehicles parked on that side of the motel.

"Got a feeling we called this one right," Bill said. He grabbed their two soft overnighters from the back seat and carried them to the door. "Time to call Savage's cop friend?" he asked.

"Not yet. The Senator wants us to play this close to the vest, for as long as possible. If we can rescue the woman without having to call in reinforcements, that will make her very happy. I promised her and Nathan we'd try to carry out this little caper with as little police assistance as possible."

"Yeah, yeah. You and your superhero theatrics are going to get my ass fried one of these days."

When they were both inside and had turned up the thermostat, Bill said, "What's the status of the rider?"

"It's been drawn up, but the only copy is at the Savage's house. She didn't want it anywhere near her office or the floor of the Senate until the very last minute. If none of her colleagues ever sees it, or even hears about it, so much the better ".

Ted walked over to the wall separating them from Room 111. "Let's see if pretty little Calli Salvio got her facts straight." He could hear shit-kicking western music twanging away before he was within a couple of feet of the partition's ugly blue and silver-striped paper. He put an ear to the wall and motioned Bill to do the same. Along with the music, they could hear voices, almost as clear as if they were in the same room.

* * *

"Stop flappin' your lips, Jumbo, and deal the friggin' cards. You're into me for a bundle and I think you're stalling' to keep me from having' time to get even."

"You're never gonna get even, Death. Don't waste those puny brain cells worrying about it. And try to clean up your filthy mouth ... it's getting on my nerves."

"Fuck you. Deal the cards."

"I'll deal the cards when I'm damn good and ready, cowboy."

Death stood, walked to the small fridge, turned around, came back, and plopped into his chair. "Man, do it! Can't you see I'm bored out of my freakin' mind?"

"Is that why you couldn't leave the package alone? Had to mess with her. Even had to cut her up, didn't you?"

"She's nothing' but a friggin' whore. And what's it to you if I got a piece of ass out of it? Gonna finish her off after tonight anyways, right?"

"No way, man. We need her to get the rest of our bread. So until then we play it by the book. Now pour us another shot of that tequila. Make yourself useful while I deal."

"It's about friggin' time, man." Death set a brimming shot of the cheap booze in front of his partner. "Down the hatch, shit face."

Jumbo jumped up, flung his chair against the wall, and grabbed Death by the shirtfront. "That's one time too much, bub. I've had it with you and your slimy mouth. You and I are through. Get your ass out of here."

Death swept the cards off the table, tore up the paper record of his losses, and said, "I ain't goin' nowhere without the rest of my money. Then I'm gonna kill that bitch 'cause no mark walks away what's seen my face, unnerstan?"

"You're not going to kill anyone, loser. Now settle down or I'm going to plug you, you worthless asshole."

Death tipped over the table with both hands, but before he could make another move, Jumbo had his pistol out and aimed. Death snarled, started forward, and was stopped by two quick rounds to the chest.

Both men watched the blood spread around the wounds until Death toppled over and hit the floor with a loud thud.

* * *

The flimsy door splintered under the impact of Bill's boot and he was at Jumbo's throat before the goon could figure out what was happening.

"Drop your weapon. Now!"

Jumbo held onto his gun as Bill continued to squeeze harder and harder. After what seemed like an eternity, the goon's body went slack and the pistol dropped to the floor.

"On your knees," Bill yelled. "Hands behind your back!" He pulled plasticuffs out of his pocket and yanked them tight around the man's wrists.

Ted kneeled next to Death, felt for a carotid pulse. "He's gone."

Bill kicked Jumbo forward and stomped on his back. "Try anything and I'll kill you right here." All he got for a response was a groan.

Ted went to the closed bedroom door and pushed it open. There was no light, no sound.

"She in there?" Bill asked, crossing over to stand next to Ted.

Ted flipped the light switch. At first they didn't see anything but the mussed bedspread. Then from behind the far edge of the bed they saw a pair of clawing fingers, then hair, and finally a face with dark, caked blood on one cheek, from eye to mouth; two black eyes stared back at them.

"Call the EMTs and I'll get the Senator's cop friend."

* * *

"Senator, she needs medical care," Ted said into his cellphone.

"What's her condition?"

"She's got a huge cut on her face and she's been beaten to within an inch of her life," he said, standing outside the hospital ER in Carson City. "The EMT guys said we barely got to her in time."

A long moment passed before the Senator spoke, her voice shaky, "Bring her back to Washington. I'll get her the best medical care available."

"I will as soon as we can, but right now, she's not fit for traveling."

"Let me speak to her, please."

"Can't do it. She's unconscious, hooked up to oxygen, and covered with all kinds of chest leads. They've had to shock her twice. Like I said, we didn't get to her any too soon."

"Listen to me carefully, Mr. Yost: I've spoken to Nathan Sorkin and told him if Joanne is not here, in Washington, before that Medicare appropriations bill goes to the Senate floor for a vote, I will add the rider."

"But Senator—"

"I know that sounds unreasonable, but I'm caught between a rock and a hard place. There's the rider, Medicare, Hygea, Wade Wilson, the upcoming election, end-of-life moral questions … all of it snarled and intertwined. And from my perspective, I can't think about any of it until I have Joanne Paige here in my presence ... not in a hospital in Carson City, not on a flight between there and here, but right here in D.C., where I can put my hand on her. Do you understand?"

"No, I don't understand. We've got Joanne, and you know we'll get her to you as quickly as possible."

"That's not good enough."

"But why, Senator?"

"I don't trust W. W. Wilson," her voice came in gasps. "I still think he'll find a way to hurt her."

"What more can he do, Senator?"

"She's still alive, Mr. Yost. Need I say more?"

"Senator, I'll do my best to explain that to the doctors but—"

"But in the meantime, I'll arrange to have a medevac plane ready and waiting at the Carson City airport."

"There could be a problem with the local police," Ted said. "They've already interviewed Bill and me once."

"You won't be bothered by them again."

Chapter 43

W.W. lay in bed on his back, eyes wide open.

3:00 … 3:05 … 3:10.

He'd gone to bed early, had been trying to sleep for hours. At this point, he didn't dare take a sleeping pill or his mind would be like mush the rest of the day. And if ever there was a time he needed to stay focused, this was it. What happened today was crucial to his future. He either stayed on top or he would be down for the count.

He stared at the 50-inch television monitor on the opposite wall and realized he'd had on an old John Wayne western, with the sound on mute. He picked up the remote and clicked it off.

3:20.

Just as his eyes began to droop, the phone rang. He grabbed the cell from the bedside table.

"Wade?"

He recognized the voice but for a moment he couldn't connect it with a name—his mind refused to focus. Who? Then it came to him just before the silence became awkward.

"What's going on, Levi? Why the early call? Good news, I hope." When the line remained silent for a long moment, he knew it was going to be bad, really bad. Levi Black was the kind of man who took care of things, quiet and efficient. No fuss, no muss. If he was calling at this hour, it had to mean trouble, trouble with a capital T.

"The guys who lifted the broad messed up. Messed up bad."

"What do you mean they messed up? The girl's all right, isn't she?"

"Yeah, the whore's alive, but just barely. The big problem is that one of our men is dead." There was another long pause. "The other's being held in the Carson City jail."

"The woman?"

"Word is, on a medevac plane bound for Washington."

"Shit!"

"Yeah, that pretty well describes it."

"I hope you've covered our asses. I don't want any of this landing on my doorstep." Wilson's hands were shaking; he couldn't get them to stop. "I put out damn good money and made it very, very clear how I wanted this to go down. Now look what's happened. Keerist!"

"It is what it is. If you're blaming me, forget it. It got away from us. Either face up to that, or run."

"Hell! I'm not running. And if it sounded like I was trying to dump this on you, I'm sorry. Thing is, I'm drowning here and I need your help, Levi. Do you think the jailbird will talk?"

"Sure he'll talk," Black said. "He'll do anything to save his friggin' neck. Wouldn't you?"

"But he doesn't even know me."

Black roared with a laughter that made W. W. shiver. "It's like dominoes, Wade—if they get back to *me,* who do you think'll be next on the list?"

W. W. could barely recognize his own voice. "Is there any way we can make this go away? Can you make the jailbird … disappear?"

The silence that followed stretched out longer and longer until Wilson thought they had been disconnected. He was about to hang up when he heard a long breath at the other end.

"It can be handled," Black said. "But it's going to take a bundle of hard cash to grease all the wheels, and get the right dude to make it happen."

"How much?"

"My guess would be somewhere in the neighborhood of a quarter mill. Certainly no less."

"You've got to be kidding."

"No, I'm serious. Not only that, once this is over and done with, you and me are finished. You don't know me and I don't know you. Ever! That's the deal, Wade. And no dickering."

Wilson gave it about two seconds. "Done!"

"You'll get a message in the usual way."

W. W. clicked off the phone and slowly put it back on the bedside table. The sheet beneath him was soaked in sweat; he couldn't remember ever being this scared.

He forced himself up, walked out the bedroom, down the hallway, and across the living room to the wet bar. With shaking hands he poured a couple of inches of Maker's Mark into a cut-crystal tumbler and tossed it straight down. His stomach turned into fire, threatened to reject the liquor.

Wilson grabbed the edge of the bar to steady himself, fought back a painful spasm, then turned and ran for the bathroom.

Chapter 44

"Senator, we're about an hour out," Ted said into his cell phone. "The doctor says she's holding her own, doing better than expected."

"What about her heart?"

"They think it was mostly dehydration and shock that pushed her into cardiac arrest. The on-board doc says she appears to be physically strong."

"Good."

"Yeah, but her emotional status is iffy. I won't minimize the situation—the wound to her face was deep and destructive. Your friend has been through the wars, and she looks it."

"I can't get my head around it," Angelle Savage said, her voice catching. "But now you know why I wanted Joanne here. Wade Wilson's an animal. He's responsible for all of this."

"Maybe not. My take: it was more an impulsive act of sadistic pleasure."

"Those bastards are going to suffer."

"Save your energy, Senator. One was dead when we got there, the other one hanged himself in his cell before we left Carson City."

"Good riddance! Saves the tax payers a fist full of money."

"Spoken like a true Nevadan."

"That's exactly who I am, Mr. Yost."

"You'll have an ambulance waiting at the airport when we arrive?"

"When they open the door of the medevac plane, the ambulance and I will be waiting." She paused for a beat. "And Mr. Yost, I'll owe you one for this. Words can never express how much I appreciate all you and your friend have done."

"I'm glad we have a happy ending here." Ted clicked off and looked over at Joanne, who was awake and listening to Bill. He was trying to distract her with complaints about having to fly back to Washington in another small jet. He was pretty funny.

Joanne's eyes were even blacker than before. She looked like a raccoon with a large dressing covering half of its face. She wasn't a pretty sight. The suture job had been tricky—the ragged cut was deep and wide and she would require plastic surgery in the near future.

Ted continued to listen to Bill complain and allowed himself a small chuckle. As far as he was concerned, it was one of the cushiest rides he'd ever had. The interior of the plane was plush—the nurse and doctor were relaxing in first class-style leather seats, sipping soft drinks. Probably one of the easiest assignments they'd ever signed on for.

* * *

Joanne tried to escape in sleep. The meds they put in her IV helped, but when she was awake, she couldn't stop crying.

The mirror she'd insisted upon had only revealed what she already knew: her face had been sliced open. Sewing her up would never take away the ugliness. How would she survive looking like this? She was ruined.

They'd loaded her onto the plane when she was asleep or she would never have allowed them to take her to Washington. To Angelle.

She could still see the look on Angelle's face when they'd met accidentally years ago. Angelle was embarrassed to be seen with her.

And who could blame her? The past was the past and the love they'd shared in Virginia City no longer existed.

Angelle was a Senator now, a big shot. Why would she want to have anything to do with a mutt from her past? And a whore, to boot?

No, she wouldn't see Angelle Savage when they got to Washington, or ever again.

* * *

Angelle and Gabe stood side by side, watching the jet land smoothly on the runway and taxi to where they were waiting with an ambulance.

She thought about Joanne and what had happened to her.

I should have been a better friend. Should never allowed her to just slip away. How many others have I hurt because of my ambition and drive?

She looked up at Gabe, took his hand, and squeezed it. "I know I have no right to ask, but when this is over, Gabe, please stay, please don't leave me again."

He turned his attention away from the arriving plane and looked into her eyes. "Do you really think I want to go?"

"Then don't."

"Angelle, I can't be with you and live the way we were before. As selfish as it sounds, I need to know I'm more important to you than anything else."

"But you are, you always have been," she said. "We can make it work. We can! Please." They looked into each other's eyes, both afraid, both wanting, wanting so much. She pulled him to her, squeezing, kissing, crying, laughing. Holding on for dear life.

* * *.

"Take me back!" Joanne screamed. She twisted against the straps that held her to the gurney. "I don't want to be here. I don't want to see her."

"Come on, Joanne," Ted said, "without her you'd be dead, buried somewhere in the Nevada desert."

She smashed at the dressing on her face, pressed down harder, used the pain to try to erase the memory of what she's seen in the mirror. Tears gushed down across her cheeks. "I'd rather be dead."

The hatch opened and Angelle came rushing toward her, a man following close behind her. She covered her eyes with her hands, her sobs tearing her apart. Angelle sat next to her and gently uncovered her face. Joanne still wouldn't look at her.

"Can you ever forgive me, Joanne?"

"You don't owe me nothing, Angelle. What happened was a long time ago, in another place." She finally opened her eyes to look back at Angelle. "I don't want to talk about it"

"You're right. We won't talk about it … now." Angelle placed a hand on her arm and pointed to the man who had come with her. "This is my husband, Gabe. He knows all about us, knows everything." She reached over and gently pushed a lock of hair away from Joanne's forehead. "It's so good to see you again."

Gabe smiled, crouched down beside the gurney, and took her hand. "Things will get better. I promise"

"Let's go home," Angelle said. "We've got lots of time to talk, to figure things out after you're settled in your room."

Joanne covered her face. When she spoke her words were muffled. "I'm so happy to see you again."

"Me, too."

* * *

Ted and Bill stood next to the ambulance, waved goodbye to Angelle, Gabe, and Joanne.

"Maybe there is such a thing as a happy ending," Ted said.

Bill laughed. "You don't believe that, do you?"

"Well, I think something good could come out of this whole business."

Suddenly the departing vehicle stopped, Angelle Savage got out, and trotted back to them.

"I have a something for you, Ted," she said. "It's for you, too, Bill. I think you'll both enjoy it very much." She handed Ted a copy of the *Washington News-Sentinel* early edition, opened to the front page. The banner headline read:

RUMOR MEDICARE FUNDING BILL
MIGHT CARRY EUTHANASIA RIDER

"And by the way, Ted," she said, "as a small thank you, I'm giving you an exclusive interview concerning everything that's happened, from the very beginning. That should give your blog some buzz, right?"

"Oh, no doubt about that."

"If we do it right, I'm hoping we can topple W. Wade Wilson right out of that catbird seat of his."

"But it might topple you, too."

Bill nodded his agreement.

"Hey, it happened. Someone has to tell the truth." She smiled. "Now there's a novel idea: 'Truth in Washington'." She waved goodbye and walked away.

Ted held up the newspaper so both of them could read it:

> **WASHINGTON**—Legislation that would legalize selective euthanasia throughout the U.S. could well be on its way to passage in the form of a rider to the House/Senate compromise Medicare Funding Bill, according to Congressional sources.
>
> This so-called 'midnight rider' reportedly has the full backing of the healthcare industry, if not a majority of House and Senate members.
>
> The White House issued a "no comment" when asked whether the President would sign the Medicare appropriations bill if it carried what has been called "death panel" legislation. He has expressed no opposition to the bill as it now stands.
>
> The funding measure is scheduled for a final vote in the Senate later today. It sailed through the House without a ripple last Friday, and is expected to receive near unanimous approval by the upper body.
>
> Sen. Charles Austin (R-IN), chairman of the Senate Finance Committee, said he had no

knowledge of such a rider. He suggested it might well be "a figment of someone's fertile imagination." He rejected speculation that such a rider was poised in the wings, that it might be the work of someone on his HHS subcommittee.

"If something like that was brewing, I certainly would be aware of it," he said.

Attempts to reach Sen. Angelle Savage (D-NV), ranking member of a select Medicare subcommittee, were unsuccessful. She has a long record of opposing any such legislation.

A spokesperson for Hygea Corporation, the leading U.S. healthcare conglomerate, denied any knowledge of a legislative rider that would authorize selective   euthanasia as an option in the end-of-life treatment of Medicare patients.

They finished the story almost simultaneously, whooped, pounded on his each other's shoulders, and finally had to calm themselves when they saw security headed their way.

* * *

Dick Abrams stared at the portrait of the President of the United States, then glanced at the folded newspaper on his desk. The Medicare money saver, the big deficit-reducing measure was out the window.

Just a few minutes earlier he got the word— there'd been no last-minute rider. Senator Angelle Savage had not followed through as W.W. had promised. Desisto was finished

And now the dreaded get together with the President was only a few minutes away.

Abrams would go to the Oval Office, sit in a chair with a false smile on his face, sip some afternoon tea, and look hopeful and optimistic. Then he would offer up lame excuses why the promised legislation didn't make it to the floor for an affirmative vote; make lame promises of a big voter turnabout—the electorate would come to their senses and vote for the incumbent—and tell lame lies about how the President was poised for historical greatness, poised to help every citizen achieve the American dream.

And the lamest action of all would be his enthusiastic report that John Armistead Tyler could still win the coming election and make his adversaries eat cake

Chapter 45

Hygea's Chicago office was on the line again. Larry Epps had tried to reach Rudge four times on his cell and three times at the office, leaving complicated messages that the CEO ignored.

He'd told his assistant he was unavailable. He wasn't talking to anybody, not after he saw the screaming banner headline on the *Washington News-Sentinel* web site.

But it was more than that.

It was supposed to be a slam dunk. All of Hygea was ready. Garrett Rudge had delivered, as promised, and it still went wrong.

Several calls verified the end result. An even more chilling confirmation—W.W. refused to take his calls.

Garrett Rudge's next stop was not going to be Washington, D.C. It was over.

But Larry wouldn't stop calling and his assistant said that with all the interruptions, she couldn't get any work done. Was he mistaken or did he notice a subtle change in her attitude toward him?

Of all the people in the world, Larry was last on the list of those Rudge might want to speak to right now. He needed time to think this through, to regroup, to know what he was going to say and do. But there was no time; he picked up the phone.

"This is Rudge."

"You must know what's happened."

"If you're referring to this morning's headline in the *Washington News-Sentinel*, then, yes, I know what's happened. If there's something else on your mind, you'll have to be less cryptic."

Larry's voice turned to ice. "Have you spoken to the other facilities? What we are to do with all the selective euthanasia candidates?

Silence. And more silence.

"Garrett?"

"Has it occurred to you, Mr. Epps, that there's no final decision as yet? Maybe that could be the reason I haven't returned your numerous irritating calls. What do you think, Larry?"

What do you think, you son-of-a-bitch!

"I think *you* better make that decision, Garrett. And make it soon."

"And what would your decision be, Larry?"

"I'd say we go ahead with our plans and not provide continued expensive care. It's the only right thing to do."

Rudge started the set of silver ricochet balls in motion. Click, click, click. "You know, Larry, we do have laws in this country. You might not agree with them, but we *are* bound by them. Like it or not, we do not act outside the legal system. Is that clear, Mr. Epps?"

"Perfectly." There was a disconnect. The Chicago office was off the line.

But Rudge saw the writing on the wall. Epps was in, he was out. It was inevitable. It made no difference that he took the high road with Epps; he'd plotted and connived and it had all failed. Come to nothing.

Hygea didn't like to lose and they would have to hang the blame around somebody's neck. He could see himself as the obvious candidate. And Larry Epps would probably be the next head honcho, or someone like him

He walked to the mirror in the far corner of his office and stared at himself—his twin sister's eyes stared back at him.

"You were right, Evelyn: I was being too ambitious, too heartless. And my failure won't stop them—they came too close to winning this time. They'll all just sit back and wait for the next best opportunity, and people like Larry Epps and W. Wade Wilson will be there waiting to help them reach their goals."

* * *

Dr. Terence Emory was standing at the computer in the ICU Nurses' Station, reviewing patient transfer notes.

"Well, that's weird," he muttered to himself.

"What is it?" one of the nurses said, moving in closer.

"Probably nothing." He pointed to the screen. "Those are your notes, aren't they?"

"Yes, they are," the nurse said.

"Della Paoli was showing signs of extremity motion before we sent her to hospice? Are you sure?"

Emory sat down in one of the caster chairs and the nurse sat down next to him.

"She *was* starting to have movement in her arms. Maybe I should have called you."

"No shit."

* * *.

Della was back in a world of sound and motion. A place where machines clicked, alarms and personnel were a constant presence. A nurse came to her bedside; *Sarah Silver* was etched on her name pin. "How are you Della?" she said, taking her hand. "It looks like you're doing better." She smiled. "We wanted to watch you a little closer so we brought you back into ICU. Do you understand?"

Della blinked once for yes.

"I know it's noisy in here and hard to get any rest. Would you like to have medication to help you get some sleep for awhile? Is that okay with you?"

Della blinked once.

Sarah smiled, pulled a syringe from her pocket, and emptied the contents into Della's IV line.

* * *

A warm sensation spread throughout Della's body. She lightened, lifted until she was spinning round and round and round, floating through daffodils and lilacs, drifting through velvet and taffeta, lost in all the softness, the grandeur.

A blaze of light brought the music. She had to get to it, get to the music.

She ran, pushed hard, burst through wisps of floating dreams.

Please, please, please don't stop.
Don't let it end before I can get there.
Louder now. Faster, faster, faster.

And then she was there, twirling, twirling; turning, turning; and singing—lost in the beauty of sound that carried her down, down, down, down into her beloved Gino's arms. And they danced, danced, danced away; lost in a universe of glittering stars.

Chapter 46

Ted Yost walked slowly up the steps to the front porch of their Sonoma house. He carried their suitcases, filled mostly with dirty clothes, set them down and started to look for his keys.

Mel, a couple of steps behind, walked over to their redwood swing, an old fashioned two-seater. The supporting chains hung from the rafters, a patina of rust covering every loop. The swing moved gently in the breeze. She leaned over and ran her hand across the bright blue and orange striped pad and wiped away the dust.

"I'm glad you didn't leave Washington while I was in Carson City," Ted said softly.

Mel reached out for his hand and they both sat down on the swing. They swayed back and forth. Back and forth.

She shifted in the seat and stared at their luggage next to the front door. "I know what you did was important, very important. But right now all I can think about is how everything in our house is torn and wasted. Everything we loved, gone!"

He squeezed her hand. "They're only things, Mel. Things can be fixed, replaced. What I'm really worried about is us."

"Me, too."

She turned to look at their garden—all of her summer flowers were long gone and every plant and shrub looked drowned from the winter rains.

"Everything needs fixing," she said, "inside and out."

"I'm here, Mel."

"Do you know how long I've been waiting for you to say that?" She looked at him with sad eyes. "Can't you see we're running out of time?"

"I know."

"You can't run off and leave me alone, ever again." Then the rest flew out in a rush before she could stop. "I know killing that legislation was an incredibly important thing to do. And I know how passionate you are about news writing … and I'm so proud of you … so very proud of you … still—"

"I promise, Mel, this time I'm home for good."

She turned and looked into his eyes. "Can I believe you—"

"I'll be here from now on, Melissa Yost. From now on it's the blog, and only the blog … right here from my study. I've even been thinking of creating more news features. And this is as good a time as any to ask if you'd like to make it a dual byline? You know, Ted and Mel Yost, or Mel and Ted Yost."

"What are you talking about?"

"Hell, Melissa, you were a damn good writer, and you're a whiz at the computer. Why not get back to it? Let's try something new together. Something fresh. "

A wide smile spread across her face. "You mean it?"

He wrapped his arms around her, drew her close. "Don't you dare think of leaving me. I can't live without you."

She laughed out loud. "We'll worry about who gets top billing later."

"Let's go in and put our lives back together again."

Her smile faded away. "I don't want to, Ted. I don't know if I can handle the broken furniture, torn books, torn pictures, torn memories. And my piano. It's all I can do to keep from bawling when I think about how totally ruined it is."

"We'll fix it, Mel. We'll fix everything. I promise."

He stood, offered a hand, pulled her up from the swing. "There's nothing you and I can't do together."

He unlocked and pushed open the front door, then picked up the suitcases and barged in before they could change their minds.

At the end of the foyer, they stopped so fast they stumbled into each other.

The living room was neat, everything returned to normal, like nothing had ever happened.

"What's going on?" Ted said, peeking into the dining room and kitchen.

Mel ran over and sat down on a new piano stool, tossed off a C major scale from bass to treble, and said, "It's perfect. I can't believe it."

They held hands and tiptoed into their bedroom; everything was back in its place—no slashed mattress, no dresser drawers emptied onto the floor.

They burst into laughter and ran into the kitchen.

On the table was a bottle of Dom Perignon, two crystal flutes, and a note.

Ted ripped open the envelope, Mel read over his shoulder.

It's the least we could do. CORPS thanks you for everything.
Nathan Sorkin
PS: Now don't be strangers

-The End-

About the Authors

Bette Golden Lamb & & J. J. Lamb have co-authored more than a dozen crime novels, plus a few other individual fiction titles as both books and short stories.

Bette is not only a writer, she's an award-winning painter, sculptor, and ceramist. She's also an RN and the model for Gina Mazzio, protagonist for their *"Bone"* medical thriller series.

J. J. has spent his entire career behind a keyboard as journalist, freelance writer, editor, and fiction author, plus, when the occasion demands, he's a competent jack-of-all-trades.

The Lambs have lived in Virginia, New Mexico, New York, Nevada, and currently make their home in Northern California. If you see them at a writers' conference, or anyplace else, say *Hello!*

www.twoblacksheep.us

Acknowledgement

To our exemplary critique group of Margaret (Peggy) Lucke, Shelley Singer, Nicola Trwst, and Judith Yamamoto, who know the very special difference between critiquing and criticizing. Their observations, suggestions, and encouragement have been an integral part of everything we write.

#

www.ingramcontent.com/pod-product-compliance
Lightning Source LLC
Chambersburg PA
CBHW021307250626
47155CB00002B/418